Fangs

for

Nothing

Mary Jean Rutkowski

Chapter 1

A tall, well-built man stood on the shores of Lake Erie, the wind blowing back his long blond hair. He hummed to himself as he fired several canisters at the rocky shoreline.

"You can't go home now," he shouted at the open water. A strange thick fog arose where the canisters broke open on the rocks. The waves washed the contents into the cold lake water. The man careful aimed each shot so that each canister would break open. He did not care if he left any evidence of his deed. In fact, he wanted everyone to know who had started this revolution. He smiled at his work as he returned to his car and drove on to the next body of water. The fog rose from the water, spreading over the land.

+++++++++

Heather stood watching Holly slip away. Her baby sister lay dying. The chemo seemed to be slowing the spread of the cancer. Yet with each treatment, Holly became more listless. She had just given her the pain medication that would allow Holly to sleep for a few more hours. Then the pain would return. The surgery to remove the cancer had left both sisters depressed and angry. Heather knew it would only be a short time and Holly would be no more. She could not even bring herself to say the D-word. It was much too painful.

On the television, The Weather Channel reported that an unusually heavy fog was blanketing the Great Lakes region on this unusually hot and muggy March 8. Highs were in the 70's with lows in the 60's. The talk of global warming dominated all of the stations. The high temperatures were combining with high humidity to intensifying the fog. The United States and Canadian governments were advising people in the affected areas to stay indoors, keep windows and doors closed, and not travel except in emergencies.

Holly stirred in her half sleeping state. Heather had just given her an injection of morphine. "Leave the window open, it's stuffy in here. I can't breathe."

"Okay." Heather pulled the blanket around Holly and tucked her in, before opening the window a couple of inches. She could always close them later. "Are you in pain?"

"No."

"Good, now get some sleep."

"Okay, good night."

Heather seated herself on a chair across the room from Holly's bed so she could be close if Holly needed her during the night. Sometimes Holly would wake in the middle of the night screaming in pain. It tore out Heather's heart to see Holly like that. She soon drifted off to sleep. When she woke up a few hours later, the fog had become so thick she believed herself to in a horror movie and half expected something to jump out at her. Bumping into furniture more than once, she made her way to Holly's bed.

Holly snored lightly. Heather leaned closely over Holly as she tucked her in. She watched her sleep for several minutes. Her breathing kept steady. The fog was thick, but it was warm in Holly's room.

MareMoo whined at the foot of Holly's bed. She wanted to go out. MareMoo is the most beautiful reddish brown and white pit bull mix having huge brown eyes and a gentle loving personality. She even liked the mail carrier. She looked like the dog from the Our Gang comedies.

"Shush girl. Let Holly sleep. Come on, if you want to go out. Meet me by the door. Okay?" The fog was so thick Heather kept walking into the walls and furniture.

MareMoo went out and came back in quickly. The fog frightened her.

+++++++++

Holly woke sometimes before dawn. A thick fog entered through an open window and chilled the house though she felt warm. She could hear MareMoo whimpering. Following the sound, she found her in the bathroom, trying, and failing to hide from the fog behind the toilet. She was just too big to hide there. The fog was everywhere.

Holly barely made it to the toilet before her stomach gave out. Her next 24 hours were a blur of puking and shitting. She was not the only one. Wherever the fog spread, people who breathed it in experienced the same thing. After 72 hours of this, life would begin to return to normal.

Holly scratched her nose. Her memory of the last few days consisted of a blur of puking, shitting, and letting the MareMoo in and out. Had she even fed MareMoo? Had she even given her water? She felt woozy, where did Heather go? Maybe she took the car. She could have gone to the grocery store for food. The thought of food made Holly sick.

"There she is!" Holly declared as she stumbled into Heather's bedroom after another round of puking.

Holly studied Heather as Heather snored in her sleep. "She must be sick too. She looks smaller than I remember, or my eyesight is going. No, she has lost a ton of weight. My illness must be wearing her down more than I realized. I better make her some coffee."

Holly ran into the bathroom at the thought of coffee. Nothing wanted to stay in her stomach. Her pants kept falling off as she tried to run. "Damn dumb ass pants," Holly tried to keep her pants on as she headed for the kitchen. They were the smallest pair she owned. "I haven't felt this good in quite a while. That right, isn't it MareMoo? Now, do I make a half a pot of coffee, or a full pot? Make a half a pot of coffee and full pot of hot water for tea, what a good idea. Should I get you food and water first? What a good idea girl."

MareMoo looked at Holly as if Holly had lost her mind.

"Want to go out girl? Okay. Hold still so I can put your chain on you, you silly girl, you." Leaving the door open so she could hear MareMoo, Holly went into the kitchen to make herself some tea, and then back to the dinner table to drink it. The tea seemed to stare at her accusingly. Chewing her lip thoughtfully, Holly ignored the whimpering at the door until it became a bark.

"MareMoo is whimpering to come in." A voice came from nowhere. "Let the damn dog in already," another voice added. Startled, Holly jumped up too fast. She propelled herself across the table. She landed head first with a loud bang and bit her lip hard enough for her teeth to break the skin. This frightened the hell out of MareMoo who whimpered louder and clawed at the door. Holly had heard the voices with her mind, not with her ears. "I'm definitely loosing it."

Breathing heavily, Holly rolled over on her back and cursed. Every time she tried to move, her pants would drop down to her ankles. Had she lost that much weight while she had been sick? She did not remember losing any weight. In fact, she remembered gaining it. As she lay there on her back, the blood from her cut lip pooled in her mouth and trickled down her throat.

"Damn. I taste good. I wonder if everyone tastes this good. Now that is a strange thought. I wonder where that came from." Looking at MareMoo who looked like she was about to break the door down, she shook her head then went to let her in.

Holly went back to sleep after she feeding MareMoo. Talking to Heather and MareMoo and avoiding food when awake because her stomach was far too queasy took up most of her waking hours. Thinking about eating anything solid was out of the question. The mystery of why her blood tasted so good baffled Holly. The few times in the past when she had cut her finger and put it in her mouth she had tasted nothing except the dirt on her finger. Her blood had never had any taste to her before. Why should it now?

Late in the day, she found herself staring at a picture of her favorite actor, Gregori Cornridge. He had the most beautiful dark green eyes framed by the longest darkest eyelashes she had ever seen on anyone. There were women who would kill to have lashes and eyes so beautiful. He had a long thin nose and his crowning glory, beautiful, sensuous lips that begged for kisses.

She had the most erotic dream about him. She could not remember much about it, except that she had bitten his neck and drank his blood. He had then drunk from a wound on her wrist then one on her chest. Then he wanted sex. His warm hands cupped her breasts. She always woke up at that point, damn. He looked so good naked, not that he was a porn star or anything. She had never seen his private parts though she could imagine them. Damn if what he did show was always very good.

"I wonder if he tastes as good as he looks? I wonder if he tastes as good as he does in my dreams. Ugh, this can't go on. I need some fresh air. I'm going to be in the back yard. And stop staring at that poor man's ass."

Heather was watching a movie with Kyle Matthews. He had recently lost his wife. In this movie, he was naked and trying to get away from someone with a knife. Good luck there buddy, you'll need it.

"No, and be careful."

Holly went to stand at the far end of the yard. Thinking of the unmarried object of her lust and muttering to herself. Once in the fresh air, the cold helped clear the cobwebs from her brain.

The stars were so bright in the moonless sky, every detail in the woods surrounding her house were as clear as day. As eyes adjusted to the night, it became unbearably bright, almost painfully so. Every sound magnified yet the air so still one could hear the movement of the insects in the trees. This was not only weird but it hurt her ears too.

Holly heard the rustling in the shrubs as a feral cat made its move on a family of rabbits. She could hear the frantic beating of the rabbit's hearts. Jumping over 18 feet, she grabbed the cat by the neck and subdued it. Its blood re-energized Holly and made her feel more alive than she had ever felt before.

After placing the cat's body under the tree and covering it with dirt, she found herself running on all fours in the body of a small polar bear. It was wonderful. Rolling in the grass, bounding through the woods, soon hours had passed. It is time to go home. For the first time in her life, Holly did not get lost. She normally had no sense of direction. Nevertheless, in the form of a polar bear everything was clear.

The run had been exciting. Changing back, Holly became saddened to realize she had gained weight. The pants and top were suddenly tight. I cannot tell anyone about this. No one will understand. They will think I am crazy or worse. She blurted out everything as soon as she entered the house where Heather waited for her. She had become concerned about Holly's absence and had been about to call the police.

"What makes you think you gained weight? You skinny, ass kissing bitch." Heather rolled her eyes.

"Sigh. Being sick has made you blind. Look how tight these pants are. You're the skinny one. You must have lost a zillion pounds."

"Come here," Heather dragged Holly to the only full-length mirror in the house. "See!"

"Hey. That hurts. Damn, we're hot. How did this happen?" Holly pushed her shirt up and stared at her flat belly. She had not had a flat belly since she had been ten years old, if then. Moreover, her breasts were perky too. "It looks like I lost about 200 pounds. It looks like I've a whole body transplant. I'm a teenager again. That's not possible. If I had lost that much in five days my skin would be all lose and floppy. It is all taunt and tight. What about you?"

"The same and you have only lost about 100 pounds. If you lost 200, you wouldn't weigh anything right now. I'm the one who lost the 200. Now what is this shit about turning into a bear?"

Holly leaped forward, turning into a bear in mid leap. She ran up and down the hall several times and frightened MareMoo who thought Holly was going to steal her food. She guzzled it down.

Heather tried several times, but unable to copy her. Angry, she bit Holly on the shoulder. "Um mm, you do taste good."

Holly bit back.

This turned into a wrestling match until MareMoo decided to join the fun. After calming MareMoo, Heather turned into a wolf.

"Ha. My animal is better than yours."

"Let's go to a bar and pick up some guys for lunch."

"There are no bars open at three in the morning. You twit."

"You're just jealous that you didn't think of it first."

"I am not. Now come and watch television with me. I want to know what is going on."

CNN had news about the alleged mad man who had passed through the great lakes and down the Atlantic coast, spreading a thick fog, which had initially made millions of people ill before giving them perfect health. On a related note, they reported that thousands of nursing homes were reporting their patients simply disappearing. The staffs of the nursing homes were unable to find any of the patients, though thousands of young people claiming to be the missing nursing home patients were in their rooms. Authorities were still investigating. Government authorities are asking citizens of the infected communities to stay inside and contact local authorities if they experienced any unusual symptoms. Holly rejected the idea.

"Oh look, I work with her." Holly perked up when a piece on how local people were handling the situation.

"Work with whom?"

"Her, that's Joanne from work, look, there's Jen and some of the others in the background. Now shush, I want to listen to this." The woman on the television looked peeved. "I'm sick and tired of all those whackos coming here looking for wooden stakes. They can all go to hell as far as I'm concerned."

"Do you think that's the proper attitude to take with them? They are customers after all."

"I'm 74 years old and I don't have to put up with their crap anymore. We are not in the business of arming murderers. Vampire hunters my ass, psychopathic idiot is what they are."

"Um, are you really 74? You look 20."

"I'm 89," the young man behind her said.

"Don't look at me. I'm only 29."

"Damn right I am." Joanne declared mightily. She smirked with disdain at the reporter who appeared to be around 35 with lots of plastic surgery.

"You look 14 and the rest of you look 18. I'm jealous." The reporter quickly ended the interview so she could find out how they did it. They did not even bother to go to the interview with the anti-vampire group, though they did show a group picture of them that taken earlier. Rumors spread that the group had been quietly converted or eliminated. However, no one knew for sure what had happened.

"It isn't safe to go blabbing about this. What happens if the vampire hunters find out about us? The ones everyone talks about on the news. Would they hunt innocent people like you and me? And what would the government do with or for us or even to us?" Holly had so much energy. She bounced off the walls until she ran up the wall and across the ceiling.

"What the hell are you doing up there? Get down right now before you destroy the ceiling. How the hell did you do that?"

"I don't know." Holly did a flip and landed next to Heather. It had seemed so natural. She hadn't thought about what she did. She just did it. It turned out to be fun and she loved it. Moreover, she would do it often.

Heather imitated her while Holly laughed with happiness. She laughed harder when Heather's blouse came down over her head blinding her. Heather had become so happy to see Holly's return to health she did not notice her own newfound health.

Soon, they drifted outside. Their neighbors were out. They all had the same high amount of energy as Holly. A small group gathered as they debated what to do. Turning themselves into the government when they had done nothing wrong was out of the question. It would be just wrong.

Across the Great Lakes region and on both sides of the border people were also coming together and reaching the same conclusion. No one would say anything to any government agencies.

Chapter 2

Vanessa Lee smacked Gregori Cornridge's head until he woke up mumbling. He's fine as long as he brings in money, she thought disgustedly. However, she would not put up with him cheating or moaning some other bitch's names in his sleep. Who was this Holly bitch anyway?

"What is it, Honey?" Gregori murmured, rubbing the sleep from his eyes. He had been having the most erotic dreams about someone he had never met, her hot little body rubbing against his way too much. He woke her just as they were about to have sex, damn.

"Who is this Holly person? And where did you meet her?"

"What are you talking about? I don't know anyone named Holly." Did he, he couldn't honestly remember.

"You don't know anyone named Holly? Are you telling me you don't know anyone named Holly? You were just ecstatically calling out the bitch's name in your sleep. You were moaning and carrying on like you were having an orgasm."

"I don't know anyone by that name." Gregori slid out of bed and headed for the bathroom. His mom had come to the States to see him and he was determined to show her a good time. She had been sick for the last few days but was starting to feel better now. "I have to pick up my mom by noon. Are you coming with me?"

"No. I think I'll go shopping."

"Whatever."

"I love you Gregori." Vanessa blew kisses at him.

"I love you too." Gregori said, thinking about the hot little chick from his dream. She would never smack him in the head to wake him up. He was sure of that.

+++++++++

"A new life," Holly pronounced. "This is what we have been given. Others deserve this too."

"But we have to drink blood. It's unnatural."

"It's against God."

"It's a couple of ounces of animal blood a day. The animal lives. You don't kill it the way you would if you were to eat its flesh. Only strict vegetarians can claim that. There are no animal killers in our group."

"What about that cat you killed?" The group developed telepathic abilities. No one could keep anything hidden for long.

"I deeply regret that, but I reacted without thinking to protect the family of rabbits it attacked."

Mumbling and murmurs spread through the crowd. Everyone knew the cat had been a menace. It killed any small animal it could get its paws on. The psychic ability of the New Life People kept growing. Every one of them could see her point. No one there were killers. They were coming to love the New Life with all its flaws and complications.

Holly placed her hands on her hips. Short at five foot two inches, she had been fat for all but a couple of years since becoming a teen. Her newfound sleekness felt strange. It would take her many years to get used to it. Everyone knew that Holly had been overweight, bald and dying just three days before. Now she had become the picture of health. Even her hair, which she lost during chemo, grew back beautifully into a rich fluffy brown with blond highlights, just about three quarters of an inch long now. Holly's petite body had curves in all the right places making her surprisingly cute. Holly did not consider herself cute or pretty. She did not feel that way. She looked 18 and soon all the people would be hitting on her. She would never have expected that complication or wanted it.

"We need to go south and spread our new-found happiness. Who is with me? Who wants to go to Disney? Who wants to go to New Orleans? Who wants to go anywhere? Who wants to get away from here?"

Throughout the crowd, children began chanting Disney, even the adults seemed to like the idea. Some has relatives in unaffected areas who they were sure would embrace the New Life. Health, youth and the longer life came with it. Who would not want that?

+++++++++

Myles Ludwig smiled at the 350 pound, 65-year-old bald man whose image shown on all the network news stations. Even the Weather Channel kept showing this image. He had been that man only two weeks earlier. Now he weighed 175 pounds and had long flowing blond hair. He looked like a 23-year-old college student. He had never had so much energy in his life, not even when he had really been 23.

He loved his new life, and became determined to find others like himself who would enjoy this new life and to give it to them. Others who would help spread his message to the rest of the world, to spread his newfound life. He had become bored and restless after he had traveled around the Great Lakes, down the Atlantic coast, the Gulf of Mexico, up the Rio Grande, and the Pacific coast until he reached the Bering Straits. Pondering his next move had brought him back to the shores of Lake Erie.

The economy would keep changing. With everyone who had reached puberty drinking blood and clear liquids, and eating solid foods only a few times a week, many food service places were cutting back or closing down. The states in the heartland were concerned. Random groups of vampire hunters were forming and heading into the affected areas. Hardware and lumber stores complained about the whackos Grocery stores complained about customers making weird requests.

Joanne and Jen from the Home Depot had joined with Dreama from the

Food Fast grocery store to form one such group. There were many others like them forming an Anti-vampire hunters group with their fellow workers. They hunted down and converted the vampire hunters. They held wild and crazy parties. No one said how people are converted. They just did it. They had a great deal of fun doing it. Their trademark was a 2010 Hummer. They did not understand what happened. No one did.

The nursing homes had finally realized that the young people found in all of the patients rooms were the patients. They just did not want to leave the home where all their friends were. No one knew what to do with them, especially when some of the women became pregnant. It was a weird and wonderful time.

Religious establishments flourished for a time, but as fear of growing old and dying faded, so did religious establishments hold on people. Without the pressing need to put food on the table, families drew closer together. Families often went feeding as a unit. The bodies of New Lifers no longer needed solid food to survive. Like the vampire bats of South America, New Lifers could live on blood alone. They just didn't like to.

The United State government tried to isolate the infected population. The unaffected portion of the country demanded it. This proved impossible when CNN reporters discovered that all of Canada, parts of Mexico, and all of the United States government were infected.

+++++++++

Holly jumped out of the car before it even came to a complete stop. She barely made it to the edge of the drainage pond before she puked. Ahhh, another perfectly good meal wasted. A beautiful thick fog soon engulfed Holly. It boiled out of the pond making it difficult to see anything. Holly continued to puke.

"Way to go Holly. This will really convince them that you're ready to come back to work." Heather stayed just close enough to Holly to keep her from falling into the pond. Holly not be able to swim and all.

Several of Holly's co-workers and her new boss came out to watch. He had only been on the job a few months. Holly had already been on sick leave when they transferred him in. It was a slow night for her co-workers, so they just stood around watching her. Some of them talked about getting popcorn to make the show more enjoyable. After about 30 minutes of this, her boss suggested she wait until she felt better before coming back to work. All of this was lost on Holly who continued to puke with gusto.

"Come on Barfy. I'll drive you home." Heather said with an unholy glee nearly an hour later.

"You take as much time as you need getting better, Holly." Holly's boss yelled. He and her co-workers were careful to stay away from her in case she had the flu or something. They didn't want to get sick.

Holly nodded dully and waving her hand as Heather carried her to the car.

"You just don't want to go back to work" Heather chided once she had Holly buckled into the car. "I'm beginning to understand your point about the new boss being a jerk."

Holly hung her head out the window and breathed in the fog. She was doing dry heaves now. Her phone buzzed at her, so she handed it to Heather.

"Hey Jasmine, guess what? Holly tossed her cookies all over the place. In fact she's still barfing." Heather smiled as Jasmine ranted and raved. Every time Holly tried to return to work, she puked her brains out for hours at a time. It didn't matter if she ate before or not. Everything in her stomach came up. Her boss always reported it to whoever was in charge of payroll. Holly's stomach did not want her to return to work.

Jeez, Heather thought, it isn't as if she's doing it on purpose. Not one would ever want to be that sick, not in a million years. "Hey, out the window with that. I have to go Jasmine before Holly falls out the car window. Okay. Later." Dropping the cell phone into the cup holder, Heather grabbed the back of Holly's shirt and pulled her back into the car.

The drive home went slowly. The fog had become so thick that it reduced visibility to just ten feet and in some places less.

Holly darted into the house so fast that she almost tripped over MareMoo. She made the bathroom in record time and barely kicked off her shoes before jumping into the tub. She spent several minutes under an icy cold shower.

"Take your clothes off and turn on the hot water. I'm giving you to the count of three." Holly stripped quickly and gave Heather her wet clothes. "I'm going to make you some chicken soup. And I brought you some clean clothes."

"Thank you." Holly grabbed the shampoo and body wash and gave herself a good scrubbing. It was one of the best showers ever. Dressing warmly, she headed for the living room to watch a movie.

Huddling under a blanket, she watched the original Dracula while waiting for the soup. No one did the part like Bela Lugosi. He was the best. He was not the scariest or the sexiest Dracula, but in some ways the most realistic. It was as realistic as a vampire movie was ever going to get. Everyone talked in full sentences. No one hissed or used only one-syllable words. No one had blood red eyes or blood dripping from their face or their fangs. In addition, no one was forced to wear a stupid rubber suit or any Frankenstein like make-up for the scene where drank someone's blood. It was perfect.

"Is he better than Mark Cornridge in Return of the Mark of the Son of Dracula's Brides?" Heather asked as she put a bowl of homemade chicken soup in front of Holly.

"Way better. Cornridge is good but the rest of the movie sucks. Come on now. Ultraviolet radiation comes from the sun, television sets, computer monitors and light bulbs. There's no way to avoid it. Therefore, any vampire sensitive to it would fry up just watching television or going to a store at night. I hate it when they try to be scientific without knowing anything about science. Don't get me started with those idiots who think Dracula was a zillion different historical figures while at the same time that he bursts into flames when sunlight touches him. Name one historical person who has ever burst into flames without someone first dousing him with something flammable and lighting him with a torch."

"You're just too picky. Besides, he has a cute ass."

"That he does. It's world class. Thank you for the soup."

If March had been unseasonably warm, April was proving that winter still had some staying power. A freak late season blizzard was predicted to bring up to a foot of wet snow. Seventy-degree temperatures tonight would soon give way to 20-degree temperatures tomorrow. Already they could hear the wind pick up in advance of the storm front. The temperature had already dropped 20 degrees.

MareMoo cowered in the hallway. She hated loud noises. That's Cleveland weather for you. You can love it or you could move somewhere else. That's how Holly felt about it.

Holly sucked up the broth from the chicken soup and then started working slowly on the noodles, vegetables, and chicken. "Let's watch the Daughter of Dracula next. We need a good laugh."

"No. Let's watch Dracula 2000. Christopher Plummer was so hot in the Sound of Music. He was quite handsome when he was younger."

"He's still good looking. Do you remember when he played the Shakespeare quoting Klingon? And he was quite dignified as the villain in several movies whose name I can't remember." Holly finished her soup as Van Helsing finished Dracula off. She could sleep through any movie if she put her mind to it. She planned to stay up. After the credits finished, she turned on the Daughter of Dracula and prepared to cringe.

The wind began to howl outside. The lights flickered but stayed on. "It's a good thing we had those wind turbines installed." Holly smiled as she settled down with another bowl of soup. God knew she loved homemade soup.

"What wind turbines?"

"The ones you had installed on the new patio out back."

"What new patio? I didn't install any turbines or any patio." Heather ranted as she made her way through the house, flickering on the porch light as she marched to the window facing the back yard and yanked the blinds up. The new patio was a huge two level thing that took up the whole back yard leaving just enough room for MareMoo to run around in and to do her business. Heather shook her head. She had dreamed about having a patio just like it the other night and now they had one. There were other parts of the dream, but she would have to wait until the storm passed before checking out those parts.

+++++++++

Gregori study the view from his mother's hotel room. It was a very nice suite. He wouldn't mind staying there.

"Gregori Matthew Cornridge. You are not listening to a word I have said. What are you looking at?"

"Just the snow, I didn't realize we were going to have so much."

Sophia moved to Gregori's side. The winds were picking up and the visibility was dropping down to zero. She poked her son's waist. "That settles it. You aren't returning home tonight. It's too dangerous."

"You're right. Besides, I've auditions in the morning. I was going to get a room anyway."

"Don't be silly. It's a two-room suite. I have an extra bed. Stay here for the night." Sophia waved her arms and smiled. "Now where are the clothes you packed?"

"In the car, I parked it in the hotel's parking garage."

"Let's go get it. You can tell me about this movie you're going to be in."

"Mum, I haven't got the part yet."

"Of course you will. My little boy can do anything he sets his mind too." Sophia pulled him toward the parking garage. She hoped he packed something warm. The wind was practically shaking the building.

Gregori shook his head. They chatted about his potential new part in a romantic comedy. He was doing a great deal of them lately.

"Ahhh, Mum, I promise to do some action movies for you. The parts just aren't out there now. Did you enjoy our dinner?" Gregori really didn't want to talk work with his mother. She would just go off on those New Lifers. She knew they were plague carriers. She did this even though she was one herself.

"Yes dear, it was delicious. Is that your car?"

"Yep," Gregori retrieved two small suitcases from the trunk. He wasn't sure what he would need to wear for the audition so he brought a selection of clothes. Sophia helped him hang everything up in the spare room's closet.

"You have to get up early. I'll iron these for you. You get some sleep."

Gregori nodded his head. "Good night Mum." As he got ready to sleep, he found himself hoping to see Holly again.

The times he spent with her contrasted vividly with the times, he spent awake with Vanessa. Was marrying Vanessa going to be the biggest mistake of his life? They had wanted the same thing when they first started seeing each other. Now, it was as if they had nothing in common.

Sophia watched Gregori drift off to sleep. After putting his clothes away, she just stood and watched him sleep.

Gregori rolled over in the bed and met Holly's gaze. "Why are you always there when I go to sleep?"

"Why not, I think you're pretty hot for a dream date."

"I think you can dream hotter. But you're the hottest thing I've ever dreamed of." Holly ran her finger down his chest. She never had such fantastic dreams before the fog. On the other hand, maybe, she had a brain tumor and this was all a dream. She hoped not.

"Ahhh, but you're my dream. Babycakes, give me a kiss."

Holly laughed and jumped out of the bed. "You have to catch me first."

Gregori laughed and chased her around the apartment, finally catching her in the suites small kitchen. He received his promised kiss and more.

Sophia frowned. Gregori kept calling out a girl's name as he slept. Someone called Holly. She remembered Vanessa bitching about him doing that. He had finally told her that the only Holly he had known was a childhood pet dog. The dog had been dead for ages. Her grandmother had named the cute little dog, Molly. She gathered as much information as she could. Gregori talked in his sleep.

+++++++++

Holly fell asleep during Dracula 2000 and dreamed of Gregori Cornridge. He was naked and chasing her around a very nice apartment. Not that she really noticed the apartment with Gregori running around it naked. Strange that she didn't dream of any of the actors from the movies she had watched that night.

She woke up in a cold sweat around dawn. The house was very quiet with only the sound of the furnace breaking the silence.

A foot and a half of heavy wet snow had blanketed the region. The snow continued to fall cutting visibility down to a few feet. To make matters worse, a dense fog had settled over the region.

From the way Holly and MareMoo stared at it, you'd have thought they had never seen snow before.

"It's foggy and snowy. Is it a snoggy?"

"A what, a snoggy, what the hell is that?" Heather frowned. Holly was always making up words. "Yes. We have to shovel it. Jasmine's bringing her grand-kids over."

"In this weather? Channel 5 says there's a driving ban for all of Cuyahoga county and Northeastern Ohio until five AM tomorrow."

Heather glared at the television. She had been looking forward to watching Jasmine's grandchildren for the last month. Picking up the phone, she called Jasmine to reschedule.

"MareMoo and I checked out the basement this morning. I know. It's a ranch style house with no basement. I'm telling you we have one now. Come on. The entrance is in the book room."

Heather followed Holly into the book room. They used it as a computer room now and before it was a bedroom. To the left of the door way, where the closet was supposed to be was a stairway, a section of which lead to the attic and the rest of it lead to the new basement. The part above ground was three feet across. The part below ground quickly widened to six feet across. The steps and banister were made of polished cedar. The smell of cedar filled the air.

Underground, the walls of the stairway looked like stone but were cool and dry to the touch. They descended about 45 feet into the bedrock the house.

The basement was 72 feet long, 27 feet wide and 18 feet deep at the walls and 27 feet in the middle. A series of Roman arches formed the walls and ceiling. Roman arches being one of the strongest designs around. A deep blue shag carpet covered the floor. Cedar paneling covered the walls except for a couple of niches. There were two on each wall. The niches showed the wall to be made of the same material as the stairway. A high definition television centered on the far wall with various pieces of comfortable furniture placed around the room. On both sides of the television were shelves full of DVD's. There were thousands of them. Along the tops of the walls were lighting panels made to resemble windows. The ceiling painted a light blue with fleecy white clouds meant to resemble a warm summer sky.

Holly had carried MareMoo down the stairs. It had been easier and faster than trying to coax her down. She placed MareMoo down by the wet bar. It was just under the stairway. Next to the wet bar were bookcases that held all of Holly's favorite authors and titles. There were bookcases with Heather's favorites also. There was a CD player and hundreds of CDs to go along with it. It was peaceful and quiet down there.

The phone rang. It was on the wall next to the wet bar. They ignored it. It wasn't anyone they wanted to talk. Caller-id was a great blessing. It was almost as good as Spam blocker.

Heather discovered additional rooms on the east side. They included a large full bathroom, and two bedrooms and a laundry room. The bedrooms were 20 by 18 feet each. Each decorated to their individual tastes. Holly's was in the south and right next to the laundry room. Heather is to the north and next to the bathroom. The bathroom was 15 by 21 feet. The bathroom had a hot tub that could fit six, along with a massive tub, a sink and a toilet. The laundry room was smaller, being only 9 by 15 feet. There was a small foyer between the bedrooms and in front of the bathroom and laundry room. It was 5 by 21 feet. They decided to open up the door and make it work with the rest of the basement.

"Do you realize that this is bigger than our house?" Heather approved. She personally thought it was a ploy to get her to clean more. She could almost never get Holly to clean.

They spent several amazed minutes watching as MareMoo slipped through a door on the west side of the room and disappeared. Following her, they found another set of rooms. These lead down to a set of stairs that lead up to the new patio outside. A warning light by the door told them the weight of the snow outside made it too dangerous to open the door at this time.

They spent the next couple of days exploring.

+++++++++

It had been just over a week since the snowstorm. The streets had just become passable a little over three days before. Two of Jasmines grandchildren, Hugo and Katrina, had been over for a visit. They were Jamaica's children. Jasmine had them while the courts finalized Jamaica's divorce.

Heather had spoiled them rotten during their brief visit.

Jasmine's other daughter, Wendy, had them tonight. This would be the first time they would really get to discuss the new basement with her.

Holly pulled up her legs as MareMoo and Trouble chased each other around the house. Jasmine's dog, Trouble, was a skinny dog with soft shiny black fur. They were in the new basement. It was warmer there.

"So you just think about things and they show up? What makes you so special?" Jasmine asked with more than a hint of doubt in her voice.

"The only thing that makes me special is having you for a sister." Holly declared as the dogs jumped over her to get to each other.

"We're not special. I'm sure other people can do this. Would you report a sudden increase in your property value? Hello. I've a completely new roof, attic, basement and some other property improvements. They just appeared out of nowhere. I didn't get permits for them, pay for them, or have them inspected or anything. My income hasn't gone up and I have no way to pay for any of this. Can you come out and raise my property tax for me? I don't think so. I mean would you?"

"I guess not." Jasmine admitted reluctantly as Heather poured her another cup of coffee.

"It seems to be a matter of getting two or more people to agree on what they want. And of course, you'll really want to have it."

"Try it tonight. What have you to lose?" Heather placed a mug of coffee in front of herself and Jasmine. Holly didn't drink coffee.

"My sanity" Jasmine replied. "Thanks for the coffee."

"Let's picture a new subbasement for you. It'll be under the existing basement but slightly larger than it."

Their minds touched. They pictured the design from a book the one Jasmine had once mentioned she liked. About 15 minutes later, Jasmine received a panicky call from Wendy.

"Mom a deep passage just opened in the basement! What am I supposed to do?" Wendy said this so it sounded like one word. She had to repeat it several times before they could understand her.

"Take a deep breathes and hit the light switch on the right side, just inside the door. Did you find it?"

"How did you know that it was there?" Wendy's voice was definitely striving for a higher pitch.

"Did the lights go on?"

"Yes, but …."

"Okay. Send Colin down first."

"He's at work. No. Mina, you come back here young lady." Thud. Thud.

Thud. "Hugo. Katrina. You two come back here. Stop encouraging her." Thud. Thud. Thud.

"Gotcha. Whoa. Where'd this room come from? It's huge." Wendy babbled as she followed Mina around. She described everything to Jasmine until Jasmine's cell phone died. Then she called back on Heather's landline and talked for another two hours.

+++++++++

Holly had become bored and restless. May sixth already, and it was proving impossible to get permission to go back to work with the government in complete disarray with so many businesses closing.

She needed to do something. In a fit of boredom, she picked up the original Dracula novel and began to read. Halfway through the novel she decided Quincy needed his story told. He is one of the four characters in the book who never get to tell their story. The other three who never get to tell their story are Dracula, Van Helsing and Lucy. No one in the original novel or later adaptations understood that Quincy was the vampire who had turned poor Miss Lucy.

He became angry when Lucy had refused his offer of marriage, and tried to woo her back at her with many little kisses, which just made her tired. Then that fool Arthur Holmwood asked that nutcase John Stewart to look in on her. Another rejected suitor and an evil man. He had plans of his own for Lucy. Van Helsing's treatments killed her.

When the Harkers returned, the fools became completely convinced that Dracula was their vampire. They never bother to look for any other vampire. They would never believe that Quincy and Dracula might be the same species.

Quincy's salvation lies in this belief. That fool Van Helsing would have staked him if his secret had gotten out. The story had to extend for a decade or more after the original novel ended.

The whole idea excited Holly. She set out to write it immediately. It went quickly with the original novel as a guide. Family advice made it possible for the finished draft to be ready in record time. She did not allow every member of her family to see it.

+++++++++

Dracula rose from his underground crypt. He shot from the earth and tasted the fresh air with a cry of triumph. It had been over a 100 years since he had last tasted freedom. He twirled around and soon realized he was still underground. How had he come to be there was a complete mystery to him? He set out to explore his new environment and to feed. He felt as confused and had no idea why his memories were so fragmented. However, they were.

Several other men rose from the ground around him. They all claimed to be the real Dracula. The four of them headed to the city center to feed, explore and argue.

Chapter 3

Holly kicked her feet as she sat on the examining table. She felt good. The best she had ever felt in all her 51 years. She looked and felt like an 18 year old. However, the doctors were worried about something. Perhaps, it was her loss of weight. She now weighed 105 pounds. Losing 120 pounds in a month would frighten any sane person. In fact, she had lost it in the 72-hour period since the fog converted into a New Lifer. Holly wondered about her sanity. Far from being frightened, she felt excited. Everything had become exciting and new to her as if she had become a newborn baby experiencing life for the first time. She felt sadness of the patient next to her. His respirator and other life support that Holly could not identify made loud humming noises. He weighed over 650 pounds. No one expected to live.

'He's a nice man who simply liked food too much.' Holly thought as she went over to talk to him. Looking him straight in the eyes, she introduced herself to him. "Hi, my name is Holly Skyhaven."

"Mine is Bruce Harwood."

Holly told about herself and about Heather. She made sure to keep eye contact with him. She hated when people would talk to her without looking at her. It was just plain rude. The events of the last few months fascinated him.

"Why hasn't this fog helped me?"

"I don't know, maybe your respirator kept most of it away from you. Or it might be because the hospital is sealed tightly against outside influences?"

"Maybe you should just bite me and change me over. That's how it works in all those Dracula movies."

"I'm not sure. I think we need a blood exchange. It works that way in all the books I've ever read. Sometimes more than one exchange is needed."

"Baugh, just bite me and let's see what happens."

"Okay. Where do you want me to bite you?"

"Um, on the neck, just like in the movies."

Looking worried, Holly did as Bruce suggested. She drank about eight ounces of his blood before carefully licking the wound to close it before sitting down again. Bruce tasted good. He tasted unbelievably good. She would have to watch herself around him. She talked to Bruce about the weather.

"Nothing is happening." Bruce whined after almost five minutes had past. "Do it again."

"Blood exchange," Holly repeated. Watching the hallway carefully, Holly cut her wrist with her fingernail and allowed Bruce to drink several ounces. She had just closed the wound when Bruce's doctor came in. Holly returned to her room to give them some privacy.

An hour later, Holly's doctor came in. Bruce watched Holly leave as his doctor came in and began examining his machines. There was something about her. Some things that made him feel better. Better than he had ever felt about himself in his entire life. It was hard to explain. He had known he had to listen to her the moment she appeared at his bedside. 'Holly is my salvation.' He thought. After their exchange, he found he could hear better, even his eyesight and sense of smell seemed sharper.

The doctor kept checking and rechecking Bruce's vital signs. Then he called in another doctor who did the same thing. Soon a large group of doctors and nurses gathered around Bruce.

"Well Bruce," one doctor finally said in incomprehensible doctor speaks. "It seems your health has made considerable improvement since I checked in on you this morning. I don't know why, but all of your vital signs are showing improvement. I am cautiously optimistic."

At this time, they heard a loud noise from the next room. It was half squeak and half shout. "What do you mean my uterus and ovaries have grown back? Isn't that like brain cells growing back? Isn't that impossible?"

Everyone looked toward Holly's room. No one knew what to say.

Bruce's literary agent, Frank TeCruzada, came in at this time. Frank having heard Bruce's life story had decided it would make a great book. Bruce needed the money to pay his hospital bills. He did not want to be a burden to his family. They weren't talking to him since he had come out of the closet during his last illness.

Frank waited for Bruce's doctors to leave before approaching Bruce. Bruce quickly introduced Frank to Holly after telling Frank about Holly's novel.

Holly reluctantly showed Frank the copy of 'Quincy" she had been working on. By the time Heather came to pick her up, Frank had signed Holly on as a client.

Everyone exchanged phone numbers.

+++++++++

Holly knocked tentatively on the door to Bruce's room. The door was open but she didn't want to just barge in uninvited. The one time she had done that his mother had been there. Good old Momma had been going on and on about how his illness was God's punishment for his sinful lifestyle and how he was going to go straight to hell.

Eventually the nurse had asked her to leave. Bruce became extremely depressed after each of her visits. Hospital officials would no longer allow Momma Harword into Bruce's room.

"Come on in Holly." Bruce called. Bruce's nurse was taking his blood pressure. He was losing about 60 pounds a day and had already lost 300 since meeting Holly.

The nurse was having some trouble taking a blood sample. She couldn't get the needle to penetrate his skin.

Holly walked quietly into his room. "Hey Bruce, you're looking good. Soon we'll have you at the beach in a little Speedo strutting around. No one will be able to take their eyes off you."

"Sure Holly, whatever you say. Has Frank gotten in touch with you yet?"

"He said he'd call Monday. He has a couple of things lined up. He didn't want to talk to me about them yet. What about you?"

"He's coming by this afternoon. He is assigning me someone to help me with my writing. They'll be coming in together."

Holly nodded. She felt comfortable with Bruce. She never felt like he was judging her poorly because of her choices or the way she had lead her life so far. He was becoming a good friend. It was just easy for her to talk to him.

They talked about the weather. Holly would have to undergo more tests before they decided whether she could go back to work or not. Her sisters, Heather and Jasmine, kept harping about that.

They talked about Bruce's family and their doctors. They had not told the doctors how Holly had converted Bruce. The doctors could wonder forever how that miracle had happened. It was funny watching them scramble for an explanation. Someday when Bruce was out of the hospital and Holly was back to work they would tell them. However, they would not tell them before then.

It was about an hour into Holly's visit when they realized they could read each other's minds without others knowing about it. Telepathy was the norm for New Lifers. After some trying, they found they could disguise their identity telepathically. They could project the identity of someone else and fool the people around them into believing they were that other person. It was a cool new power. They did not want to share it with anyone yet.

"Brucey Baby. Why won't those bitches you have for nurses allow me to see you?" Momma Harwood demanded. She had somehow gotten past security.

"Because you always put him down," Holly blurted. She picked up on Momma Harwood's fear of vampires and projected a classic Christopher Lee Dracula moment at her. It was all red contacts and bared fangs.

Bruce pressed the nurse's button frantically. He unconsciously picked up Holly's image and projected Bela Lugosi Dracula. His classic pose used it the 1931 film.

Two male nurses escorted the screaming Momma Harwood out. The police came and took her to a holding cell so she could sober up. No one saw anything unusual about Holly and Bruce.

They were still laughing about it an hour later when Frank came in with a hunky blonde dude. He looked like a Viking warrior. A well feed, well-dressed healthy blonde Viking with a suntan that came from a tanning salon. It was perfect.

"Hi, I'm Doug Bereven." The Viking said as he smiled at Bruce.

"Doug is going to help you put down your thoughts Bruce. He'll write down what you say then transcribe everything onto his computer and get it ready for publication for you."

"We're pleased to meet you Doug." Holly cut in when Bruce just kept staring at Doug. "Are you single?"

"Yes" Doug laughed. "I'm also gay."

"So is Bruce here. In a couple of days, Bruce is going to have to fight off unwanted attention from every single person in the state. If I were you, I would snatch him up before someone else does. He's the catch of a lifetime and a real keeper."

"Holly" Bruce exclaimed. Holly could just make out the serious blush he had going. His naturally dark skin coloring hid the blush from all but the most careful observers.

"See what I mean? He's a real catch." Holly nodded at Doug. "I've got to be going. I'll stop by tomorrow. Do you want me to Bruce?"

"Of course I do." Bruce grabbed Holly's hand and tugged. She bent down and kissed him on the forehead.

"Tomorrow then," Holly shook Doug's hand and whispered. "He's a real fine catch. You'd be a fool to pass him up."

Doug smiled broadly, as he shook Holly's hand. "I think you might just be right about that," he whispered back.

Frank shook his head. "I'll walk you to your car. It's getting late and there are all sorts of nut cases running around. You should have seen the woman the police dragged out when we got here. She kept screaming that her son and his girlfriend were really Dracula."

"Ohm, Heather has the car. I walked. It's only a couple of miles."

"Oh Holly" Bruce and Frank moaned in unison.

"There are vampire killers out there ready to kill any New Lifer they can get their hands on." Doug admonished. "I lost my baby sister to those lunatics just last month. Is that what you want?"

Holly stuck out her bottom lip. The boys were going to be hard asses about this. "Really guys, I can take care of myself. There's no reason to worry about me. I'll be fine." Three sets of eyes looked at her as if she was a complete idiot.

"Bruce, Doug, I'll be right back after I drive Holly home. Why don't the two of you take the time to get to know each other better?"

"Sounds good, Bye Holly."

"See you tomorrow Holly." Bruce shook his head as Frank escorted Holly home. "I know she's older than me, but I can't help thinking of her as my long lost baby sister.

She is so naive. It's mind blowing."

"I can see the family resemblance." Doug joked dryly.

"So you're going to be my scribe. Huh?"

"Yep. Do you have any family besides Holly?"

"Yeah, I got six older brothers and two older sisters. They live in Cincinnati. They wanted to stay close to our parents and grandparents. My

Momma was just here. She wanted me to know that I'm going to hell for my sinful lifestyle. I think she was the crazy woman you and Frank saw on your way up."

Doug nodded. "So you're the seventh son. Was your father also the seventh son?"

"I think so. Is it important?"

"I'm not sure. Have you ever turned into a werewolf during a full moon?"

"No."

"Then it isn't important. Are you close to any of your family?"

"No. They excommunicated me when I came out of the closet. Though Momma keeps coming around to harass me with her belief that God's punishing me for my many, many sins." Bruce shrugged casually, but his family's rejection still stung. "Good ole Momma couldn't wait to tell me I'm going straight to hell."

"Your family is Baptist? Mine's Catholic and they feel the same way."

"Yeah, they're Southern Baptist. They moved up from the South during the 1950's." Bruce nodded as Doug pulled out a digital recorder. "Where do you think I should begin?"

"At the beginning," Doug laughed as Bruce began not with his birth but with the birth of the universe.

+++++++++

Holly placed a steaming hot cup of tea in front of Heather and her other sister Jasmine. Tea being one of the few things most people could still tolerate. It was already August 8 and there was still no word on when she could go back to work.

"My ovaries, uterus and fallopian tubes had grown back, but not my intestines or stomach. No one can tell me why. I don't think they know why. Is that enough sugar? Is that too much information?"

"It's fine. I wasn't listening."

"You know what the worst part is? I can get pregnant now. Birth control doesn't work for us now. The microbes that made us New Lifers keep neutralizing them. At least I won't get my period. Freaky huh?"

"Will you sit down? You're making me nervous. When can you go back to work? Did they say when you can go back?" Jasmine sipped her tea. It was just like Holly not to ask about work. "And why are you worried about getting pregnant? You have to find a man first. You have to have sex first. Then you can worry about getting pregnant."

"Yes, I did ask. No, they want to do more tests. Have you read Quincy yet? You've been promising." She ignored the jab about finding a man.

"Yes, it is quite good. I blushed in several sections."

"You said that about my last novel and it was crap."

"No, I mean it. It's good. You've got to get it published."

"Before you give it to all your friends and let them read it." Telepathy was a bitch when it came to keeping secrets. "I talked to Frank, the agent Bruce helped me get. A couple of publishers are interested. He said he would get back to me tonight."

"Cards or scrabble?" Heather asked, changing the subject. Jasmine did not like Bruce for some reason.

"Scrabble, but you're going to have to help me. I can never think of any words."

"Are you feeling well? You hate Scrabble."

"Do not. I just have a hard time thinking up words." Holly stuck out her bottom lip. Why did they have to make everything so difficult? On the other hand, maybe it was she. She didn't want to think about going back to work. Every time she got within a mile of the place, she lost the contents of her stomach. Laying out the board, she reached into the bag and pulled out a tile. "I've got an E."

"I've got a Q," Heather smirked.

"J," Jasmine sighed. "Do you want me to keep score?"

"What do you think?"

Holly stared at the letters she picked, and then checked the dictionary to see if it was really a word. It was. "Lemures, that's a double word score and I've used all of my letters."

"It's not spelled that way."

"Yes it is."

"No it is not. It's spelled with just a -s."

"That's the monkey. This is the ghosts of the dead in the ancient Roman religion."

"Let me check it out. Damn, she's right." The phone rang.

"Wait. I think that's Frank now. Hello? Yes. It is. It has. How much? That much! Wait. Tell Heather so I can make sure I'm hearing you correctly."

Holly handed the phone to Heather, whose eyes grew large. After a brief exchange, Heather hung up. "Frank will be over tonight to go over the paperwork and get your signature. He thinks you might be able to get a movie deal out of it."

Holly fainted.

"The ghosts of the dead in the ancient Roman religion," Jasmine muttered to herself.

+++++++++

Holly gazed around the room intently. She found herself sitting on the bench of a water fountain. Everything gave a peaceful and calm feeling.

A man approached her. He reminded her of someone she had seen before, but she could not place him. He had wavy shoulder length black hair, bushy eyebrows and deep-set, glacial blue eyes. Tall, he was perhaps six feet four inches. Holly continued to watch him, as he seemed to survey the room the room without moving.

"Tell me about you" Holly encouraged. "What kind of vampire are you? Are you the kind that needs an invitation to enter a home? You just cannot enter. Am I right? Can you turn people? And if you can, how do you do it?"

Dracula gazed at the young woman before him. There was something odd going on here. He could not quite put his finger on it. He knew that normally when around women he would just seduce them and suck them dry. He had no such urge here. In fact, he found the idea revolting.

"To answer your question, yes I can turn people. I'm the kind who turns everyone I bite. They turn quite quickly. It usually takes only a couple of hours. I am the first of my kind. I need an invitation to come into a residence before I can enter it the first time. I can enter it freely after that. The invitation cannot be revoked."

"Why do you turn people just by biting them? All the other vampires I've talked to tell me a blood exchange needs to be done. Some say the change may require more than one exchange. Why are you different?"

"I don't know. I guess they based the movie on the book. Everyone he bites turns into a vampire in Stoker's Dracula."

"Actually only poor Lucy is turned. I think Van Helsing is a quack. I think that's why Dracula had Mina drink his blood. It's the only way to turn someone." Holly pulled out two paperbacks and handed them to Dracula.

"Here I want you to read these. They will offer you a different perspective on the story. I think you'll like them."

Dracula barely looked at the titles as he stuffed them into his coat pocket. "How will this help?"

"Find the qualities you admire in these characters and see yourself as having those qualities. What have you got to lose?"

"I repeat. How will this help?" Dracula gritted his teeth. This was useless.

"You believe your bite turns people right away because it is in the book. Am I right?"

"Yes. That's how it is in the book."

"No it isn't. It took many months for poor Lucy to die. In fact, Van Helsing's blood transfusions probably killed her. You can't have much of an appetite if everyone you bite turns. The only one we know of for sure who you bit in the book is Lucy. Otherwise there would have been vampires running around all over the place in the book and there aren't." Holly reached down and played with the water in the fountain. "I must repeat. Lucy is the only one turned in the book. Now one else is turned. I guess you're not much of a vampire. Are you?"

"I am too." Dracula frowned. "Lucy is really the only one turned? What about Mina?"

"She went on to have a child and to lead a normal life. Well as normal, a life as one can have when living with a bore like Jonathan Harker. Tell me more about you."

"I burst into flames when sunlight touches me. I'm more than 2012 years old. Do you have any more questions?" He hated to ask, but felt compelled to. He really liked this young woman. She disliked Harker as much as he did.

"Why?"

"Why what?"

"Why do you burst into flames in sunlight? It's not in the book. In the book, you walked around in broad daylight. You wore a hat and clothes, of course, but otherwise you were unprotected. This idea that sunlight destroys vampires is a movie thing. It's not in the original novel." Holly wondered mildly what he would look like without his clothes.

Dracula looked blankly at Holly. "That is in the book?"

"Yes, you really need to read it. Can you handle all this reading?" Dracula nodded his head. "That's my boy. I'll see you in a couple of weeks."

Dracula woke up. He had the Anointed Dracula in his hand and two other books in his coat pocket. He had no idea where the books had come from or why he had been dreaming of them, or even whom the young girl who had given them to him was. How strange, he thought as he started to read.

+++++++++

Holly gazed around the spacious dining room in awe. She had never been is such an upscale restaurant before. Bruce took her hand as they followed Frank and Marlene TeCruzada to their table. She clung to him, half expecting someone to object to her being there. Surely, someone is going to be coming over and tell her she had to leave, and then escorting her out. It would be so embarrassing. Frank pulled out a chair for her and smiled encouragingly at her.

Marlene smiled encouragingly at Holly and Bruce. They both looked so nervous. They were like little children invited to play with the big kids, shy and nervous. It was so cute. Marlene had to hide her smile behind the menu. She tried to look interested in it while watching Holly and Bruce.

Holly stared at the menu. She didn't have the slightest idea of what she should order. Nothing looked appealing, yet at the same time everything did. Everything was so expensive.

"Do you want me to order for you?" Bruce leaned closer to Holly and pointed out a couple of items he thought she might like. "Look chicken, you like that. Don't you?"

"That's not chicken. Its steak," Holly squeaked.

"The chicken looks good. I think I'll have that."

Bruce patted her leg under the table. "Now what kind of side dish do you want?"

"Salad."

"Fries or a vegetable?"

"I want a salad, but fries will be okay."

"And to drink?"

"Water."

"Um."

"Water, I have to drive home tonight."

"Okay," Bruce ordered her and himself a screwdriver when the server took their orders for steaks and fries. Frank had scotch bourbon with his surf and turf. Marlene had wine with hers.

They talked all about the things Holly and Bruce would have to do when they went on tour. "If we go together," Bruce explained when Frank looked doubtful, "then Holly won't be so nervous."

"That's a good idea, Frank." Marlene took a sip of her wine, batting her eyelashes at Frank in the way that always annoyed him. "And she should take some of her family with her. That way there won't be any gossip about her and Bruce."

Frank studied the nervous pair in front of him. They would need someone to coach them too. He mentioned this briefly as their server arrived with their food.

Holly nibbled on her food and very slowly sipped her drink. She knew alcohol would help her relax, but she did not want them thinking alcohol was the only way to loosen her up. That path would only lead to trouble and ruin. "Bruce! You stop that. I told you...."

"Not to push it," he finished. 'But I can't help myself,' he thought to her. Their mind touched often lately. They developed a strong telepathic bond. It was such a strong bond that none of the other New Lifers could hear them when they communicated that way. The others heard only silence. Bruce and Holly often chatted that way.

"We can do this." Bruce smiled as Holly announced this. "We work very well as a team."

"Then it's settled. Bruce and Holly will do this as a team. Isn't that right Frank?"

"Yes my darling wife." Frank said while mentally calculating the growing cost of the tour. It was beginning to add up.

"Then it's settled. This way we'll save money. It would cost twice as much to send them on separate tours."

"Except for the details," Holly and Bruce said together.

"I'll work that out. I want to see you go out and about town together. Out to dinner or lunch three or four times a week. I think I can arrange for your first interview to be close by. I have something coming up in Cincinnati. Is that okay?"

"Yes master."

"And cut out the group act. It's getting creepy."

"Yes our master." Bruce and Holly laughed loudly to themselves, while fighting to keep a straight face.

+++++++++

Myles listened to the television. Both stories appealed to him, but Holly's story felt stronger to him. Her book was ready for publication and she had a movie deal. Bruce's book would be published a month after Holly's.

Perhaps they'll make it into a movie. Perhaps not, actors were a good vehicle for spreading the New Life to the rest of the world.

It would help their cause that Holly appeared young and fresh. She could be everyone's sister or daughter. Someone they could relate to and trust. Myles smiled. By sending out telepathic inquires, he knew he would soon be able to contact her.

+++++++++

Bruce and Holly bounced around the downtown area. They had never spent any time in Cincinnati before and wanted to make the most of it. "It is getting late, but the bars are still open." Holly laughed at something Bruce said. She turned toward a bar named the Lemures. "The night is young."

Bruce swore as Holly disappeared around the corner. He could hear her distinctive squeak of fear. Something was wrong. He mentally sent out a distress to any New Lifer in the area.

"You bitch. You and your kind think you own the world. Well, you don't." He had Holly by the throat. Holly squeaked again and clawed the man's face.

She grabbed the wrist of his free arm and bit him, drinking deep and fast. Holly licked the wound and it closed quickly. When he let go, she kicked him in the balls. A small group of New Lifers and police suddenly surrounded them.

A man flashed his badge at Holly. "It's okay miss.

We'll take care of this," indicating the men. "You're free to go."

"Thank you officer," Bruce wrapped his arms around Holly and led her from the alleyway. Heather joined them there. Bruce shook his head before Heather could say anything.

They walked a short way before meeting Myles Ludwig.

Chapter 4

Gregori felt ill. He had developed a cough that would just not go away. His chest hurt all the time. He had a hard time just trying to catch his breath. His head throbbed. He tried to ignore it. It only got worse.

"Darling, you need to see a doctor about that cough."

"I did Mum. I saw one this morning." He glanced at his mother. Since the fog, she had become younger and healthier. His mother now looked 20 years younger than him. This had become disturbing trend with everyone he knew getting younger. He glanced outside at the late November snowfall. They were expecting only four or five inches.

"What did he say?" Sophia became concerned. He looked tired and older than his years, his black hair streaked with gray. The dark shadows under his dark green eyes made them look sunken. She thought he had been worrying too much and he needed to lose weight. He always ate junk food. It was killing him.

"She had some tests done and said she would get back to me with the results. I've an appointment with her in a week to go over the test results. Do you want more tea?"

Sophia bit her lip. If the doctor said she would see him in a week to go over the test results then it must be serious. Otherwise, she would just give him the results over the phone. She did not like to think of anything being seriously wrong with her baby boy. "No, darling, I'm okay. Where is Vanni? I haven't seen her in quite a while."

"You know how she feels about the city. She wanted to do some shopping out in the country. A new shopping center just opened not far from where we live. Are you going to finish your sandwich?"

"No, I'm not hungry. Do you want it?" Sophia sighed. Gregori still has a good appetite.

"Yes, please," Gregori loved food. He especially loved junk food. He had to work hard to keep his figure, though he only did so while working a job. He did not have a job now. It had been a few months since his last job. It was definitely showing.

Handing over her sandwich, Sophia smiled. "Are you still having dreams about that girl?"

Gregori choked on his sandwich, and glared at his mother. The dreams were becoming more intense over time, more vivid.

"I'll take that as a yes." Sophia had done some investigating. She had so far been unable to determine who Holly was or why Gregori kept dreaming about her. It was only a matter of time. Sophia would find this person and have it out with her. Another gold digger, Sophia knew for sure, just someone out to get Gregori's money. She had to be like Vanessa in that. Sophia knew that no woman could possibly be good enough for her baby boy.

"What are you talking about?"

"I'm sorry darling. I learned about her when you came to visit me a couple of months ago. You do know that you talk in sleep. Don't you?"

"Do I?"

"Yes, you kept calling her name out. I told Vanni she was a girl you had a crush on as a teenager, but she died in a car crash. And also, the name of a childhood pet dog. Is it all right that I did that?"

"I love you Mum."

"I love you too, darling. You will tell me what the doctor finds. Won't you?"

"Of course, I will."

"And I need you to tell me everything you remember from your dreams about this Holly."

+++++++++

Holly bounced around happily. Myles had asked her to help spread the New Life to Europe. She would get to travel and to prove herself worthy. It helped her that the studio planned to make her new book Quincy into a movie. Better yet, her publisher planned to release her first novel she wrote years ago, Fangs for Nothing. She could now officially quit her cashier job. She could say goodbye to waiting on cranky customers, though some of them were nice and she would miss her fellow employees. Writing would be her full time job now.

She was officially going to Europe to promote the book and movie. While Holly preened for the press, others would be aiding those who wanted to receive New Life. Excitement filled her household. They would arrive in New York on November 23. She hoped Frank had secured the rooms. She hated the idea of sleeping in the lobby. She planned to take as many family members as she could. No one had been out of the state in years, and Holly had never left the country before. New York would be her first stop, then Europe. She would get to do the Dracula tour while she was there. She had always wanted to do that.

What do I pack? Holly thought excitedly. Whom would they pick to be in the movie? Holly's thoughts were all over the place. She was just too excited to concentrate. It was so confusing. She was not use to being happy. It was going to take some time to get used to the foreign emotion.

"Oh look," Holly peer at the television. "It's Joanne from work." Holly turned the volume up and smiled. It was nice seeing someone from work. She remembered when they had gone to the strip club for her 70th birthday. It had been a blast. Turning up the volume, Holly watched Joanne interview a scientist.

"So you're saying that histatins are the reasons that wounds heal when we lick them." Joanne leaned close to him and placed her hand on his arm. She is a real passionate woman, and a lover of all things male.

"That's right, Joanne. Normal human saliva as well as the saliva of animals naturally contains histatins. The saliva of New Lifers contains 1000 times the amount of histatins found in normal human saliva." The scientist gave

Joanne gave him her warmest smile. "There is still work to be done on the connections being a New Lifer and the amounts of histatins and complex growth factors a New Lifer body produces."

"How long until something definite is known?"

"We are positive that histatins are the major healing factors in New Lifers. I've seen New Lifers lick a wound and not only was it completely healed. There will not even be a scar. That's the work of super powered histatins. The rest is up to conjecture."

"Well," Joanne smiled at the camera. "We hope to be hearing more from you Doctor Smith on this exciting discovery. Thank you for your time."

"It was my pleasure." A voice comes over the picture, "And today on celebrity gossips."

"Do you think I'll meet any celebrities while I'm in New York?" Holly mused as she turned on the Weather Channel.

"Not that ugly asshole, Gregori Cornridge," Otto sneered. He thought Gregori to be an over rated hack. He had no idea what his Mom and Aunts saw in that strutting peacock.

"He doesn't strut and happens to be a fine actor with a fine singing voice. Steven Gram isn't a better actor though he is a better singer. And neither is Anton Wilkinson."

"Yes, he is. You and Mom are just horny for Gregori. Don't take that purple thing." Otto grimaced.

"You can go to hell." Holly placed the purple thing on the pile of things she planned on taking.

"Suit you," Otto shrugged as he passed Nicole in the hallway. Nicole and Otto were expecting their first child in late February.

"Let me help you or you'll be at this all night."

"Thanks Nicole, I could use some help."

Holly had finally finished packing two hours later. She gazed at the television. She kept blanking out and missing the local on the eights. Damn that Weather Channel, they were always playing such hypnotic music. One minute you were watching some storm system hit the Midwest then poof; you were daydreaming about a Caribbean vacation or somewhere else where it is warm and sunny.

"That snow storm had better miss us. I don't want our plane delayed for any reason." What was that about Yellowstone Park? Holly focused on the television. It was hard to concentrate with MareMoo licking her feet, so she turned the volume up. The park moved up to a higher earthquake alert category. Earthquakes had forced the park to close for the first time in recorded history. The surrounding towns and cities were on alert. Be ready to evacuate at a moment's notice. Park Officials were optimistic that the park would reopen soon. They expressed gratitude that this was happening during the slow winter season, and not when the park had millions of visitors who would need to evacuate.

Holly tried to remember everything she had ever heard about the Yellowstone supervolcano. If it went up, it would be the largest eruption in recorded history. It would be 100 to 1000 times more powerful than the eruption of 1816. That eruption prevented summer of 1817 from coming. The volcanic winter killed more crops and people then the eruption itself. The complete middle part of the United States would become a vast wasteland of volcanic ash. The breadbasket of the world would stop existing. The loose of life would be catastrophic. Billions of people would die worldwide from the resulting famine and ice age, which could last a decade at the best, centuries at the worst.

"Those are some nice depressing thoughts. When did you get so cheerful?" Otto plopped down on the couch. He and Nicole would be taking care of MareMoo while everyone else went with Holly for the book and movie tour. They hoped to be away no more than a month.

"The same time I became the life of the party. Must you be so annoying?"

"Yes, I do have to be annoying." Otto grabbed the controller and changed the channel. Grunting he turned on a Dracula movie. Not the good one, but the one from the 1970's with Mark Cornridge and a bunch of people who went on to bigger things. Dracula rose from his underground crypt like a superman.

+++++++++

Sophia Cornridge stared across the lobby of the expensive hotel she had been staying at since the beginning of the plague. Some called it the New Life, but until she returned to England, it was the plague to her. She could have chosen to stay with her son, Gregori. Nevertheless, the English government was paying her rent. Why should she hide out in the country?

Gregori liked staying in western New York State with his girlfriend Vanessa Lee. His home was more than a three hours' drive from New York City. Vanessa had made him move out there when they announced their engagement more than a year ago. Vanessa hated the City.

Sophia loved it. Sophia wanted Gregori to be happy, but she really hated Vanessa. Vanessa was a gold digger and a slut. The television blared news about the fat middle-aged cancer victim whose vampire novel a major studio planned on making into a movie. Sophia felt certain that this Holly was the same one her Gregori had been dreaming. She did not like her anymore then she liked Vanessa. She knew the woman had a crush on Gregori. He had done more than a few movies with nude scenes in them. Why couldn't nice young girls chase after him? Why is it always gold diggers? Perhaps if he had done fewer nude scenes he would have better luck. The fog had not affected Gregori and Vanessa. They lived too inland for the fog to reach them. They did not have the plague.

"Maybe you'll get to meet him," Bruce chided.

"You act like it's the equivalent of getting the bubonic plague. I want to meet him."

"I don't want to meet him." Holly became distraught. They knew how much she hated meeting people one on one, in groups, or at all. The interviews would be okay. They were coaching her on what to say in them. Good think they did not know about the erotic dreams she had been having about him. "I can't believe you told people I had a crush on him. Why would you do that?"

"It's the truth. Beside they asked, do you remember your first crush? Think about those dreams you've had about him."

"That doesn't mean you have to tell everyone. I'm so embarrassed. I could just die."

"It's good copy." Frank added. Frank was all about good copy and the press. It did not matter to Frank if it was good or bad press, as long as it was press. It is what made him good at his job. One could easily get tired of Frank.

Holly turned and found a woman staring at her from across the lobby as they reached the receptionist's desk and signed in. Good God, she thought, is that Gregori Cornridge's mother?

Sophia stared at the young girl who could only be Holly Skyhaven. Sophia was just stunned. She had pictured her as an old fat gold digger, but here was a young girl who was embarrassed because someone in her party told the press she had a crush on Gregori. Holly felt too embarrassed to even meet with Gregori, if Sophia heard them right. Sophia held Holly's eyes for a few moments, then Holly turned away blushing.

"That's his mother over there." Holly stated as they got the key cards to their rooms. She looked at the floor. "Why do you always have to publicly embarrass me?"

"I don't always embarrass you. Sometimes you do it yourself. Look, she's coming this way."

Frank placed a steadying hand on Holly's back. She was okay once she gets to know someone, but the first meeting was hard on her.

"So, you're the one with the crush on my little boy?"

"It's been over a year. I hardly thought of him that way since I became sick. I've been too busy writing to think about anything else." Holly blushed from head to foot. Her answers seemed lame to her. I could definitely die right here and now, she thought.

"And you're wondering if he tastes good doesn't count?"

"I wonder if everyone tastes good now. When I'm hungry everyone looks like a tasty treat to me, even Frank here."

Sophia laughed. Gregori had gained weigh recently and to Sophia he looked like a plumb little sausage. She worried about his health. He smoked too much. "I think we're going to be good friends."

"You think I can get you back to Europe?"

"That would be good."

"I don't have to meet him?"

"Not if you don't want to." Sophia found herself crossing her fingers behind her back. Those two needed to meet.

"I'll believe that when I see it." Jasmine announced to no one.

"I don't want to."

"I do," Heather chimed in.

"Will he be in the movie?" Sophia prompted.

"That's up to the director, and whether he wants to be in it."

"And the list you gave the director?"

"Just a suggestion, I have no visual imagination so I used pictures of real actors to help me visualize each character. She can pick any actor she wants for the part. I have no say in it. I just get a copy of the DVD when it comes out. I don't even have to go to any of the premieres"

"Are you really? You're not going to the premiere?"

"I'm not big on movies. I prefer books to movies. I like vampire romance novels." Holly frowned. She could not remember the director's name. "Anyway, he worked for her before. I remember her saying on one of the DVDs how great he is to work with. She really likes him."

Sophia tapped her foot. "Is there something wrong?"

"I can't remember the director's name. I know I should know it, but I'm drawing a blank."

"Laura Sanders," everyone sighed in frustration. Holly and names is like water in a sieve. They went straight through without leaving a trace of their passage.

Sophia looked into Holly's eyes and thought of a waif who needed protection, a child in need of a mother. "I've been stuck here for far too long. Let me show you the town tonight."

"Do you know where I can get some inexpensive cigarettes at?" Heather inquired. Everyone else made coughing noises.

"Well, yes I do. What brand do you smoke?" Sophia followed them to their room, chatting about all the places to see while they were in New York. While Holly put her stuff into the room, Heather and Sophia plotted to get Gregori and Holly together.

"He needs to find a good person to share his life with."

"She needs to get out and meet people."

"But we have to go slowly. I have to win her trust first."

"True, we don't want to push them apart before they can even get together." The joy of conspiring was something both women loved.

Sophia joined Holly and Bruce's tour group.

Myles went by the name of Charles Gregory for the tour. He disliked Sophia Cornridge, and hated her son. However, he could do nothing about it.

Sophia doted on Holly. Moreover, Holly loved the attention.

Chapter 5

Holly and Bruce slipped into the bar and grill. With all the fuss about Holly's book, people were forgetting about Bruce's book, The Sleeper Has Awaken. Bruce looked pleased. He had finally shaken Holly's keepers and had her all to himself. Holly's phone rang. Bruce, who had taken it from her purse, shut it off. "Wait up for me."

They had to cross the crowed section of the bar. In a game they had learned back home, Holly projected the image of a 1950's movie actor causing some of the males around her to turn around. Bruce decided on a 1960's actor. In this way, they could lure unsuspecting people to them. A couple of males followed Holly out the back of the bar. After Holly and Bruce had feed on them, they placed pleasant memories of sex with dead movie stars with them. They would pick which actor from the person's memories. They never took enough blood to hurt them.

Heather wanted them to be careful. She did not want them doing anything that would endanger the group. When they reentered the bar, Jasmine and Heather grabbed Holly and dragged her to a corner both. Sophia acted as lookout.

"Mum?"

"Gregori darling, what are you doing here? I thought you and Vanni were going ring shopping?" Again.

Gregori said nothing. He kept staring at Holly. She was the girl from his dreams. She had been having sex with him in their dreams. In the dreams, they shared each other's blood and bodies. She is real, he thought, dumbfounded.

"Gregori, are you going to answer me? Where is Vanni?" Sophia watched her son watching Holly. Her sisters were lecturing Holly about safety. Holly had no time to notice that anyone was staring at her.

"Vanni didn't want to come to the city. You know how she hates it. She had things she wanted to do besides spend time with me. Who is that girl? Do I know her from somewhere? She seems awfully familiar." It couldn't possibly be the Holly from his dreams. She was only a beautiful, horny dream.

"That's Holly Skyhaven, darling. They are making a movie out of her book Quincy. You wanted to be in it, remember?"

Gregori took a deep breathe. He remembered wanting to be in that movie, but he had pictured Holly as being old and fat, not young and attractive. He had told Vanessa that morning before he left for his doctor's appointment.

"Do you want me to introduce you to her?"

"Yes, I would like that."

Holly glanced at the good-looking man standing next to Sophia. She had never imagined she would ever miss being fat. Yet she did now. I had been her shield against the world. Without it, she felt naked. It kept good-looking men from looking at her. It also kept ugly men from looking at her, the ones in-between too. If they did not look, she would not have to deal with them. It had worked for decades. It did not exist anymore. Holly returned her eyes to Heather as Bruce explained what had happened.

"Hey! Have any of you seen Marilyn Monroe go by? I think she's a Marilyn Monroe impersonator. Marilyn Monroe is dead. Isn't she?" The young man looked confused.

"Yep, Marilyn Monroe is dead."

"Nope, we haven't seen anyone fitting that description."

"Sorry, I haven't seen anyone like that here. But you're right, she is dead."

"I think I saw your impersonator leave with an Elvis impersonator," a young man said. "I'm sure they left by the rear exit."

"Thanks," the man said as he headed for the rear exit.

"See," Bruce smiled. "You were worried about nothing. We were careful. We always are."

"Teach me how to do that, and then I'll believe you."

"Okay."

Gregori cleared his throat, and held out his hand to Holly. "You must be Holly. My Mum hasn't stopped talking about you." As soon as their hands met, Gregori exhaled. Her touch was the same as it is in his dream. It felt spooky and strange, yet also erotic in an indefinable way.

"That's very nice of her. I'm pleased to meet you. These are my sisters, Heather and Jasmine. This is Bruce. He's not a sister. We were just going to have a bite to eat. Do you want to join us?"

"I'd love to," Gregori smiled. This was the first good thing that had happened to him this night.

As soon as they got their food, Holly began to fret about her upcoming book Death is Only the Beginning. It was a new defense mechanism for her to ward off people. If she was always too busy writing, she would not have to deal with them. Dealing with people was Jasmine's job.

"Oh, that's lovely." Sophia smirked. Holly rocked back and forth on her seat, trying to catch the flow of the conversation. She needed to get several more pages done before she could allow herself to think of partying. She leaned over and looked at Gregori's food. "That looks fattening. It must be delicious. Is it?"

"Oh yeah," Gregori watched her carefully as he ate. She looked cute and smelled wonderful, exactly as she had in his dreams. "You're not eating?"

"Oh, no," Holly said. "I can only eat a couple times a week. We found the fried chicken gizzard place. It was on the Food Network. They have the most marvelous deep fried hamburgers there. I want to go tomorrow and try one out."

"Deep fried hamburgers?"

"I saw it on the Food Network." Holly repeated.

"They took the whole burger, bun, burger and toppings. Then they dipped it into a batter mix. After it's completely coated, they slipped it into a hot deep fryer until it was a golden brown."

"It sounds delicious. Can I join you?" Holly was a woman after his heart, someone who liked food. Vanessa hated food. She ate only when she was starving to death.

"I thought you and Vanessa were going ring shopping tomorrow?"

"Not now mother. How about it can I join you?"

"Sure, if you want to come. I'm okay with it. What about you guys?"

"Sure, if you want him to come, I don't see a reason why he shouldn't come. Isn't that right Bruce?"

"Um, right."

Holly frowned. What exactly had Heather meant by that? It was something dirty, no doubt. Bruce and Heather snickered.

Gregori beamed. He grasped Holly's hand, looking deeply into her eyes. She's putty in my hands, he thought.

Frank coughed loudly. He had finally found his little group. "Mind if I join you?" Frank slid onto the bench seat without asking to join them. He watched Holly blush and pull away from Gregori. Honestly, he had to watch out for that girl all of the time. She was far too trusting. Bruce glared at Gregori. Holly was like a baby sister to him. He never wanted anyone or anything to hurt her, especially not someone like Gregori Cornridge. He went through girls the way other men changed their underwear.

Holly hyperventilated. All this testosterone was making her tense. She was ready to forget about tomorrow and just jam something down her throat, preferably something fattening. Was she the cause of all this male posturing? It had to be Heather. She's far more experienced than I am, and far more beautiful, Holly thought. This calmed her mind somewhat. It always did.

"You didn't answer your cell phone, Holly." Frank needed her to stay focused on the present situation. "Do you have it on you?"

Everyone but Holly stared at Frank. Holly looked angrily for her phone. It was not where it was supposed to be. Where could it be? Things were going so well. Then, poof, everything went right down the toilet. It was the story of her life.

"Really Frank, it isn't as bad as when Bruce forgot her at that gay bar. You do remember that, don't you Bruce? It had taken all night to find Holly. Bruce had taken Holly's phone. There Holly's puking her guts out at the edge of the pier. We were lucky the police didn't arrest her for public intoxication. It's a good thing she didn't fall into the lake. She can't swim."

"I haven't had any alcohol since then. Bruce, did you take my phone, again?" Holly fumed. She liked Bruce, but he was always getting her into trouble. He had left her that night at the bar so he could hook up with that cute boy who turned out to be Doug. It had been so foggy out that night. After she had thrown up, the fog seemed to boil up from the lake. She hadn't been able to see and had twice almost fallen into the lake. "And I'm taking swimming lessons now. We won't have to worry about me falling into the lake anymore."

Now that Bruce had lost all that weight, he looked like a movie star, only so much more handsome. He had short curly black hair, deep brown eyes that were so dark they were almost black and framed by long eyelashes and thick eyebrows, and a dark chocolate complexion that was completely clear of any blemish or imperfection. There were women out there who would kill for Bruce's skin tone.

"Bruce, please give me back my phone." Bruce handed it over, and Holly turned it back on. "There are 15 new messages? How long have you had my phone? Never mind, I don't want to know."

Gregori moved closer to Holly. He sensed the tide turning his way. He moved as close to her as he could without actually touching her. Her guardians were very uptight tonight. He didn't want them biting his head off.

"Your mother said Vanessa and you were going to pick out rings tomorrow. Have the two of you picked a date yet?" Jasmine picked at her food. The deep fried hamburger place sounded like a bad idea to her. She had to admit that she hadn't seen Holly so excited about anything in years.

"No," he said, glaring at his mother. "We are not picking out rings tomorrow, or any night. I do not care what that bitch has been telling everyone. Please, let's not talk about it."

Everyone frowned. He was either lying or on the rebound, but something serious had happened.

"Oh dear," Sophia fretted. "What happened darling?"

"I'd rather not talk about it in such a public setting." He had come home unexpectedly after a doctor's appointment filled with bad news and found Vanessa in the shower having a great deal of fun with another woman. It was so embarrassing it made Gregori's heartache, and his head throb. Why was this happening to me? He kept asking himself. His thoughts filled with pain.

"Greg-ums, I told you Marissa doesn't mean anything to me. It is just sex." Vanessa had suddenly appeared. Myles Ludwig, who had been looking for Bruce and Holly, had followed Vanessa into the bar and grill.

"Woe, information overload here. I'm sure most of us do not want to hear this." He did not want this bitch converted ever. He telegraphed this message to other New Lifers. They agreed. Sophia tried to argue with this, but gave out when she realized how embarrassed and hurt Gregori was by her betrayal. "Maybe you should go home and thing this over."

"Um, okay, sure," Vanessa looked confused. She looked imploringly at Gregori.

Gregori was angry, and embarrassed. He refused to look at her. He felt horrible. It was bad enough she did it. She had to announce it to the world. What had he done to deserve this? Nothing, except for his dreams about Holly, he had always been faithful to her.

"I'm sorry, Greg-ums. Really, you're blowing this all out of proportions." He wouldn't dare throw her out.

"I'm telling you this Marissa means nothing to me."

"Is the girl called Marissa White?" Myles inquired and he studied a television set. The bar and grill had five running simultaneously.

"Um, yes, why do you ask?"

"She's on Entertainment Tonight telling everyone about her great love, Vanessa Lee. She says the two of you planned to get all of Gregori's money by knocking him off. She says it's your idea. Oh, look, she had photos of the two of you together."

Everyone in the bar, Vanessa included, gaped at the barely censored photos of the two nude women. The pictures left nothing to the imagination. How could Marissa do this to me? We had it all planned out? Damn, I look good, Vanessa thought.

Gregori could have died right there. God, this was the worst thing that ever happened to me. This was far worse than the pimples he had in high school. He thought desperately. He felt something touch his wrist, glanced down. He saw Holly gently caressing his fist from the knuckles to the wrist and back again. It was a soothing gesture, and it calmed him more than he would have thought possible at this point. He stretched out his fingers, and her touch delighted him. He grabbed Holly's hand and took a deep breath. When he looked up, Vanessa was gone.

"I would like some tea. Does anyone want anything?"

"Shouldn't we leave?"

"No, we should not leave. Please bring me one ice tea." Holly asked the server who had appeared out of nowhere.

Everyone settled down, and the rest of the meal went smoothly. Heather invited Gregori up to her and Holly's room. Everyone in the group, including Gregori, accepted it. Gregori drove them there, and brought a small suitcase with him. He planned to get a room for the night until his mother talked him into staying in her room. He could sleep in her spare bedroom. He had done so before.

Around 12:30 in the morning, Gregori had a coughing fit in the small kitchen area of Heather and Holly's room. Sophia approached him there, fighting back the panic she was beginning to feel.

"Mum, Am I the only one here who's not a vampire?"

"New Lifer, Darling, no one likes to be called a vampire."

"Mum, when did you stop calling them plague carriers?"

"Since, I have gotten to know Holly and Bruce. Aren't they the nicest couple?"

"They're not a couple. She's straight and he's gay."

"Whatever you say, Darling, I say they're a couple."

"Mum, please, why won't you just tell me? Am I the only one here who is not a New Lifer?" Gregori felt frustrated.

"Yes, you are. But I love you just the way you are."

"Why?"

"You're my son. That's why."

"No, I mean why wasn't I converted like everyone else? It isn't fair."

"You live too far from water. The fog only seems to have affected those who live close to water. Life isn't always fair sweetie."

"Can I be converted?" Gregori wanted to pull his hair out. His mother seemed to be talking in circles and it was driving him crazy. His head throbbed. It felt like someone was doing a drum solo inside his skull.

"Why would you want that?" Sophia was curious. He had not shown any interest in converting until tonight. What had changed?

"I don't know. It's just that I haven't been feeling well lately. I didn't want to worry you. Can it be done?"

"Oh honey, this isn't going to change anything between you and that slut. You need to work through this some other way."

"No Mum, I mean I am really not feeling well. I am ill. All those years of smoking have finally caught up with me."

"Cancer," God say it isn't true. Sophia pleaded silently.

"Yes," Gregori looked away as he said this. He had just learned the diagnosis the day he caught them together. He could not even bring himself to say her name. It had been one blow after another that day.

Sophia threw her arms around Gregori and held him tightly to herself. She was so short he could rest his chin on the top of her head. She just cried. This could not be happening to her little boy. He could not be dying. She was sure of it. Converting would save him, the way it had Holly, Bruce and countless others.

"Please Mum, do it for me."

Everyone listened as Sophia told everyone what Gregori had told her. Sophia could not convert her own son. Many reasons went into her decisions, but mostly it was the sex. The act of biting someone was very, completely and highly erotic. It would be like incest if Sophia converted Gregori. Gregori himself wanted Holly to do it. She had one so in his dreams and he felt safe with her.

Holly explained how she converted Bruce. Bruce explained how it felt. Both felt Gregori should think about it. Holly did not feel safe. The act itself would change her. She felt sure of it. Holly hesitated. Gregori looked so hopeful, so trusting. She wanted to help him. Bruce had been following her around like a puppy ever since his conversion was completed. Bruce is gay and Gregori is straight. Would Gregori be worse than Bruce who just wanted to protect her? It was nice and flattering, but she did not want that with Gregori, did she? She did not want another person following her around. Not even one she had a crush on. Did she even really love him? Bruce could do it. She explained this again, but everyone encouraged her to convert Gregori. Holly took a deep breathe. Gregori might not be afraid, but she was.

"I'll bite you on the neck, and drink a couple of ounces. We'll wait a few minutes, and then I'll cut my wrist with my nail and allow you to drink a couple of ounces. I'll close both wounds. Is everything clear to everyone? Does anyone have any questions?"

"Yes, why do you keep delaying? Get on with it already."

"Don't be in such a hurry. You don't know how you'll feel about this later."

"You don't think I can handle it. Do you?"

"You can handle it just fine. It's me I'm worried about."

"Everything is more than clear. You'll be fine. Will you just do it already?" Heather wondered if, perhaps, she shouldn't do it. Holly looked to be on the brink of a panic attack.

"Like now," Gregori hissed. He though he knew what it would feel like from the dreams.

"Sit down on this chair, and tell me when you are comfortable."

Before he could reply, Holly leaned forward, licked his neck and sank her teeth into his neck. His blood flowed like sweat nectar setting her senses on fire. She had never wanted anything so much in her entire life. She had to fight her instinct to drain him. He tasted the same way he did in her dreams. That helped her relax.

Oh my God, Gregori thought as he pulled Holly so close she is straddling his lap. Every part of his body became so hot. It was the most erotic feeling he had ever had with his clothes on, and his Mum in the room. He wanted to take her right there. The only thing stopping him was the presence of so many spectators. He held her as tightly as he could, and moaned. God, it was just like in his dreams.

Heather became concerned. "Holly, what are you doing?"

"She's trying to stop. You make her keep doing it." Gregori sounded desperate. His voice husky, his eyes closed in ecstasy. "God, this is good."

Heather snorted, and several others giggled.

Holly pushed away. She was breathing hard and fanning herself with her shirt. Gregori's neck was clean. "I warned you. People act weird when I bite them."

"I am not acting." Gregori pulled her back, kissing her roughly above the left breast.

"Go for it," Heather encouraged. "It's your big chance to lose your virginity."

"Wait," Bruce interrupted. "I'll get the camera so we can save it for prosperity."

"I did not say anything about you biting me. Now stop it. Your mother is now looking at me as if I'm raping you. Bruce, you can go to hell. They have a special place reserved for you there."

Bruce laughed, "You first honey".

"Don't look at her Mum, and no cameras."

Gregori rested his head on Holly's shoulder. He watched everyone start to leave. Soon they were alone. He watched Holly as she cut a deep wound on her wrist and brought it to his mouth. Her blood tasted like hot and spicy nectar to him. It made him even hornier, if that was possible.

After he had his fill, he watched her lick her wound closed. He wanted to lick some of her more interesting anatomical parts. He did not feel any embarrassment over what he was thinking or feeling. They were alone.

Gregori cupped her shoulders and pulled her tightly to himself as he suckled her nipple. She moaned softly and kissed the top of his head. She could not think when he touched her, especially not when he pulling her pants down. Oh my God, she thought, I'm not wearing any underclothes. Holly helped him remove his shirt, and pants. He was wearing underpants, silky tight briefs.

Soon she was straddling him on the chair. Moaning and carrying on in ways that Holly would normally find embarrassing. He slipped them to the floor, missionary position. Holly moaned loudly. She nibbled on his chest and bit him deeply, before rolling him over and straddling his hips. He thrust his hips vigorously with each new position, penetrating her deeply, his moans co-mingling with hers.

Gregori was truly amazed. She had said she was a virgin, but he had never truly believed that she really was. She was so tight. Every penetration was like slipping on a velvet glove. She even knew where he liked to be touched. He had died and gone to heaven. Somehow, they wound up in Holly's bed. He fell in love. He wanted it to go on forever.

He loved biting and sucking her blood, and did so many times during the night. It was so very erotic. Who thought blood drinking could be erotic? Gregori thought dreamily.

Holly woke early the next morning, exhausted and very sore. Gregori pressed her tightly to his bare chest, and nibbled on her shoulder in his sleep. She felt sore in all the right places and some not so right places. Last night had been the happiest of her life once she realized everyone had left the two of them alone.

She had at least 60 pages to go on her new novel she was working, but she wanted this moment to last a little longer. It was only 4:44 am. She could wait until six am to get up.

Gregori draped his leg over her. Buying his face into her short brown hair, he murmured stay. How could anyone be so paranoid about making love when making it left him feeling so warm and protective of her? He adored her. He could see himself marrying her and them having a bunch of kids together. He felt sure his Mum would approve.

Holly rolled off the bed and flew into the bathroom. Frank is going to kill me, she thought as she slipped into the shower. I have to finish that book. Gregori Cornridge is just too much of a distraction when I've work to do.

Gregori rubbed his hand over the spot on the bed where Holly had been. It was still warm, but where could she be? Listening carefully, he could make out the sound of running water. He followed the sound to the shower in the hotel's luxuriously appointed bathroom. The sight in front of him caught his eye. He stood watching her scrub her face and neck before climbing in with her. He grabbed some body wash and began massaging her back and shoulders.

"Easy Babycakes, I'm not going to eat you." Gregori pulled her back into his chest while reaching around her to wash her breasts. He cupped one in each hand, thumbing each nipple slowly.

Holly tensed, then relaxed. What could he do now that he had not done the night before? He had filled her with desires, pleasures and passions she had never experienced before. Even if she lived a thousand million years, she would never forget that night.

Gregori's right hand traced a soapy line from Holly's breastbone to her soft curly pubic hair. His mouth found an interesting spot on her neck as his left hand made its way to her right breast. "Relax Babycakes. I just want to wash your hair." The deft fingers of Gregori's right hand found the hair in question. It wasn't on her head either.

Moaning loudly and frantically wiggling her butt against his groan, Holly put her legs around his and reached around his hips. She grabbed his butt for support. Her last coherent thought for quite some time was Frank was going to kill me for not finishing that book. Screw Frank.

Sometimes later, they dried each other off and went to look for some clothing. Holly could not stop laughing as the pants Gregori wore the night before kept falling off. They had been painfully tight on him the night before.

"This is not funny. I've got nothing to wear."

"But I like watching them fall down. It reminds me of when I first felt better after the fog. Everything fell off. No, I didn't run out and buy new clothes. I'm still wearing the same clothes I wore when I was fat."

"How?"

"I changed into one of my animal forms. When I changed back the clothes I was wearing fit perfectly." Before Gregori could protest, Holly threw herself to the ground. When she touched the ground, she was a very large black dog.

Gregori gasped. Could he do that? It took him only a minute to realize how easy it was to change. It was so much fun. When he turned back, his clothes fit. They worked their way through his small bundle of clothes in no time. He was reluctant to return to his home in western New York for more. Vanessa might still be there and he wasn't ready to face her.

Holly had to face Frank. He had called several times while she was in the shower. Then a couple of more times while they changed shapes. She was in big trouble with Frank, no two ways about it.

Heather opened the door to the suite and sighed. "I'm sure they're fine. Holly never answers her phone." They had been out early having breakfast and had let Holly and Gregori sleep in.

"But Gregori always answers his. I'm so worried." Sophia wrung her hands as she entered the suite's sunken living room.

Gregori ran out of Holly's room and jumped over the couch like Superman. He scooped his mother into his arms, laughing like an overexcited six year old. "I'm so sorry Mum. Holly showed me something wonderful."

"Oh, I'm sure she did." Heather said knowingly.

"Yes. She taught me how to change into animals. I changed into a dog, wolf, bear, and a tiger. It's so cool." Gregori place his mother on a chair before plopping down at her feet.

"And a lion," Holly added as she entered the room much more slowly than Gregori had. She was sore from using muscles she normally didn't use. Oh hell, she had never used those muscles until Gregori. "Frank's been calling all morning. I had better call him back. He's on speed dial."

He answered right away. "Holly. Where the hell have you been? I've been calling you all morning."

"I was taking a shower."

"For two hours?"

"There is a great deal of me to wash. I'm a big girl." Holly replied with dignity while leaving out the part about Gregori helping her shower.

"That's a complete crock of shit." Frank steamed, expressing the exact sentiment that Heather, Sophia and Gregori were thinking. "Let me talk to Heather for a moment."

"That's not true, Frank. I have very big body parts."

"You had very big body parts. You don't now. You're a skinny little thing with boobs. Now put Heather on."

"Boobs are body parts. And they are big."

"Heather, now," Frank bit off each word.

"He wants to talk to Heather. Besides, I can't talk to him when he's being so unreasonable." Holly huffed. Turning to Gregori, she gave him her exasperated expression. "And you had better tell me where you hid my entire collection of tee-shirts buster."

Gregori smiled. "No. You're lucky to have grabbed that one. It isn't feminine. You should wear those itsy bitsy spaghetti strap tops. Ouch. Mum. Why did you hit me?"

"Oh Gregori, don't be such a pig."

"Mum that's not fair."

"If she wants to wear tee-shirts then you should let her." Turning to

Holly, she smiled. "You look lovely dear. Where did you get it?"

"I got it from the county fair. It was a couple of years ago. I've one with bats on it, but the wolf is my favorite. Your son hid the bat one on me along with several others. And he had better return them."

"Awe, isn't she cute when she does that?"

"Does what?"

"Ummm, crinkle your nose and stick out your bottom lip." Sophia smiled. "You do look quite cute when you do that."

"I do not." Holly said without steam. Her nieces were always saying she was the cute Aunt. Holly didn't believe it but it wasn't worth arguing about. She stuck out her bottom lip and pretended to pout for a couple of minutes. "Are we still going to the deep fried place? I'm hungry."

"Okay. First, you have to teach me how to turn into animals. I want to change into an owl."

Holly nodded. Leaping onto the couch then off, she turned into a snowy white owl. After some practice, Sophia turned into a barn owl. Gregori and Heather kept turning into fruit bats. They were large fruit bats, but they were not owls so it was a little disappointing for them. The sensation of flying was indescribable. It was both exhilarating and exhausting. It took a great deal of energy to get off the ground and stay in the air.

Sophia knew she should be angry with Holly. The girl had had unprotected sex with Gregori the night before. How could she become angry with Holly when Holly made Gregori so happy? She had not seen him so happy and energetic since he got his first part in a high school play. He played Captain Hook.

Gregori laughed as he lunged for Holly. Holly made an ungodly noise that fell somewhere between a squeal and a shriek as she barely escaped his grasp. Heather snorted at the two of them and went to answer the door.

Gregori was feeling so much better. He looked like he had dropped 40 or 50 pounds of fat and had become all hard muscles. Yet weirdly his face had filled out. His eyes and cheeks were no longer sunken. He seemed to radiate health. Sophia watched him chase Holly around and laugh.

He finally caught her by the dining area and tickled her into submission.

Sophia was shocked to realize that her beautiful baby boy had become an incredibly handsome man. When had that happened? Did Holly realize how lucky she was that he loved her? He loves her. Where did that come from?

Bruce glared at Gregori as he entered the suite. He was convinced that Gregori was not good enough for Holly. It wasn't something he could give concrete reasons. It was just a belief he shared with Frank.

Heather watched Holly squirm out of Gregori's grasp to run and hide behind Bruce. "Frank wants Holly to finish her current novel before the deadline which is less than a week away."

"Yea, you're right. I've got at least 60 pages to go. I had better get to work on it." Holly trudged to the refrigerator. She could at least get herself a glass of orange juice to drink while she worked.

"You don't have to work. I'm more than capable of supporting you." Gregori frowned as she moved away from him.

Holly bit down her first reaction to his offer, joy. She was not a disciplined worker. No, she had to earn her own money and not mooch off him. "Thank you for your kind offer Gregori, but I have to earn my own money. I have my family to support and I plan to do that with my own money. Not yours."

"All right," Gregori sounded sullen. He wanted to support Holly. He was the man and he didn't care how old fashioned that sounded. He knew his mother approved of Holly not wanting his money. It rubbed him the wrong way. Holly was not Vanessa. Vanessa had only cared for his money and not for him. Holly cared for him. A fact that made him wants to protect Holly.

Holly sighed. "I dreamed about Dracula last night. He looked like the gorgeous hunk from the Return of the Mark of the Son of Dracula's Brides. You know, Mark Cornridge."

"Mark Cornridge? Why would you dream of my ex-husband?"

"I don't know. I dream about Dracula a great deal. We just talk in them." Holly frowned. What was it to her?

"Mark Cornridge? You're dreaming of my father?" Gregori gasped. He knew what kind of womanizer his father was.

"Is he really your father? I thought he is just some guy with the same last name."

"Someone who has the same last name," Gregori repeated stupidly, his eyes wide with disbelief.

"You know" Holly elaborated. "It's like the Keatons. There is Michael, Buster, Diane and Elijah. None of whom are related to each other. It's just one of those Hollywood things."

"Who's Elijah Keaton?" Sophia asked suddenly curious.

"He's my sister Jasmines son-in-law. He's married to her youngest daughter, Bobby Joe. They live in Connecticut. They're moving to Southern Italy in April. It's a missionary thing." Holly had no interest in missionary things.

"Oh."

"They're expecting their first child in February."

"Now back to the point, Mark Cornridge is my father."

"Which explains why you're so sexy?"

+++++++++

Gregori steamed as Doug straightened his tie. "Why is she wearing that sluty outfit?"

"It's not sluty Now hold still. Besides some idiot name Gregori Cornridge told her, he liked her in spaghetti strap tops and dresses. There you go." Doug sighed. Gregori was so agitated over Holly's choice of clothing he couldn't even get his own tie tied.

"I meant she should wear them for me. Not for everyone else and certainly not for Myles Ludwig."

"She is wearing it for you. Trust me. I was with her when she picked it out. Every other sentence from her mouth was; do you think Gregori will like me in this? Ask your Mum, she was right there. Isn't that right Mrs. C?"

"Isn't what right? You look very nice, Gregori."

"That Holly spent our whole shopping trip asking if Gregori would like her in this or that outfit."

"It's true." Sophia glanced at the mirror. "Does this make me look too young?"

"Yes Mum. That is not a proper dress for my Mum to be wearing. And why am I wearing this suit again?"

"Because the one time Holly saw you in it she couldn't stop drooling." Doug smiled. "She thought you were the hottest looking man in the universe. If you want to win her back, you have to show off the goods."

"Why'd she break up with you in the first place?"

Bruce studied Gregori's ass. No doubt about it, the man had great assets.

"How should I know? She's crazy." Gregori huffed. His ego still stung from Holly flatly refusing his offer of marriage.

"Well," Doug smirked. "Someone threw himself at her and begged her to marry him. So naturally, she freaked. There was that time when she was talking to Anton Wilkinson and you thought she should just shut up. You do know that all New Lifers can read minds. Isn't that right?"

"She said she needed to get to know you better." Heather entered the room so quietly that everyone jumped when she spoke. "You scared the hell out of her by proposing so quickly. You should have waited a month or two." Heather twirled around so everyone could see her new dress. A white floral spaghetti strap number in the same design as the red one Holly had picked out. Holly had hers altered to be shorter. Heather gave Gregori a quick hug. She laughed as the people swore at her for sneaking up on them.

"You know if you'd quit pouting you could win her back in a heartbeat. She adores you and you know it."

"Sure she does."

"You should've been there when we picked out her dresses. Every other word out of her mouth was will Gregori like me in this?"

Gregori sighed in frustration. "Then why is she with Myles Ludwig and not me? And does she really like me in this monkey suit?" He did look nice in it.

"He wants us to promote the New Life in Europe." Bruce tore his gaze from Gregori's ass and looked at Doug. "He thinks she'll be a great spokesperson. I'll make an okay one. And you look totally hot in that suit."

"You're fucking beautiful. And I wouldn't mind doing just that with you. However, Holly really does prefer you naked. Do you want us to break Myles Ludwig's legs for you?" Heather asked cheerfully. She hadn't been in a bar fight in decades.

"You know Gregori," Bruce backed away from Gregori as he contemplated his next statement. "Your Mum and Heather are wearing the same dress as Holly is, but in different colors. I don't hear you saying they're dressed like sluts."

"Mum! He's right. You can't go out in that thing. It shows everything." Gregori blushed from his head to his toes. His Mum was wearing a black version of the dress he had seen Holly wearing earlier. It was even shorter and more revealing then Holly's.

Sophia twirled around like a schoolgirl and laughed. "Do you like it? Let's go before all the good seats are taken."

"Jasmine's holding our seats. We had better hurry. I think Myles wants Holly for himself."

"I'll kill him with my own hands."

"Now Gregori, you know Heather is only teasing."

"No Mum, I don't. That bastard had better keep his hands off my Holly. He has no claim on her."

"That's the spirit. Now let's go and enjoy dinner." Doug wondered vaguely if Gregori was any good in bed.

"Did she really keep asking if I'd like her outfit?"

"Yes," everyone shouted at once.

"It does look nice on her. Maybe I'll ask her out later." Gregori mused as the entered the dining room. He frowned when Sophia ran ahead and hugged Jasmine rather enthusiastically.

"That's a good idea." Bruce replied absently. He found himself wondering how good Gregori was in bed. He checked it off as something he would never have firsthand knowledge.

"I've saved us the seats on this side of the table. Holly went with Myles to discuss something. They wouldn't say what." Jasmine said innocently. She only had eyes for Sophia and had no idea how her words were affecting Gregori.

Gregori stared blindly across the room at Holly and Myles. She was sitting on Myles's lap. Gregori sat down hard when Myles ran his hand over Holly's stomach toward her breasts.

"Just take a sip of water and cool down." Doug whispered.

"Fine," Gregori grabbed the water glass as Myles whispered something into Holly's ear making her laugh. Splinters of glass flew everywhere as Gregori's hand crushed the glass. What he had really wanted to do was crush Myles's throat.

Myles frowned. Holly was no longer in his arms. She was across the table fussing over Gregori Cornridge. How had she managed to cross the room in the blink of an eye?

Gregori blinked. He was suddenly so happy. Then Holly stroked his hand and made little whimpering noises.

"Oh Gregori, you have to be more careful. He doesn't know his own strength." She informed the server who came to clean up the glass. "He's only been a New Lifer for a couple of nights."

"It isn't a problem miss. We'll have this cleaned up right away." Eight minutes later and it looked like nothing had happened.

"Let me see. I don't see any blood." Holly kissed the palm of Gregori's hand. "She's right. I need to take better care of you until you become use to being a New Lifer that is."

"Who's right?" Gregori pulled Holly onto his lap. He never wanted to let her go.

"The server, she thinks that as your maker I should be teaching you these things. I promise to do better from now on." Holly breathed in the scent that was Gregori. His scent being a mixture of strawberries, chocolate and whipped cream. She loved his scent.

Doug and Bruce quickly blocked the seats closest to Holly and Gregori. With the help of a few other partygoers, they managed to force Myles to sit at another table.

"How do you plan on taking care of me?"

"When I can't even take care of myself," Holly kissed Gregori's fingers, taking time to suck on each one.

"So would you like to do something after this? Maybe we could go to an all-night coffee shop or something."

"Or something would be nice. I know just the place." He leaned toward Holly for a kiss. Holly was more than happy to give him one.

Doug winked at Sophia. Everything worked the way they had planned it. He could practically hear the wedding bells.

+++++++++

Sophia watched Gregori watch Holly. Holly worked on her book. It had taken more pages then Holly had thought to finish it. Frank would be coming over to inform them of Bruce and Holly's itinerary. It had change, again. They now would be traveling down the Atlantic coast to Florida and would spend a week at Disney, with a possible stay at Universal Studio Theme park.

They were having trouble getting overseas visas for the group. Fear of the New Life being rampant in Europe, Africa and Asia. The Europeans were becoming concerned. News of the New Life spreading to Middle America did nothing to ease their fears. Cincinnati had been one of the first non-New Life cities converted. It had spread like the plague from there. Perhaps Heather is right. New Lifer did sound like someone going to prison for the first time, and with a life sentence to boot. It sounded like a bunch of murders. Sophia mused quietly.

"There, it's done." Holly enthused. She had been so full of life this last week. "I can't wait to show Frank. When will he be here?"

"That reminds me. The police want to go over what we were doing the night Vanessa disappeared."

"But we told them everything."

At that time, CNN reported that Vanessa Lee had been located. She had returned to her family in South Forks, Indiana. No one in the group believed they had heard the last of her.

CNN also reported a rash of pregnancies among the nations now youthful nursing home residents. The pregnancies were both disturbing and funny.

Chapter 6

Holly stared out the window of the plane. She missed MareMoo. They
had been able to visit home for only two weeks. Now they were flying to
Orlando, Florida.

MareMoo had been so happy to see them. Holly had not wanted to go to
Florida. She had wanted to bring MareMoo with them, or stay with her. That
had not been possible. She had obligations.

The quick tour felt like it was taking forever. Holly began to feel tired all
the time, again. It frightened her enough that she went in for a checkup. The
family doctor had run a battery of test on her. He had promised to call Holly
on her cell phone when the test results came in. Otto and Nicole, Heather's son
and daughter-in-law, were watching MareMoo while they were away.

Disney here we come. Heather had wanted to drive. She had told Heather
to go ahead. Holly wanted to fly. Vanessa Lee had disappeared. Running back
to her family home, but not bothering to let anyone know of her plans. It had
taken her parents over two days to get her to come forward. In the meantime,
everyone the police interrogated everyone whom seen with Vanessa the night
she disappeared. Holly hated Vanessa for that.

"Auntie, Auntie," come here. At three, Mina could be quite demanding.

"You should be taking a nap young lady. Where's Mommy?"

"No, come sit with me." Mina was definitely turning into a little dictator.
Holly heard laughter coming from behind her.

"Don't encourage her. Now where is Mommy?"

Mina grabbed Holly's hand and pulled toward the back of the plane. She
did not want a nap. She wanted her Auntie, and she wanted her now.

Katrina ran up the aisle toward Holly, and darted behind her.

"And where is your mother? Is anyone watching these kids?"

"Auntie," Mina persisted.

"Watch out," Katrina yelled as her brother Hugo barreled into Holly.

Gregori, Frank, Doug and Bruce all laughed. Sophia chased after the
children, clucking her tongue.

"Let me help you Mrs. C.," Doug grabbed Hugo.

"Quit teaching your sister bad habits or no Santa Claus this year."

"I've been good. It is Katrina's fault."

Doug moved quickly to stop him. Hugo could spin all kinds of wild tales,
and he was never to blame for anything. One could only take small doses of
Hugo, or they would go insane.

"I'm coming. I'm coming. Hugo, I'm giving you to the count of three to
get back to your seat right now young man, or no candy for you." Hugo's
grandmother, Jasmine came tearing up the aisle. "And no giving lip to your
Aunt, young man."

Holly sighed, bringing Jamaica and Wendy, and their children had been

Jasmines idea. Jasmine loved her children, and grandchildren. Holly remembered the argument well. Yes, both girls would be helpful in making sure Holly dressed properly and behaved herself but Wendy had just given birth on Christmas Eve. It was too early for her to be traveling with a baby. Holly was just grateful that Jasmine's youngest daughter and her husband Elijah had not been able to make it. She didn't need another person telling her what to do.

Sighing heavily, Holly picked Mina up and head down the aisle to where Mina's mother was feeding Lucy. Smiling triumphantly, she plopped Mina into her father's lap. Colin just looked at her as if she was crazy.

"I'm not baby-sitting unless I can use it as an excuse to miss some of the interviews. Baby-sitting is for grandma, not Auntie."

"Auntie, color with me."

"Not now Mina. It's time to go to sleep. It's nap time for you, young lady." Colin tried to look stern. He did a good job of it.

"Auntie, it's time for our nap time"

Doug had decided to help with Jamaica's children. Jamaica's ex-husband had run off to South Fork. Hugo did not want to listen to anyone. He gave Aunt Holly a dirty look, so Holly headed back to her seat. The flight had just begun and already there was chaos.

"Auntie, you come back here." Mina was definitely getting bossy.

"Auntie doesn't have to come back here. It is nap time for you, young lady." Wendy had her hands full.

"Oh, there you are. Gregori has been looking for you." She gave Holly a knowing look.

Holly rolled her eyes. How could he miss her on the plane? There's nowhere to go on it. Why does this woman think I'm going to become her daughter-in-law when just last week she said that Bruce and I make the perfect couple? Holly pondered. What am I missing now?

"Okay, is he in his seat?"

"Yes dear, he is. You look tired, perhaps you should get some rest before we land."

Nodding her head in agreement, she headed back to her seat. She did not see Gregori. Holly covered herself up from head to toe with a blanket and passed out.

Gregori watched Holly slip under the blanket. He knew she did not mean it to be, but everything she did was cute to him. Nodding to his Mum, he slid under the blanket with her, and held her while she slept.

+++++++++

Jamaica fretted while Holly and Bruce did another interview. They were developing a flare for it, but to Jamaica, it seemed so un-Aunt Holly like. Aunt Holly never did anything. Wow, that good-looking hunky actor who followed Aunt Holly around like a puppy dog, what's with that? Aunt Holly had always been the cute Aunt. He was a movie star. What was going on here?

"It's going well," Gregori whispered into Jamaica's ear. "I've been coaching her on her interviewing techniques."

"Wow, she is doing really well. Did you coach Bruce too?"

"Holly insisted. Were those kids yours who had been running around on the plane?"

"The two older ones are. Do you have any kids, Gregori?"

"I never married. My Mum wants me to have a couple." They watched as Holly and Bruce did several more interviews. Between every interview, Jamaica would run in and re-do their makeup. Finally, at 3:30 in the afternoon it was over for the day.

Holly skipped over and hugged Jamaica. "This is going so smoothly since you started helping. My clothes have been perfect every time. Thank you, thank you, thank you, you are a life saver."

Jamaica hugged Holly back. This was definitely un-Holly like behavior. "I'm glad I could help."

"But I'm taking you away from your job and the kids. How will I ever be able to repay you for this?"

"With money," Bruce said. "Let's go back to the hotel and enjoy the afternoon off. Has the director's plane come in yet?" She was coming in with Yoshi Kenwood, and Kyle Matthews.

"It is delayed by customs in London. However, they finally got permission to take off. It will be landing tomorrow." Everyone checked their cell phones. Bruce had Holly's cell phone again.

+++++++++

Laura studied the photo on her cell phone. She had talked to Gregori the night before and he had sent her photos of Holly. She looked cute in the photo, curled up in Gregori's arms the way she was. Was Holly in bed with him? She would have to get the whole story from Gregori. Laura's daughter, Hanna stared out the window. To Laura, Holly looked to be about the same age as her daughter. Hanna turned 14 years old. Could Holly really be 52? Her cell phone rang. Gregori sent her more photos. In these, Holly was awake. She looked older, but not much.

Kyle and Yoshi joined her. She showed them the photos.

"Can I see them, mom?" Laura handed the phone to Hanna who stared at the photos. "I've seen her on a pod cast. They showed the before and after photos."

"The before and after photos of what," Yoshi asked.

"Before she got the New Life, She's fat, old and dying of cancer."

"Hanna!"

"But mom, those were her own words from her first pod cast. Here I'll get it on my phone. See," Hanna handed her mother the phone. "I've got other stuff on my laptop. Let me pull it up for you."

Laura looked at the photos and showed them to the others. "Why do you have this on your laptop?"

"Everyone I know does, mom. It's real big thing to down load stories about them. The CNN say they had something to do with Cincinnati, Ohio being converted."

"Them?"

"Holly and Bruce, mom, or any New Lifer,"

Hanna shook her head. Mother would never be with it. "She lost, like, 120 pounds, and he lost 475. They both wrote books."

"Four hundred and seventy five pounds, how the hell much did he weigh?" Kyle and Yoshi just stared at Hanna.

"Six hundred and fifty, I think. They say he was dying when Holly converted him. I found it. Here sit together so everyone can watch." Hanna arranged the three so they could watch her laptop screen. Hanna fiddled with her phone. Sometimes she could get late breaking new casts and updates.

Laura was fascinated. She could tell it was also holding Kyle and Yoshi's interest. Bruce's pictures were graphic. She was glad his life had turned around. Holly seemed shy. Though she did not have Bruce's screen presence, she was making a go of it. Kyle and Yoshi thought she was cute. Holly's later videos showed someone who had grown in confidence.

"They say everyone affected by the fog looks like a super model." Hanna offered. "I think that's why the videos are so popular."

Kyle pointed to one of the woman. He watched a tall blonde-haired woman who kept fussing over Holly.

"Who's she? Is she Holly's mother?"

"Which woman? Nope, it's her older sister, Heather. Their parents have been dead for a couple of years. Heather had been taking care of Holly during her illness. Heather lost 188 pounds. It's on the videos, somewhere." They watched the videos twice, before piping up again. "Let me download this to laptop. You have got to see this."

Hanna worked quickly and they were soon watching the new video. Afterward no one could think of anything to say, so Hanna played it again. It showed Gregori Cornridge telling the world how and why they had converted him. His doctors shared a link, and were more than willing to pronounce him cured. There were no more tumors in his lungs or anywhere else in his body. Holly, his mother, and several others were with him. He looked gorgeous. He had always been gorgeous, but Laura had never seen him look that good. His skin and eyes were clear, and his movement's fluid. He positively glowed.

"See mom, everyone is beautiful over there, even aging actors."

"Hey, he's younger than me. Are you calling me old?" Kyle protested.

"Yes, you are. We love you anyway. Right mom," Hanna winked at her mother, who just shook her head.

"Who are we going to meet at the airport?"

56

"Just some studio guys, I hope you're not too disappointed."

"Nope, I would have been surprised if it's anyone else."

Everyone settled down for the long flight, Hanna picked up her copy of Holly's second published book, Fangs for Nothing. It wasn't as good as Quincy was, but it is still worth reading. She finished it just as the plane landed at the airport.

+++++++++

Gregori smiled at Heather as they passed in the hallway. Holly had been avoiding him. He needed to find out why.

Holly hid in her room. Her doctor had not called, but she was constantly tired. There had to be something wrong with her. Gregori deserved someone healthy. Someone better, sexier, smarter, and younger than her.

Gregori looked at the necklace he had purchased for Holly. It was a journey pendant. He hoped she liked it. It would look lovely on her.

"Oh, Gregori, we need to talk." Holly yawned.

"Am I boring you?" He loved to tease her.

"Never, you're the most interesting person I've ever met. My brain is just overheating."

"I love you."

"We just need to talk. This is important." Holly gazed at Gregori's cheekbones. It gave the illusion she that was looking at his eyes when she wasn't. If she looked him in the eyes, she would never be able to say what she had to. "I feel we're moving too fast here. I don't ever want you to feel trapped in our relationship." Holly leaned toward him and inhaled deeply. She closed her eyes. He smelled so incredible, so real. She could not remember ever being so happy. It frightened her. She simply did not know how to handle the emotion. "I mean it. If I ever become one those needy bitches, you tell me. Do you think I'm becoming needy? You will tell if I am?"

"Holly? Where do you get these ideas from?"

"I get them from books. You have your life and I have my own." Holly babbled until Gregori backed her up against the wall. He leaned over her, both hands planted against the wall to prevent her escape. "I mean it."

"Yes, Holly," Gregori purred in his slinky voice, the one Holly always found irresistible. "Holly?"

Holly inhaled deeply. She would never get enough of his smell. "Yes?" She asked, reaching out to touch his chin with her fingertips. He needed a shave.

"Did I tell you I love you? Cause, I do. I don't think I can tell you that enough." Gregori handed Holly the necklace.

"Gregori, you don't have to buy me anything. Your Mum loves jewelry more than I do."

"I know you don't like jewelry. Nevertheless, I think this will look lovely on you. Will you please try it on?"

"Okay, but promise me, you won't buy me anymore gifts."

"Okay," he promised, his fingers crossed behind his back.

"Holly, Holly," Bruce came flying into the room with Holly's cell phone. "It's your doctor. You're pregnant."

"Give me that phone. Hello, yes, I'm she. How far am I along? Four weeks? Really? Is that why I've been so tired? Can you e-mail me that information? Thank you." Holly gave the doctor her e-mail address while Gregori place the necklace around her neck. "Could you please tell the father? He's right here." Holly handed the cell phone to Gregori who put it on speakerphone, with the doctor's permission.

They listened intently as the doctor explained the difference between a regular pregnancy and a New Lifer pregnancy. It amounted to speed. New Lifer pregnancies lasted half as long as regular ones. Four weeks would be the gestational equivalent of eight weeks. Holly knew this from Nicole and Wendy's pregnancies. Pregnant New Lifers ate like teenage boys. They also slept a great deal and were cranky.

"Thank you doctor, I'll be sure to pick up those vitamins for her." Gregori closed the cell phone and placed it into Holly's purse. "We need to tell the others."

"This great news calls for a big celebration. Let's get everyone together."

"Oh my God, what am I going to do now? I can't take care of one baby, let alone two. I have no patience."

Holly look as if she was about to flee. Everyone in their group picked up her misery and shock. They filed in quickly to help ease her tension. Twins were not, after all, the end of the world.

+++++++++

Laura greeted Marco. She had not recognized him at first. He had been out of shape and was getting up there in years. Now Marco was young and healthy looking. He looked 19, not 54. Hanna was right. Everyone looked like supermodels. Everywhere she looked, she saw young, healthy, happy airport personnel. She breezed through customs in record time. Everyone was so cheerful. She could not remember a time when the customs officials were ever so cheerful. What did they know that she did not? Soon everyone was reunited. They all had the same experience.

"Why are you complaining about that? Will you look at that poor man over there? They're really after him." Everyone turned around in time to see the police handcuff a young man and lead him away. He had been on the plane with them. No one else at the terminal seemed to notice.

Their driver appeared and introduced himself as David Frank. He and Jorge Mikhail would be doing all the chauffeuring for them. Jorge was seeing to their luggage at that moment.

Laura and Hanna picked up some nice souvenirs and new bikinis at the airport.

"Where will we be meeting the others?" Hanna was anxious to meet some New Lifers. She wanted to lose 50 pounds. She only needed to lose 20.

"The Universal Grand Hotel, some of the executive will be meeting you there at 5:30."

"In the morning?"

"In the afternoon, it will give you just enough time to unpack." Like most New Lifers, they preferred the afternoon and nighttime hours to early morning or noon hours. The intense early morning light tired them out.

"Will we get to meet Holly and Bruce?"

"Yes, I believe they will be joining you there in a couple of nights."

"Good."

Laura frowned at Hanna. What was with those questions? She turned away, and watched all the good-looking people go by. She was looking for any sign of imperfection. When she got to the hotel, she found some, but soon realized she was looking at tourists from overseas and Middle America. The areas the fog had not been able to reach. It also seemed to have only limited effects on teenagers. How strange, Laura mused.

+++++++++

Holly expressed confidence that Laura Sanders would make a wonderful movie, and all the cast choices would be perfect. That she would get a deluxe copy of the DVD when it came out. She hoped everyone would buy her new book, Poor Dear, She Must Have Told Him, and would go see the movie of Quincy when it came out. Holly deferred all other questions to Laura Sanders.

Kyle smiled. The press conference went the way they usually did. Everyone had smiled on cue. No one asked Yoshi if his parents named him for the video game character. No one asked if Gregori parents named him after Rasputin. However, he personally had asked him that question about a million times since they meet.

Laura announced Kyle to be playing Quincy, Angel Sanders to be playing Van Helsing, Yoshi as Harker, and Gregori as Dracula. None of them had ever played a part in a horror movie before. They were all looking forward to it. The rest of the cast had yet to be decided. Several well-known actors were under consideration for the parts.

Bruce expressed confidence in his new book, Only by Invitation, and announced which studio was picking it up. He also announced that he was currently working on his next book, which was still untitled.

Kyle found himself walking with Heather as they headed to a restaurant. They talked as they watched Gregori fuss over Holly. She was wearing the diamond pendant Gregori had given her earlier that night. The two of them held hands whenever they were together. Nevertheless, strangely no one in the press or entertainment industry bothered them or took their pictures.

"Holly's not a people person," Heather explained. She expected Holly to bolt at any moment. "She has a commitment phobia. She prefers books to people."

"Gregori seems quite found of her. Have they known each other long?" Kyle had never worked with Gregori before though they had met before.

"We met him a month ago in New York. He joined our group shortly after his mother did. Will you be doing anything tonight? We're celebrating New Year's Eve and Holly's pregnancy tonight. Do you want to join us?"

"I'd love to join you."

"Wonderful, I'm looking forward to it." Heather's eyes twinkled as they walked into the diner.

Sophia chatted quietly with Laura. Sophia looked about 22 now. It was hard to believe they were about the same age. They spent most of the diner engaged in small talk.

+++++++++

Heather watched Kyle's deliciously tight ass as he headed back to the bar. He kept trying to get her drunk. Little did he know, when she was younger, Heather could drink anyone under the table. She never got drunk when she was young. She was young again. The night was full of possibilities.

Kyle was about Holly's age. He worked hard to stay in shape. Image is very important in his business. It got harder every year. Heather approved of the way he maintained himself. Kyle returned with their drinks. "Have you known Holly long?"

"She's my younger sister. I've known her all her life." Kyle wasn't the sharpest tool in the shed. He could project intelligence in his movie performances, and that's what counted.

Kyle felt slightly embarrassed. Hanna had told him that on the plane ride over. He was having trouble remembering things lately. The memory enhancing drugs were not working. "Aw, I'm sorry. I forgot. It's the glow of your splendid beauty. It makes me forget everything."

He's definitely full of it, Heather thought, but he's so easy on the eyes. Kyle Matthews was tall with short blond hair, big blue eyes and a well-kept body. Even without being a New Lifer, Kyle was a hunk. "Don't worry about it. Here, sit down closer to me so we can watch the rest of the drunks."

Holly trundled past. "Honestly Gregori, its only tomato juice. Will you quit pestering me about it?"

"Baby, I'm only thinking about our babies."

"That," Kyle observed," is going to get old fast." He smiled broadly, as he moved closer to Heather. In college, he could drink everyone under the table. He was going to get lucky tonight.

Yoshi and Jamaica came over with more drinks. "Mind if we join you? We were hoping you'd tell us how Aunt Holly converted Gregori. "

"Sure, feel free. Why do you want to hear that old story?"

"We just do," Yoshi, Kyle and Jamaica loudly responded. Heather sighed and went into the whole story for them. Jamaica hadn't changed into a New

Lifer, and no one seemed willing to do it for her. Kyle was particularly eager to hear about it.

Heather had just finished explaining how Holly had done it when Hugo ran up waving his arms. "Aunt Holly locked herself in the restroom and won't come out."

"Let your grandmother take care of it. She's just mad because Gregori keeps asking her what she's drinking." Everyone knew Gregori didn't drink. He did not want Holly drinking while she was pregnant, or any other time for that matter. Hugo ran off to find his grandmother. He loved telling on others.

"Doesn't he trust her?"

"Not since that incident in New York."

"But that wasn't her fault." Jamaica and Yoshi protested at once. They were always finishing each other's sentences. It was so cute it made Heather want to puke.

"You did this to me. I'm going to look like an apartment complex because of you, a townhouse, and a freaking skyscraper. And don't call me baby, I'm older then you, you thug."

"Wow, Aunt Holly's really upset about something."

Heather downed her drink as she rose from her seat, and handed the empty glass to Kyle. "I'll be right back."

Katrina kicked Gregori's ankle. "You're bad. You made Auntie Holly cry. You take a time out."

"Oh my God, I'm so sorry Gregori. Katrina! Stop kicking him this minute and say you're sorry." Jamaica pulled her away before she could kick him again.

"It is okay, Jamaica, really. I probably deserve it."

"Mommy, he made Auntie Holly cry. He's bad. You make him take a time out."

"Honey, Auntie Holly cries at the drop of a hat these days."

"She does not. You need a time out too, Mommy."

Heather sighed as she turned into mist and slipped into the restroom. Holly threw her arms around her as soon as she rematerialized.

"He said I'm getting fat."

"He said he wanted a sip of your drink. Look at you. You've lost 10 pounds since we left New York. Now come out and talk to him." Heather held Holly for a few more minutes. "Come on, everyone is here to celebrate your pregnancy." She opened the door and called Gregori in.

"Babycakes," Gregori hated seeing her so distressed. Nothing could unbalance him the way her tears did.

Holly wrapped her arms around him. "You must think I'm some kind of crazy woman. I'm sorry."

Gregori wrapped his arms around her. "Babycakes, I love you, all of you, even the crazy parts."

"I'll try to behave like a sane person." She clung to him like a life raft. "Just don't tell anyone that I'm not."

Heather sighed and slipped out of the restroom.

"There is nothing to see here. Everyone can go back to getting drunk."

Hiccupping, Holly emerged from the restroom a few minutes later. "Sorry about that, it's just my hormones getting out of control. You can go back to getting drunk. You can forget about this." Holly determinedly made her way to the bar. She needed another tomato juice, and maybe some mozzarella sticks. For some reason, those were the only thing she could keep down. She ignored Gregori. He looked worried as he followed her.

The bar tender smiled at her as he handed her an unopened bottle of V8 juice. "The mozzarella sticks will be right up."

"Will you open this for me?" Holly asked as she handed Gregori the bottle to open. "Do you like mozzarella sticks, Gregori?"

"Yes to both," Gregori smiled weakly.

Heather and Kyle turned their conversation to sports. They both liked basketball and football, but were only so-so on baseball and soccer. Around two in the morning, they drifted over to the bar where Holly kept feeding mozzarella sticks to Gregori. That crisis was over for now.

Kyle asked Heather if she would transform him.

She said she would think about it. She didn't want to make a commitment on their first date.

Heather and Kyle said goodnight to everyone after a heated discussion over whether she should transform him and which cities sports teams were the best. They headed for his room.

"Do you want to come in for a nightcap, or how about a piece of me?"

Heather responded by pushing him against the wall and gave him a big smooch and rubbing her hands all over his body. Several people stopped to watch as she slid one hand over his ass and the other over the bulge in his pants. They paid the voyeurs no mind.

"Maybe," Heather murmured as they separated.

"What else do you have in mind?" Kyle opened the door. They were stripping as they passed through the doorway, and naked before they got to the couch. Giggling and laughing, they got whip cream from the refrigerator. Whip cream never tasted as good as when you were licking it off someone you really liked. Heather really liked licking it off Kyle. He felt the same way about her.

It was during the shower that Heather bite him and drank his blood. He drank from her while they were on the bathroom floor. There was also the kitchen floor and table. The carpeting in the hallway felt exceptionally soft against their bare skin. They did it everywhere except the bedroom.

Heather and Kyle were very happy the next night, though no one saw them until after one pm.

+++++++++

Dracula rose from his underground crypt. He shot from the earth and tasted the fresh air. It had been three months since he had first tasted freedom. He was beginning to become accustomed to the strangest, and the fragmented nature of his memories. The books the female kept giving him were helping there.

Harder to accept was the others who kept throwing him into the sunlight and calling him Flameboy. It was degrading. Nicknames were needed so everyone could tell who was being talked to or about with so many Draculas hanging around.

Several other men claimed to be the real Dracula. There were nine now. There were several women claiming to be Mina and Lucy. Regrettably, there were also several Van Helsing and other of his ilk out there and they all wanted to see all the Draculas dead. It was something they would all have to deal with. It would not be a simply task.

+++++++++

Myles studied the man in front of him. Marco and his fellow custom officers had kept him from joining the others. They needed to know what they had to do to spread the New Life to Europe. They had been in contact with their counterparts in Europe. Several of those had relatives who were sick. They all wanted to know if the New Life could help their relative too. After a brief discussion, Myles laid out his plan. Did the others agree with it? Did they think they could implement it? They did. It would be. The New Life was going to Europe.

+++++++++

Holly ran down the sidewalk, easily dodging pedestrians. Bruce, Doug and Gregori followed her, cursing her out. She stopped in front of a music store and waited for them to catch up. It was very foggy out, and getting hard to see. Holly had no problem with it, but the boys were having a hard time of it. They were trying too hard. One had to trust one's instincts then everything would be clear.

Holly took a deep breath and held it. Negativity filled the air. Here in Atlanta the Anti-New Life movement was still strong. New Lifers just called them goons. Holly could feel that several of the goons were nearby. She relayed this to the others. The fog seemed to intensify forcing them to enter the store.

"Okay, you win. I'm sorry I dragged you out tonight." Holly wanted to see if she could find an old soundtrack from a Dracula movie. It had been out of print for years, but she still felt hopeful. The goons were getting closers. Holly felt sure they could handle two or three, but not a dozen. She let the others in her group know where they were and what was happening.

One of them grabbed Holly's arm, without thinking she grabbed the back of his head and pulled him closer. Before he could make a sound, she bitten him and drank his blood. Gregori was there in a flash, wanting to tear the man's head off. However, cooler heads prevailed. Holly and the babies needed the blood.

Myles had arrived and convinced Bruce to convert the young man, not kill him. They did the same with the other five in the store.

The police arrived shortly after that, summoned by store security. What the goons should have known was they had been the only non-New Lifers in the store. The police had been investigating them for weeks. They had no sympathy for the goons, since the entire police force was New Lifers. The telepathy made police work that much easier.

Chapter 7

Mark Cornridge swore at his cell phone. He swore at his useless son and his bitch of a mother. It wasn't even seven o'clock in the morning and he was totally wasted.

"What's the matter Honeybees?" Veronica Sedum asked as she rubbed Mark's shoulders. "Won't he answer his phone?"

"No. That bastard won't."

"I thought you were married to his mother." Veronica's twin sister, Nymphea Pink Sedum, asked innocently. She thought Gregori was hot and a good person. His father on the other hand was a drunken, lying, freeloader. Her sister completely adored him. Nymphea had no use for him. Veronica loved him. Nymphea loved his money. "And why should he? All you ever do is curse him and his mother out then demand that he send you money. I wouldn't answer your calls either."

"You know I was married to her. You are the one who insists I send her the alimony checks." Mark pushed the words out through his teeth.

"Such that they are, she deserves more than you send her." He really was all right when he wasn't drunk. He hadn't been drunk for the last ten years.

"Momma, why are you and Poppa fighting?" Angeline Sedum Cornridge demanded. She is the illegitimate offspring of a then 58-year-old Mark Cornridge and a then 15-year-old Nymphea Sedum. Angeline would be six on August 8, a month and a day before her mother and Aunt's birthday.

"Because Poppa doesn't know when he has a good thing. Plus, he expects everyone to clean up after him." Nymphea glared at Mark who lay on a chaise lounge sipping red wine for breakfast for God's sake. "Pay the last $1,000,000 you owe her and get it over with already."

"Gregori can do it. He makes enough. I certainly don't have it."

"Gregori had a brain tumor and lung cancer." Angeline nodded sagely. "It was on the news this morning. He became a New Lifer and was cured of it." She had already talked to her half-brother on her cell phone. It made her happy that he had found the woman of his dreams. She wasn't going to tell her father any of this. He would just get mad. "He looks really good. Isn't that right Auntie Ronnie?"

Everyone turned to Veronica who tried to look innocent. A job made difficult by the skintight two-piece bathing suit she was wearing. "Why, yes dearest. The news did mention that he had lung cancer. His condition had kept him from working most of this year. He hoped to get back to work now that the fog had cured him. He's doing a movie called Quincy." Gregori had looked happy, Veronica added to herself.

"What else did it say?" Mark gritted his teeth together so hard, he almost cracked them. Why hadn't his only son confided in him?

"That he broke up with Vanessa Lee. She was sleeping with another woman. They were going to kill him for his money. I saw that on Entertainment Tonight about a month ago."

Nymphea frowned at her daughter. Clearly, the news was not something Angeline or her sister should be watching if they were showing stuff like that.

Mark frowned. His Gregori had been deathly ill and no one bothered to tell him. Gregori was a New Lifer now, yet he had to hear it from his daughter who found out about it from an entertainment news show. Without thinking, he called his agent, Zagreb Coreopsis. The last time Mark had seen Zag he had been a balding, overweight, hard drinking but totally great agent. Since becoming a New Lifer, he had gained hair and lost weight. He was still a great agent and a hard drinker.

"Mark baby, how are you doing? Damn I wish that son of yours was one of my clients. He's hot."

"And I'm not."

"You said it, not me. To be honest with you, no you're not. How can I help you?"

"My son was deathly ill and no one told me about it."

"He didn't tell anyone about it. Sophia didn't find out until the night he was converted. From what I understand, the cancer had so far advanced that no treatment could have saved him. It had spread to his brain."

"Oh my God," he looked at the packet of cigarettes on the table next to him.

"Look, I'm coming down south soon. What with the supervolcano and all, several major productions are heading your way. Maybe I can get you a bit part in one of them." Zag was doubtful, but Mark was one of his clients.

"Maybe if you become a New Lifer more parts will open up for you." Then again, he could be wrong. Mark didn't have a tenth the talent of his son.

"Do you think it will really blow?"

"Yep."

"I do need a job Zag. I still owe Sophia money."

"You mean you're finally going to pay her off. Gregori turned 18 only 21 years ago."

"I paid off his child support. This is back alimony." He pushed Veronica's hand away as he stood up and began to pace. "When will you be down here? Soon?" He made a choking sound as Angeline showed him the morning paper. Gregori and Sophia pictured with some other people. Sophia hadn't been that sexy and beautiful when they had been a young married couple, and certainly not since then. This New Life stuff worked miracles.

"I've got a better idea. The little chick who converted Gregori is carrying his child. Now everyone tells me Gregori and Holly are going to marry. I don't have a date, yet. Would you like to attend the ceremony if I can arrange it?"

"Yes," he couldn't take his eyes off the picture of Sophia even when Angeline pointed out Gregori's girlfriend. "Are they in New Orleans now?"

"For a couple of weeks, they head for England when they get their permits. Europe doesn't like New Lifers."

"New Orleans," Mark sighed.

"They should be there for Mardi Gras." Zag smiled. He knew he had Mark right where he wanted him.

"Now you're not going to start any trouble. Are you?"

"No. I just want to see her and pay off my debt." He crossed his fingers.

"Does everyone have passports?"

"Yes."

"Okay. I'll work out the details. Let me get back to you."

"Okay. Later." Mark stood listening to the dial tone.

"Poppa?"

'We're going to a real Mardi Gras sweetheart."

+++++++++

Heather pretended to be interested in folding clothes while watching Kyle work on the new television set. It was a new high definition flat screen. Now that Gregori had taken over Holly's care, she could focus on Kyle. Kyle being almost as good as a bowl of fresh strawberries dipped into a bowl of dark chocolate with a side of whipped cream, almost.

Kyle turned from the television and smiled at her. "You know that just because she lives with Gregori, it doesn't mean you don't have to keep an eye on her. Mardi Gras is coming up and Myles wants her to go with him. Gregori's been ignoring her lately."

"Has he? I haven't noticed any drop in his attentiveness." Heather frowned. Did Kyle never wear underwear? He had only two briefs in a weeks' worth of laundry.

"She spends all her time writing. Gregori spends all his time going over manuscripts. She spends more time with Bruce, Frank and Doug then alone with Gregori." Kyle grabbed the remote and turned on the television. He flicked through several channels. The images on the screen were clear and beautifully detailed.

Heather shrugged. Holly and Bruce were writers. Doug was their scribe. Frank was their agent. Kyle and Gregori were actors. They were always reading manuscripts. She saw nothing exciting about them doing their jobs. It would have been weird if they weren't doing those things.

"I'm telling you that Myles is making a grab for Holly. He wants her for himself."

"Have you talked to Gregori about this?" Heather gave up on the laundry and gave Kyle her full attention.

"You know how he feels about Myles Ludwig." Kyle laughed. "I'll talk to him as soon as I can. Mardi Gras is in what, a week?"

"Yep, it's a week from tonight. So you had better talk to him soon."

"We should invite Otto and Nicole for the holidays. They could bring the dogs and drive Gregori completely insane. What do you think?"

"Sounds like fun, but I don't think he can get off on such short notice."

"Hah! I talked to him this morning. We'll pick them up at the airport on Thursday morning." Kyle punched the air. "I've finally got one on you. I'm the king of the mmmmmm….." He couldn't finish his sentence with Heather kissing him so vigorously. He knew how to make her happy.

+++++++++

Holly gasped. She just woke from a sound sleep to find Myles Ludwig naked and on top of her under the covers. Why wasn't she screaming?

"Come to Mardi Gras with me. You've already spent enough time baby-sitting that fool. Come on, you need a break from him."

"Myles, the fool is the father of my babies. If he doesn't kill you, Bruce, Doug, or Frank will. Oh my God, you are naked. My whole family will kill you."

"Not if you don't tell them. Come to Mardi Gras with me."

"I can't drink. I'm pregnant."

"So, don't drink. You don't have to drink to have fun. Like now, let's have sex."

"Myles," Holly tried to shout but it came out a throaty whisper. She tried to escape him, but he had her pinned to the bed.

"Come on, it isn't like you're marrying what's his name. Now is it?" Myles lowered his face to Holly's neck for a quick bite. His right hand pulled her left thigh against his hip as he drank her blood.

Holly moaned as Myles teeth pierced her skin. Without any thought on her part, her treasonous hips shot up to meet his. Holly's brain went into overload. It there was one thing she had learned from Gregori, it was that she loved sex and couldn't get enough of it. It didn't hurt that Myles has the built of a blonde haired, blue eyed, well-endowed Norse God. If Holly hadn't already been pregnant with Gregori's children, she would have been glad to have Myles's instead. Hell, she'd be glad to have Myles anytime Gregori was too busy for her which was all the time lately.

"So, you'll go with me to Mardi Gras?" Myles asked as their bodies still quivered from their third orgasm.

"Sure. Why not, it sounds like fun." Holly's voice came out sounding funny, like she felt drugged or something.

It was a week later and Holly found herself running after Myles on a crowded street. Men shouted drunkenly as some equally drunken young women exposed their breasts and tossed cheap beaded necklaces down to them from second and third floor balconies. Everyone had a beer or two.

Exhilarated, Holly grabbed a good-looking young man by the hips. He had actually been a freshmen college student in 1969, the Summer of Love. They slipped into a doorway for a little necking.

Myles swore like an enraged dockworker, a job he had once done while working his way through college. Holly had been just a few feet behind him, and now she was gone. How could anyone disappear so fast? Backtracking, he found her feeding on some young man. It took Myles only a minute to realize he had gone to college with this young man. He had been a drug dealer back then, if Myles was remembering correctly.

Holly stumbled out of the doorway and over to Myles. "I think he's doing more than beer. He's a werewolf." The only way a vampire New Lifer could get drunk or high was from drinking the blood of a werewolf New Lifer. Tommy was a werewolf. He was a werewolf high on drugs and alcohol.

"Yes," Myles smiled. He found watching Holly feed almost as exciting as having sex with her. "I think I went to college with him. Why don't you give me a minute alone with him?"

"Okay."

Myles walked over to the man who was still in the doorway. "Hey Tommy, it's been a long time."

Tommy's eyes widened. "I'm sorry dude. Is she your girlfriend?"

"You could say that." Myles sunk his teeth into Tommy's throat and feed well. The police never could figure out what happened to him. They chalked it up to an over excited college professor celebrating being released from the bounds of old age. Tommy could not remember anything about the night including how he ended up in the hospital.

"You didn't kill that poor young man. Did you?" Holly tried to focus on Myles while encouraging a group of young men in front of her to drop their pants. She had no luck with them. They would have had to put down their beers in order to pull their pants down. There was no way they were putting down their beers.

"He'll be fine though he might need to feed more heavily than usual. Let's go to the lake. I've heard they're having fireworks this year."

"Cool. I love fireworks. Let's feed a couple of more times along the way." Holly ran ahead jumping up to join a group of women who were displaying their breasts and throwing beads. She joined them for a few minutes. It gave her a real thrill when the men expressed loud appreciation of her bare breasts. No one had ever admired them that way before. At least she could not remember anyone expressing admiration of her breasts before. Holly found it so exciting that she did it over a half dozen more time before they reached the lake.

Myles and Holly lingered by the lake. They admired the fireworks and fed lightly on the party goers

Holly got very drunk doing this though the drugs the partygoers ingested only added flavor to their blood. Drugs ingested in any manner just didn't affect New Lifers. They couldn't get high.

Bruce and Doug followed Gregori closely. It would do no good to try to talk to him. Once he had learned from Heather that Holly had gone out with

Myles, all Gregori could think of doing was to kill Myles.

Bruce sniffed the air. Holly had come this way some hours earlier. "She's heading to the lake to watch the fireworks." Bruce announced a moment before the first fireworks went off.

"Which lake?"

"Lake Pontchartrain," Gregori growled as they headed north. "Oh great, just fine, we're in the part of the city furthest from where they're headed."

"She came this way for sure. I think she feed on couple of people along the way." Bruce frowned. "They were drunk and probably werewolves." Bruce pushed through the crowd and started running toward Holly as quickly as the press of the crowded streets allowed. Holly's scent became stronger. Another round of fireworks went off above them.

Bruce stopped abruptly as they reached a clearing causing Gregori and Doug to run into him. "Oops, the hot dog she had earlier just come back up. There's going to be a fog."

Gregori rubbed his nose. He could feel the change in the air, which always preceded a fog. First, the air became increasingly humid, followed quickly by a drop in temperature. He watched Bruce sniff the air, then take off running again. They soon encountered a rich, thick fog. At the center of the fog, they found Holly leaning over a railing. She was vomiting her guts out into Lake Pontchartrain.

Gregori grabbed Myles and repeatedly punched him in the face.

A police officer appeared out of nowhere and demanded to know what was going on.

"This man got Holly sick. She's mister Cornridge's fiancé and the mother of his unborn children." Doug explained. "She's way too trusting most of the time. A trait sometimes gets her into big trouble. Plus, I think he drugged her."

Gregori stopped beating Myles and went to Holly's side. She looked quite pale and ill. Rubbing her shoulders, he kissed her on the top of her head. "Babycakes, it's time to go home."

"Officer, that man over there is doing more than beer. You should arrest him." Holly pointed out a young man in ripped jeans and a Grateful Dead tee shirt who was smoking something while chugging beer. Even as they watched, he turned green and started puking. Only half of his puke made it into the lake.

Gregori pulled Holly into his arms. She had finally stopped puking.

"Can I take her home now officer?"

"What about my nose?" Myles demanded as a trickle of blood slowly flowed from on nostril. It stopped.

"Is it true Miss that this gentleman lured you here under false pretenses?"

"Yes officer." The fewer words I say, Holly thought, the better. She wasn't willing to admit she wasn't paying attention. Not since Gregori took her into his arms, anyway.

"I did not." Myles protested loudly. He gritted his teeth. He could tell from the way the officer looked at Holly that he wasn't going to win this one. "I simply took her out for a pleasant Mardi Gras party. Mister Cornridge never takes her anywhere." Myles added spitefully.

"I think Mister Cornridge should take his girlfriend home. In fact, I think you all should leave now." The officer added politely as more people started to puke.

Gregori scooped Holly into his arms with no further discussion and took her directly to their new home with the others following them closely.

Home being a three story Victorian manor that Gregori and Holly picked out as being a perfect place to start a family. Gregori wanted alot of children. For the time being, Bruce and Doug lived on the top floor, which was really the attic. Sophia and Jasmine shared the first floor. Gregori and Holly had the second floor while Heather and Kyle had the third. The basement was for everyone.

+++++++++

"What do you want Mark?" Sophia gazed frostily at her ex-husband. He had appeared on her doorstop unannounced with two children. The two girls were now sleeping in the guest bedroom next to Jasmine's room.

"I want to give you the money I owe you plus some extra." Mark fidgeted. Gregori had purchased a very nice home. "Will 200,000 dollars cover everything?"

"Where'd you get that kind of money?"

"I got an advance on my next movie." Actually, Zag had given him most of it.

"What you mean is another Dracula flick? Right," Sophia had long ago resigned herself to the fact that Mark only wanted to do horror flicks. He was like an overgrown kid in that respect. That couldn't be right. Horror flicks never pay that good.

"It's an adaptation of a book by a well-known science fiction author. I'm playing a minor character. I forgot the name." He hedged. "I hear Gregori is playing Dracula."

"Yes. He's doing Quincy. It's an adaptation of the book of the same name. What's the name of the movie you're making?"

"Quincy? I've never heard of it. Who's it by?"

"Holly Skyhaven, your son's girlfriend, Jasmine is her sister." Sophia pointed to Jasmine while whipping out her cell phone. Truly, the man was getting stupider by the minute. "Let me talk to Zag about this. He must know who you're playing." Sophia had Zag on speed dial. They talked often about Mark and his career. Though she would never admit it, she still cared enough about Mark to worry about his health, which was not good. Zag answered by the second ring.

"Hey gorgeous, how can I help you today? I know. Gregori needs a new agent."

"You can keep on dreaming, sweetie. I'm calling because Mark's here. He says he's in a movie but can't remember its name or the name of the character he is playing. I hope you can clarify things for us. You can. Can't you?"

"He's getting too old to play Dracula. That hasn't stopped some people. He's either going to play Van Helsing or Renfield in the Dracula Tapes by Fred Saberhagen. He may play Dracula if, and only if, he becomes a New Lifer."

"How did he take being offered those parts?"

"With embarrassment, he wants to be Dracula. To be honest with you, his memory is going. He's done too much alcohol over the years."

"Will he command more money if he becomes a New Lifer?" Sophia phrased her questions carefully. Mark's two daughters were sleeping in the next room. She didn't want to wake them or upset them.

"Easily double or triple what he's getting now. When he's healthy and not drunk he's almost as good an actor as Gregori. Almost. Drunk, he's not even a tenth as good as Gregori. Do you remember how good he was before the booze when the two of you were first married?"

"Yes."

"I tried to convert him. He isn't ready to come out of the closet yet."

"Let me take care of it. I'll get in touch with you in a couple of nights, sooner if there are any problems."

"Later then."

"Later." Sophia closed her phone and licked her lips.

Mark watched Sophia lick her lips. He knew from experience that he was getting himself into big trouble. The signs were all there.

"Whoa. Sorry. We didn't know you had company."

"It's okay. This is my ex-husband, Mark Cornridge. His five and three year old daughters are sleeping in the next room." Sophia smiled gaily. "His agent wants me to convert him. Do you want to help?"

"Don't I have a say in this?" Mark spared a glance toward the room where his daughters were sleeping.

"No," Sophia shook her head. "Honestly Mark, you look like a beached whale. I'm surprised Sea World hasn't called saying one of theirs was missing."

"That's not funny, you bitch." Mark was very sensitive about his weight.

"Let's convert him the painful way." Jasmine shocked everyone with that statement. She was always the gentle, peaceful one.

"I'm sorry." Mark gasped. He could feel his heart pounding against his ribcage. Zag had set him up. This had been his plan all along. "I just wanted to pay off my debt."

"You owe me alimony for the rest of my life. How do you expect 200,000 dollars to cover all of that?"

"That's back pay." He eyed the people circling him. "Are you going to introduce me to your friends?"

"This is Kyle, his girlfriend Heather, her son Otto and his wife Nicole.

Their triplets are sleeping in the stroller."

"I'm pleased to meet you." Mark tried to think of ways to stall them, but his mind went blank. "Who'll take care of my daughters while I'm undergoing this procedure?"

"I will." Bruce said from the doorway. He was trailing an angry Gregori. "Hi guys. Does anyone want to help Gregori beat up Myles?"

"We're going to convert Mark here. Do you want to help us?" Nicole felt excited. This would be her first chance to feed since giving birth just after midnight that morning. Her doctors had been wrong when they said she had another five weeks before her delivery. Man was she hungry.

Gregori and Myles stopped glaring at each other and turned their attention to Mark. The way they licked their lips frightened Mark. He watched Gregori set Holly on the chair between Sophia and the stroller holding Nicole and Otto's newborn triplets. The triplets had been born that morning. Hospitals really should not push women out only a couple of hours after giving birth. It could not possibly be healthy for the mothers or the infants. As that pleasant thought passed through his mind, everyone in the room took turns biting Mark and giving him an exchange.

He woke up some 72 hours later with much the same people watching him. He was sitting cross-legged on the bathroom floor with his head propped up by the toilet. The toilet bowl felt cool to his feverish skin. "How long have I been out of it?"

"Three nights."

"I've got to call Ronnie and Nymphea. They must think I've deserted them." Mark buried his face in his hands. Physically, he felt fantastic. Emotionally, he felt like shit.

"They're in the hospital." Otto said bluntly. "They were leaving town when a heavy fog hit. The police told us they must have gone off the embankment and rolled the car a couple of times. I'm sorry. The last we heard they were in a coma."

"The police told us when they came to check up on Myles. It seems that someone broke his nose." Nicole smiled. Everyone had wanted to be there when Gregori had beaten the crap out of Myles. Myles had so deserved it.

"Where are Angeline and Little Nymphea now? Is someone watching them?"

"Bruce and Doug are watching them." Myles said while keeping an eye on Gregori. "The police just called. Veronica Sedum and Nymphea Pink Sedum have disappeared from their hospital rooms. They don't know what happened to them. They don't seem to care one way or the other about what happened to them. At least they called."

"But my girls are okay?" Everyone laughed as Mark quickly stood up and his jeans and underpants just as quickly fell to the floor. They spent over an hour teaching him how to turn into animals. Mark turned into a snow-white

Arctic fox.

They fog grew into a soupy mess which shut down the city and made travel impossible. Veronica and Nymphea's disappearance was low on the police's to do list. The fog was causing other problems. Problems they would have to deal with soon or later. Jasmine explained all of this to Mark when Angeline and Little Nymphea burst into the room. "Poppa, you're finally awake."

"Yes honeys."

Just then, Jamaica and Yoshi burst into the room waving their marriage license and the paperwork needed for Yoshi to adopt Jamaica's children. It's a good night.

+++++++++

Myles Ludwig stared across the table at Mark Leo Cornridge. The resemblance between him and his son was remarkable. However, he found Gregori to be the more personable of the two. Gregori had beaten him up. He had deserved it, of course. There was also Mark's drinking problem.

Mark stared back at Myles. "I don't have a drinking problem. I haven't touched an alcoholic beverage since before Mardi Gras." Not since Nymphea and Ronnie dumped him and the girls. "Alcohol makes me sick since I've been converted." Mark hated that he sounded so defensive but just the smell of alcohol made him want to vomit.

"Plus you have two small children to take care of."

Mark nodded his head glumly. He had no idea where Ronnie and Nymphea had gone to the night they disappeared from the hospital. He had been undergoing his conversion at the time, which was the only reason no one blamed him for what happened to his girlfriends.

"I think it is very mature of you to take full responsibility for your children."

"I wanted to earlier, but alcohol kept me stupid. Their mother and Aunt were dead set against it. They thought I favored Gregori." Mark smiled at the irony. He could count on one hand the number of time he had seen Gregori since his divorce from Sophia. He asked the Gods why he had ever left her.

"Because, you think she is way too bossy. She actually expected you to stop drinking and pay the bills."

"And help around the house, and, be a good father. In short, all of the things I still have to do now but without her help." He looked across the room where Little Nymphea and Angeline were getting to know their half-brother and his girlfriend. The girls looked like Gregori except both had his blue eyes not Gregori's green. Following Mark's gaze, Myles smirked. He did that a lot. "The guys will be really fighting over them when they get older." Choosing to ignore that comment, Mark smiled.

"Gregori will make a fine father. I wonder if Holly understands how lucky she is to have him."

"So you finally agree with me on something." Sophia whispered into his ear causing him to jump. He hadn't heard her approach him. As usual these nights, Jasmine was right next to her. The two were always together.

"You've done a wonderful job raising him Sophia. I'm sorry I wasn't there to help you. I missed so much."

"It's not too late to get to know him."

"Tell him that. He won't ever look at me now. Not that I blame him."

Sophia blinked. She had never heard her cocky, brazen, drunken ex-husband sounding so defeated. She wondered if the television special showing him to be a drunken, womanizing lazy ass bastard who had deserted his wife and child to sleep with a teenager was finally getting to him. Hell, even Sophia had thought the girl to be over 30. Smoking really does age some people.

"I'm going to be heading to England with Zag. He's got some movies lined up for me."

"Who'll be watching the girls while you're working?"

"He's arranged a nanny service for me. A couple of elderly women agreed to watch them on the set. With my luck, they'll become New Lifers and lose interest."

"Or worse," Sophia laughed. "They'll look like teenagers and get you into trouble again."

"Have I ever told you how beautiful you are you when you laugh? You have the most beautiful smile."

"No," Sophia sat down across from him.

"That's because I'm a fool."

Myles and Jasmine made their way across the room to where Holly, Gregori and the girls were playing video games. It was best to let Mark and Sophia work things out in their own way.

"I knew that when I married you. Everyone told me repeatedly. I love you anyway."

"Even now?"

Sophia nodded. "It was your drinking and womanizing I couldn't take. Don't say you're sorry. It's too late for that."

"I am anyway. But the press always said I was a sorry excuse for a human being."

"It's harsh, but true."

"The girls tell me I'm going to be a grandfather. When is Gregori due?"

"Holly's due in April. New Life pregnancies are half as long as normal human ones. Can't you say her name?"

"I don't think Gregori want me to say her name. I don't want him to beat me up the way he did Myles. I didn't know he could be so possessive."

"There's a lot you don't know about him."

"But you didn't know that either."

"I have to admit, it took me by surprise. It's a part of him that he never showed before."

"He's never been in love before." Mark smiled.

His only boy had found happiness. "Now if he can only hold on to it."

"He will." Sophia crossed her fingers under the table.

"I love this song. Let's dance. It might be a long time before we see each other again."

"Won't you be going to Gregori's wedding? You've missed so much already."

"Will he let me come? Does he want me there?"

"I'm sure he does. I'll talk to him. I want you there." Sophia took Mark's hand, leading him to the dance floor.

+++++++++

The next month and a half was a blur of interviews. Holly woke several times from a horrible dream. Everyone knew about the dream, and several others had shared it. Everyone thought it was interesting, but no one felt it was important. Telepathy kept bringing their dreams to come together.

Chapter 8

Holly sat with Gregori and Sophia. The cream of cheddar and broccoli soup is good. It made her feel all warm inside. It was the best soup ever, except for the homemade soups Heather made from their mother's recipes. "Remember when we had the deep fried hamburger? It was so good."

"It made you sick, as I recall." Sophia did not approve of Holly's eating habits. It was the only complaint she had about her.

"It sure did, but it had been worth it." Holly had only been able to eat a half of the hamburger. Gregori had eaten the rest, along with his own. They both loved food. It kept them together.

"Didn't you sleep well, Babycakes?" Gregori frowned.

"Not really. Heather and Kyle stayed up all day watching slasher movies and discussing popcorn. He loves it with butter and cheese, and she hates butter and cheese."

"They spend a great deal of time together, don't they?"

"Yes, he wants her to move in with him." Holly tried to concentrate on the soup. She could keep food down it she concentrated on it. Holly was 12 weeks pregnant. With the accelerated New Lifer pregnancy, she was really at 24 weeks gestation. Everything was going well according to the doctors. She had not gained much weight. The doctors wanted her to gain more. Holly had a hard time keeping most food down.

"Will the others be joining us soon?" Heather did not like cream soups, so they went to a different restaurant. Gregori did not understand what Heather had against cream soups.

"Soon, Heather wanted to pick up something back for Otto and Nicole. Baby clothes, I think. She's always thinking of others." Holly wished she were as considerate as Heather. Heather always thought of others first. It made Holly feel like a selfish clod.

"You are not." Gregori hated when Holly put herself down. She did not seem to realize that she had many fine qualities of her own

"Name them," Holly replied, picking up his thought, as she finished her soup. It was so yummy like Gregori.

"You're a kind and good person. You don't start fights and seldom finish them. You see the good in everyone. You love people. And you still believe in happy endings."

"Will we have a happy ending?"

"Yes, we will. Don't you doubt it for a minute?"

"See what I mean. Those two are hopeless optimists." Heather slid into the seat next to Holly. How Holly could eat cream soups was beyond her. "Frank just got word. We can pick up our visas tomorrow. We'll be in London by the weekend."

"Will I get to do the Dracula tour?"

"Yes Holly, for the zillionth time, you will get to go on the Dracula tour."

+++++++++

Gregori and Myles waited for the others to join them at the dock. Holly wanted to send some souvenirs back home before they departed. She had become fussy during the final preparations. Myles gazed at Gregori and shook his head. He knew that Gregori did not really understand Holly. Nobody did. "Holly is a polar bear."

"What?"

"She's a polar bear, or maybe a grizzly bear, I think. She's like a bear in that most of the time in that she just wants people to leave her alone. The only exception is during mating season." Myles leaned back and watched Gregori carefully. He wondered what kind of animal Gregori was. One who loved togetherness and snuggling, no doubt? He wondered how Gregori was in bed. "She's pregnant now. She just wants to hibernate and be left alone."

"That's stupid. She needs people more than ever right now. She's hardly a bear of any type." This man is so full of shit. He never makes any sense. Gregori glared at Myles. What is the man doing? He remembered clearly the trick he had played on all of them during Mardi Gras. The fuck head would pay for that. Gregori ground his teeth. Holly was carrying his children. She would not ever leave him. The thought of her leaving him made him ill. Gregori was more than a bit of a bear himself. He would have preferred being a wolf right now so he could rip Myles's throat out.

"I'm just trying to explain why she seems so distant recently. She's not planning on leave you. Sometimes this is just a bit much for her. There is an incident in her youth were she lost someone she loves. She's just afraid of losing you too." Myles played with the lid of his soft drink. He loved her as if she were the woman he would never have. He loved taking her to bars and getting her drunk and watching her feed. They had a very complex relationship. Gregori was destroying that relationship. Maybe he's doing drugs. New Lifers aren't supposed to react to drugs, but maybe he found a way. If he feed off werewolves who did drugs, then it was possible for him to get high. "Tell me about this supposed childhood incident."

Myles went into great deal about the event that shaped Holly's personality. "And that's why she likes being alone. She's worried about delivering in Europe. She'd rather be back in her home town for the birth."

"There are good doctors in Europe."

"I didn't say there weren't. But this is her first pregnancy." Myles had to be sure Gregori was the right person for Holly. Frank had insisted. Besides, he wanted her for himself. "She wants to nest."

Gregori hissed.

"I just don't want to see either of you hurt. She is very vulnerable right now. Holly just not sure of what she wants at this time."

"And she told you all of this?"

"Not all of it, she told me you keep buying her stuff and it's making her feel guilty. She loves gifts, but feels she has nothing to give you in return. I told her she thinks too much."

Gregori nodded his head slowly. He loved buying Holly stuff. Holly gave him love in return. He didn't need gifts from her. This incident from her youth was something that made him think. A polar bear, he could almost hear her grumbling bear like as she guarded their children. It made him laugh.

'You know Gregori,' Gregori heard Holly's voice in his mind, 'I might be a bear, but Myles wants you for himself. Am I going to lose you to him?'

'Of course not,' he thought back. Gregori laughed at that.

"I hear them coming, time to put on our happy face."

Heather and Kyle came in laughing. Holly, Bruce and Doug followed a few minutes later with Sophia. Sophia looked concerned about something. She smiled bravely at Gregori.

Holly gazed at no one. She avoided looking at anyone. She was hungry and tired, but so was everyone else.

"Is anyone willing to bet that Holly spends most of the voyage with motion sickness?" Heather loved making those kinds of bets. She had a wicked sense of humor.

Chapter 9

Gregori pulled Holly unto his chest and rolled away from her side of the bed just as a wooden stake is plunged into the bed. It would have gone straight through her heart.

A cry of unimaginable fury erupted in the room. Gregori dragged Holly from the bed, keeping himself between her and their attacker.

Not fully awake, her heart pounding, Holly silently urged Gregori to turn to mist and escape. She would follow.

The man screamed as he tried to pull the stake out of the bed. It had gone through the mattress and become jammed on a spring. "You bitch, I'll kill you. I'll kill you. I'll kill you for leaving me. I will."

"I've never met you before." Holly protested. She had never met this man in her life. It scared her that someone might be using her image to lure men for feeding.

Bruce had heard enough. He grabbed the man's head and snapped his neck. Doug appeared at his side. "There were two more outside. The ship's crew has them. Is everyone okay?"

"Yes," Holly's voice is barely a whisper as she clung to Gregori's back. She had never been so frightened in her life. She was sure she would vomit. This was getting to be a bad habit, she thought.

Gregori pulled her around, stroking her hair as he held her to his chest. "You're not going to throw up on me, Babycakes." Cupping her face, he kissed her forehead.

Kyle pushed the door open and entered. Heather, Jasmine and Sophia followed. "Is anyone hurt? They captured two outside our door. They say there were ten in all." Kyle surveyed the room. It took all of his will power not to lock at Holly's bare ass. Mercifully, Doug pulled out bathrobes for Holly and Gregori. Doug had been looking at Gregori's ass.

"Thanks Doug," Gregori smiled as he put his bathrobe on. "Mum? Are you and the others okay? This guy almost got Holly."

"Yes, we heard them before they could cause any mischief." Sophia watched them take the body out of the room. That goon almost had Holly.

Bruce stood by the door talking to the captain of the Princess Ayala. They gestured toward Holly and Gregori several times before approaching them.

"The ship is secured but I think it best if everyone stayed in their rooms tonight. This will be a problem for you. They broke the lock on your door. I'm arranging another room for you. It will be an upgrade at no extra charge to you. You will not be able to move in until around midnight tomorrow. Is this acceptable?"

"It'll be more secure than this one." Bruce gazed steadily into Gregori's eyes.

"Security will be our number one priority from now on. I can guarantee it."

"That's very kind of you. Isn't it Gregori?"

"Yes."

"We really do appreciate anything you can do, Captain." Holly gestured to the bed. "This is such an unexpected, truly terrifying thing. No one could have predicted it." Holly said as she pushed Gregori into a chair and sat on his lap.

"We'll discuss this tomorrow. I must look into a few more things tonight in order to insure everyone's safety." The captain bowed as he exited the stateroom.

"I don't think I'll be able to sleep."

Little Nymphea and Angeline tore into the room.

"Bad men are everywhere," Nymphea yelled.

"Everywhere," Angeline looked fearfully around the room.

Mark followed them in. He surveyed the room.

"Stay in my room," Sophia volunteered. "Jasmine and I are going to be playing cards all day. I'm up three games."

"Plenty of privacy," Jasmine added. "Good, then it's settled."

+++++++++

"No, you don't understand. I'm not rejecting you."

"Then what are you doing?"

"Explaining all of the good reasons why we shouldn't get married just because I'm pregnant." Gregori gave her a narrow eyed, tight-lipped look. He did not understand her position at all, or was simply refusing to accept it. It was hard to tell from his general look of dissatisfaction. He might have had gas for all Holly knew. "Look, every couple I know who married because of pregnancy now hate each other's intestines. They had very bitter, angry divorces. Do you want that for us?"

"No, but it'll be different for us."

"How?"

"How what?"

"How will it be different for us?"

"It just will be. We will not get divorced. Why do you have to argue so much? Just agree with me all the time and everything will be fine."

"If I just agree with you all the time I wouldn't be Holly. I'd be someone else." Cupping his face in her hands, she rubbed her nose gently against his. He is so sweet and smells so wonderful, Holly thought.

Gregori sighed. He tugged at Holly's hand and placed a kiss in the middle of her palms. He could never make her just do whatever he wanted. Despite his image and reputation, women were not just putty in his hands. He loved Holly and just wanted to be with her.

"Holly, will you please marry me? Let me make you happy."

Holly looked into his deep-set piercing green eyes and knew she is lost.

"Yes, I will marry you. However, no diamonds, I mean it. Anything with diamonds is going to your mother. And uncross those fingers."

"Yes master," Gregori laughed.

+++++++++

Sophia and Holly walked around the upper deck of the ship. This was how they would get to Europe if some more paperwork goes through. They passed the captain, whose name, Liam Delena, Holly somehow managed to remember. Holly did not want to give birth in Europe. She felt cranky and irritable. Sophia chalked it up to Holly's pregnancy. Twins were very demanding, even before birth. Gregori's insistence that they marry before Holly gave birth only added to Holly's strain.

The salt air stung Holly's eyes making her blink. How could Myles try to steal Gregori from her? She thought bitterly. She would never try to steal anyone from him. He called me a polar bear. Frank set this up. Why would Frank do that? Why was she so slow at picking things up? Holly lifted her face to the moon and sniffed the air. She felt hungry all the time now. It was too warm for her. Holly glanced at Sophia to see if she agreed. As usual, Sophia looked cool.

They entered the restaurant where Jamaica and Gregori were talking. It was cool in there. They were discussing Quincy. Laura picked Jamaica as Mina. Even Katrina had a small part in the movie. She would play one of Lucy's child victims. They were very excited. Otto and Nicole had brought the triplets, and the dogs, Trouble, PahGoo and MareMoo down to see them. Wendy and Colin were taking care of the dogs and the children.

"Oh Gregori, feel here," Holly smiled as she pressed Gregori's hand to her belly. Holly leaned over and kissed his forehead. "They always become so excited when they hear your voice. I was so worried. They've been so quiet lately."

Gregori felt the tiny feet kicking outward and smiled. It was a miracle. It was his miracle. "Just like their Mommy," he pulled Holly onto his lap, and listened to her laugh. She had a little girl laugh. He loved it.

Jamaica became excited. Aunt Holly and Gregori make such a cute couple. She had the perfect wedding dress in mind for Aunt Holly. She had designed it herself. They had to pick a date. The dress was finished. The only thing that she still needed to do was fit the dress. Jamaica had designed a lovely white dress with white embroidered flowers, just the way Aunt Holly liked it. She had been discussing it with Gregori when they had come in. Jamaica showed her drawings to Sophia, while Holly and Gregori smooched.

Sophia loved the drawings. She had a date picked out for the wedding. Gregori and Holly just needed to okay it. Sophia thought of Holly as the daughter she never had. Of course, with the New Life, she could try for more children. People in nursing homes all across the affected areas were embarrassing their children and grandchildren, and sometimes even great grandchildren by getting pregnant.

Gregori studied the drawings of the wedding dress Jamaica wanted Holly to wear. It is an off the shoulder A-line with embroidered white roses and flowing white sleeves. "Do you think white is the right color? Holly's so pale she'll blend right into it."

"How about we make it a very light purple? It could be almost white," Holly suggested. They were all sitting in Jamaica's stateroom.

"Do you want it the color of your ceiling?"

"Yes, exactly."

"Or pink," Nicole added.

"No, never pink," Holly shook her head to get the image out.

Jamaica pulled out a photo album. She had just finished the dress that morning. Therefore, a color change was out of the question.

Holly gazed at the dress. It was dazzling. How had Jamaica finished it so quickly? A frown creased her forehead. "What other surprises do you have for me?"

"Well," Nicole smiled wickedly as she pulled out the paperwork. "We did go to the trouble of filling out an application for a marriage license and filing it out. The doctors have already submitted the necessary tests."

"I haven't signed anything yet."

"Sure you did. Do you remember when Frank had you sign all those contracts last week? Why did you think one of them had Gregori's signature on it?"

Holly gazed blankly at the paperwork. She had trusted Heather to read the fine print for her. Now she sensed that that had been a mistake. She remembered

Heather insisting she read what she signed. She hadn't bothered to, though. She turned and smacked Gregori. It was his signature on it. He was in on this little conspiracy.

"Hey, I told you to read the paperwork. But no, you've got to just sign everything." Heather smirked.

"The captain has agreed to perform the ceremony." Bruce announced. He had to do something to get Holly back on his side. "Though I think Elijah wanted to perform it. He's coming in with Bobby Joe tonight."

"But, I always wanted to be married in Los Vegas by an Elvis impersonator." Holly dreamily played with Gregori's hair.

"What?" Everyone exclaimed at once.

"Explain yourself," Sophia demanded.

Otto just chuckled. He knew his Aunt Holly was batty.

"An Elvis impersonator, that way I could tell everyone that I was married by the king."

Jamaica snorted, and Myles rolled his eyes. Myles still thought no one was good enough for Holly. Frank had agreed with him. He wanted her for himself. Though to be honest, he also wanted Gregori for himself. Myles went both ways. No one cared what they thought. They all remembered how Frank had talked Myles into trying to steal Gregori from Holly, after their plan to steal Holly from Gregori had failed. It was a strange and very dirty trick for them to have played on the couple.

"Ha, ha, that's a good one. Now let's get serious here," Jasmine demanded. "Gregori's relatives will be here tomorrow and we still have some paperwork to fill out and last minute details to see to."

"Are Elijah and Bobby Joe coming? We don't have time to add a Klingon theme."

"Yes, and don't worry about. I'm sure they'll understand."

"You have to try on the dress. It has to be fitted tonight or it won't be done."

Holly grabbed Gregori's hand. She tried her best to look fierce. She failed miserably.

Sophia smiled broadly. "Try on these shoes, dear. We need you in them to check the length of the dress. Wow, you're shorter that I thought. And you've got such tiny feet."

Jamaica hurried Holly into the dress while Gregori and Heather finalized things. The crew of the Princess Ayala was most helpful in arranging things. It was going to be wonderful.

Holly tried to stand in the six inch stilettos. She felt dizzy just looking down. She prayed for a short ceremony with little movement required on her part. "Why do I need 12 inch heels for? Are you trying to kill me on my wedding night?"

"Six inches, sweetie, now hold still. Jamaica needs to work on that hem."

Holly gazed into the mirror. It was like watching a movie. Somehow, she did not recognize the person Jamaica was turning into a Princess. The Princess could not walk, but she was still a Princess.

Jamaica fretted. Aunt Holly was the equivalent of six months pregnant with twins. She did not even look pregnant. To Jamaica, it looked like Holly was wasting away. Aunt Heather claimed that Holly had gained 27 pounds, but she could not see it. It could be that Jamaica was used to seeing Aunt Holly being over 200 pounds. Now that Holly weighed only 122 pounds, she looked undernourished. A quick glance around the room told her that all of her family members looked that way. They had been fat all of their lives.

+++++++++

Dracula rose from his underground crypt. He shot from the earth and tasted the fresh air. He had finally found a resting place where the others could not find him. It was getting painfully degrading when the others kept throwing him into the sunlight. They thought it was funny when he burst into flames. They thought calling him

Flameboy was funny too. It was degrading. Not all of the Draculas participated in this game. The one called Erik never did, nor did his brothers Simon, Brad and Couch Potato. It was a big game the Minas were trying to stop them from playing.

Regrettably, there were also several Van Helsing and other of his ilk out there and they all wanted to see Dracula dead. They enjoyed the throw Flameboy into the sun game. They would have to be dealt with and it was not proving to be a simply task.

+++++++++

Holly paced all evening. She missed going bar hopping with Bruce. How was a girl to feed if she couldn't get out occasionally? The ship personnel were getting cranky about feeding her. She fed three times a night now. The government had decided to help pay for the trip.

The cast of Quincy was here and settled in. Gregori's family from Europe settled in and started complaining about the short notice and the nighttime hours that everyone kept. Mark and the girls were in the cabin next to Gregori and Holly's. Mark spent a great deal of time in Jasmine and Sophia's cabins. The wedding ceremony would start in one hour. Myles, who she tried to remember, was going by the name of Charles Gregory, stopped in to see her. He had an important mission for her when she got to Europe though he would not give her the details. She would have to tell Gregori as soon as she had a chance. She did not believe in keeping secrets from him, not that she could keep a secret anyway. It always backfired on her. She hated that.

Holly knew she should be angry about the way they had handled the wedding. She was angry with herself for being so naïve. With telepathy, everyone knew what everyone else wanted. It made things simpler in some ways and more complicated in other ways.

She had wanted to marry Gregori. She had wanted it for years. It was just not something she could believe in. It was a fairy tale. Fairy tales do not come true. Only the truly demented could believe any fairy tale would ever come true. Holly was giving herself a headache. She had never been so happy before. Even the weather was on her side, it was foggy.

Gregori look handsome in his tuxedo like a Ken doll come to life or maybe a G. I. Joe action figure, they were better looking than Ken any way. His long curly black hair framed his huge green eyes, long lashes and nose, and sensuous lips.

Holly remembered very little of the ceremony. She was too happy and excited to think clearly. All she could do was gaze into Gregori's eyes.

The reception was equally hazy. Everyone danced and no one tripped. Those who drank too much threw up over the side of the ship. The fog from that lasted over a month. The honeymoon cruise went well, with everyone seeming to work overtime to keep the wedding party happy.

Kyle proposed to Heather, but she was not for it.

Her choice disappointed Holly, but it was her choice. Holly liked receptions.

The only incident occurred before the wedding. The captain had the situation well underhand and none of the good bothered the wedding guests. Two of the anti-New Life goons posed as crewmembers. They caught them. They had been converted and taken back to shore. Converting them seemed to take the fight out of them. The crew sent them to unconverted areas to help people accept the change.

The city suffered a power outage starting that night, and the fog was especially thick during it. The power outage and the fog lasted a month. Only the goons complained, and by the end of the month, there were no more goons in the city.

Chapter 10

Doug pushed MareMoo's face away from his. Her constant licking was peeling the skin from his face. Why was she here? Holly had told her nephew that she would take care of her and PahGoo so he could get a break. Between the dogs and the babies, he was exhausted.

Doug knew this was important. Something had happened during the night, something that involved the captain of the ship, Charles, Holly and Bruce. MareMoo and PahGoo whined at the door, while Doug searched the cabin. He remembered bits and pieces of the night before. He and Bruce had stayed out till just before noon. They had returned to the cabin when the captain and Charles had dragged Holly into it. She had had both dogs with her.

"Are you hungry girls?" He remembered Holly asking him to watch MareMoo and PahGoo so they would not bother Heather and Kyle. Heather and Kyle had had a hot date that morning. While he settled MareMoo down, they had argued about some kind of mission. It was at that point that Charles had looked at him and he had become tired. The next thing he remembered clearly was MareMoo licking his face and PahGoo scratching at the door.

Doug grabbed their leashes and took them to the designated pet area on the ship. The sun had not yet set. Did Gregori even realize that Holly was missing? Who else was missing? "Hurry up girls. We've important stuff to do. People's lives could be in danger."

MareMoo whimpered in agreement.

Doug hesitated at Gregori and Holly's door. Gregori was very possessive of Holly. He would kill anyone who tried to hurt her.

"What do you want?" Gregori stared blurry eyed and half-naked. He answered the door as if he had the world's largest hangover. That wasn't possible. Gregori did not drink alcohol and hadn't in years.

"I'm sorry to wake you. Is Holly with you? It's important."

"I think she's in the bathroom." Gregori frowned. Holly's spot on the bed had been cool when he woke up.

How long had she been up, and where was she?

"Bruce is also missing. I think the captain and Charles took them both onshore."

Gregori and Doug searched the cabin. Holly was gone. Her jewelry was where she left last night, right next to her cell phone on the dresser. MareMoo pawed at the door, whimpering.

Doug picked up the jewelry. "Holly wouldn't have left without these unless she thought …." Doug trailed off. He could only think of negative things to say. It was not the time for such speculations.

"Holly dislikes jewelry."

"But she adores, loves and worships the man who gave her these. We know who he is."

Gregori took the jewelry and cell phone. He put it into his jacket pocket. "We should let the others know something's happened."

They pounded loudly on Heather's door. It took forever to wake her and Kyle, but soon, a large group had gathered in the main dining area of the ship. A thick fog seemed to come from on shore and soon surrounded the ship. By midnight, no one could see more than a few feet in front of themselves.

Bruce carried Holly into the dining area around 1:17 AM. They were both exhausted. Bruce did not want to hand her over to Gregori. He was too tired to think straight.

"Give Holly to Gregori before you both fall over," Doug said, guiding Bruce to a seat. Bruce blinked at Doug. He handed Holly over without another argument, and let Doug guide him to a seat. "I need caffeine."

Holly snored, and cuddled in Gregori's arms. He sat down with her in his arms and waited for an explanation. He did not think Bruce was awake enough to form a complete sentence. Everyone on the ship seemed to be waiting for an answer. Telepathy is a bitch when it came to keeping secrets, but apparently, someone knew how to keep them.

After three cups of hot black, coffee, Bruce felt ready to tell his story. "It was the captain and Charles. They insisted that Holly and I convert some of the custom officials here. The Officials in Orlando had an agreement with them. We met them in some warehouse. They had their aging parents and grandparents with them. We spent the entire night converting them. They wanted to know the secret of the fog. Holly knows how to make it. She taught them." Bruce started into his fourth cup of coffee before continuing.

"The police came and we had to hide. Someone at one of the nursing homes must have alerted them. It was too late by then. We converted them. The ones first converted took us through a bunch of warehouses and finally back to the ship. I think they felt bad that they had tired us out. The ones we converted told the ones who had not been to stop pushing us to perform more conversions.

They knew Holly's pregnant. It worried them. I don't think anyone told them, they just knew." Bruce threw his words out. "I need more coffee. I need it now."

Doug and Frank fed him. He needed his strength to finish telling them what happened. The coffee helped too.

"Holly told me they had slipped into her room after she had fallen asleep. Charles had done something to make sure Gregori didn't wake up too soon. He did the same thing to Doug when he picked me up. Holly brought the dogs along with her so MareMoo wouldn't wake Gregori. Charles had insisted on it." Bruce ended his story. He was too exhausted to continue.

No one knew how to respond to this, Holly shifted in Gregori's arms. She was hungry again, but too tired to wake and feed herself. Gregori, with the help of the ship doctor, made her feed anyway. When she was strong, enough to feed on her own, Kyle stepped in to replenish Gregori so he could continue feeding her. Yoshi volunteered next. The doctor kept a close watch on the proceedings. Before they took them to the infirmary,

Gregori slipped Holly's rings back onto her fingers.

+++++++++

Bruce opened his eyes just a crack. Doug sat reading a book to Mina, Katrina and Hugo. Doug is so good with children, Bruce thought. He adored him. Doug was the most beautiful man he had ever met. Bruce saw him as a Nordic God. Doug is a tall golden blonde-haired man with well-sculpted muscles, and large blue eyes framed by long eyes lashes. How had he gotten so lucky to get such a wonderful man as his partner? The man he wanted to spend the rest of his life. Bruce closed his eyes tight, lest the tears of happiness spill out. He let his happiness lull him to sleep. He was sure Holly would be okay. Gregori would have killed someone by now otherwise.

Doug read to Mina, Katrina and Hugo. He loved children, and wanted to adopt a couple with Bruce. It would be difficult, but Doug knew it would be worth the effort. He loved Bruce, and wanted to spend the rest of his life with him. Nothing and no one would ever be able to come between them, not even those twits Frank, the captain and Charles.

Holly sat up abruptly. She had the strangest dream in which someone she did not know kissed her. Then Bruce beat him up. Holly was glad Bruce had beaten the strange man up. Whoever he was, he was a creep. Holly looked down at her fingers and smiled when she saw her rings there. Gregori reached over and placed her necklace around her neck. Tears welled up in her eyes. Holly sniffed once and flung her arms around Gregori's neck. "I love you."

"I love you too Babycakes."

Bruce sat up abruptly. He had a dream in which some strange man tried to kiss Holly. Then he beat the strange man up. It was a matter of principal. Only Gregori could touch Holly that way. He looked like one of the people they had converted the night before. His name was Tom or Michael, or something. Bruce could not remember. Doug got up and sat down on the bed next to Bruce.

The captain, Liam Delena, came into the infirmary. Charles, Laura, Hanna, Morgan Tyler and Tom Michaels followed him. They watched Gregori and Holly smooch. Bruce and Doug were also kissing. Tom Michaels was to be their European contact. His grandson and namesake had arranged the little outing the night before. He had to be harsh with his grandson, Thomas. Thomas had pushed their guest, Holly and Bruce too hard. Holly's distress had filled the room, but Thomas had kept pushing them until he and the others had intervened. He was sorry for that. He had had to punish his grandson. However, it had been necessary.

The ship's doctor, Keyshia Milton, approached the captain. She shook her head at them. "Gentleman, I don't know what you guys are doing, but you've almost killed these two people. One of whom, I might add is the equivalent of 28 weeks pregnant." She understood the need to act fast, but to kill the two people they needed the most at this time was unacceptable.

Morgan Tyler shook his head, as the ship's first officer, it was his job to point things like that out to the captain. He had brought up the risks of the mission several times, but they pushed ahead with it anyway.

"I know Keyshia, but it didn't work and we have to know why?"

"It worked all right. It was just weak. So weak we were able to pass it off as just a normal fog." Tom said. The infirmary was better equipped than any hospital he had ever been.

"Captain, they need time to rest. You'll kill them otherwise."

"Captain, perhaps Keyshia is right. I could ask them about it when they are feeling better. If we did the whole area after we leave, we might be able to divert attention from ourselves to others, perhaps even to those goons."

"We need to know how to make it stronger."

"I'll get us the information captain. We must be patient or risk losing everything."

"You had better."

+++++++++

Holly dangled her feet over the edge of the climbing wall. Gregori peered up at her and Morgan Tyler with a bird like motion of his head. They peered down at him like hawks. As the ship's first officer, Morgan had come to talk to her about spreading the New Life to Europeans.

"Persistent, isn't he?"

"Yes, but he just worries about me."

"You mean he's afraid of losing you?"

Holly chewed her bottom lip thoughtfully. She had never had any man who had been so afraid of losing her. Hell, she had never had a man before period. Gregori had become more possessive since the mishap onshore. She had been so frightened that she had lost him after that incident. Holly had been certain he would never forgive her, though there had been nothing she could have done at the time to change what happened. She was coming to understand that Gregori loved her so much that nothing would ever change his love for her. She and Bruce had almost died doing the captain and Charles's order. Gregori continued tilting his head back and forth. He looked like a bird of prey surveying his next meal. "I'm not going anywhere."

"I don't know that." The captain and Charles had taken her right from their bed while he slept. He was going to be royally pissed off about that for a very long time.

"Yes, you do."

"Her family will kill her if she leaves you. They don't want to take care of the twins."

Gregori smiled at Morgan. The smile never reached his eyes.

"You wanted to tell me something."

"Ask you something, really," Morgan returned Gregori's empty smile.

"What is it?" Gregori's continual staring started to get to her. She was not made of very stern stuff.

"Will you tell us in your own words how you made the fog the first time? The kind we made is very weak and only a few people were turned by it."

Holly nodded and looked up at the moon. Holly needed a few moments to put her thoughts together. Bats and owls wheeled overhead. It was a midair ballet. They were newly converted people from the ship. They were learning new skills. She stretched out her arms and found Gregori perched on the climbing wall. They were face to face. Holly inhaled sharply as she gazed into his eyes.

"Cough, cough, I'm still here." Morgan knew if he did not interrupt them now, he would get nothing from Holly.

Holly felt herself falling into Gregori's eyes. "I'm not sure how exactly I did it. I'll tell you what happened the first time I did. I hadn't eaten any solid food when I went to the bar with Bruce. A gay bar served drinks mixed with small amounts of werewolf blood, and some bitch kept hitting on me. It was dark in the bar, and I don't even remember what she looked like. She was very drunk and reeked of beer. When I got up trying to get rid of her, she followed me to the restroom. I used people's own fantasies to hide my identity. She bought into it. After drinking her blood in a stall, I felt tipsy. I went to the bar and ordered a couple of drinks. I wanted to get drunk. I saw her couple of times, but she avoided me. I must have been projecting a male image because a gay man kept calling me Cary Grant. He was so drunk that drinking his blood made me drunk. I went to the bar and had a few more drinks. Then I ran out of the bar, stuck my head over the rail and threw up into the river or maybe it was the lake. I can't remember. The fog just appeared after that."

Gregori hissed his displeasure.

"That is before I knew you. I've changed since then. I don't do drunks anymore." Holly peered into his eyes. He was so possessive he frightened her sometimes. She was used to it being only her, Heather and MareMoo. Things kept changing. It was unsettling.

Gregori soften his expression. He loved her, but had to admit his fear of losing her the way he had Vanessa might still drive them apart.

"I'm not going anywhere." Holly kissed Gregori fully on the lips as he pushed off the face of the climbing wall. He carried them over the top of the wall and he landed on top of her. Holly continued to stroke his arm as she kissed him.

"I hate to ask this, but what about New Orleans?"

"Charles tricked me. He said he knew of some safe people who would let me drink their blood. He said they didn't do drugs or anything. He said they weren't werewolves. They were all drunk. They were all werewolves. So was I after the first person. Charles thought this was funny or something. I threw up in Lake Pontchartrain after I don't remember how many people. I must have hit an algae pack or something. I think there has to be some sort of bacteria in the water for the fog to form effectively. The police would recruit new areas by having people they converted go to new towns and throw up at sewage treatment plants."

"Bacteria? Sewage treatment plants?"

"I think polluted water is the best. The Baltic Sea should be the best for trying this out. I heard it is one of the most polluted bodies of water in the world. It's also why law enforcement officers prefer using sewage treatment plants when they send converted goons out to convert unconverted areas."

Morgan smiled. Polluted water, sewage treatment water, water that is full of bacteria that would explain why their pure fresh water approach did not work. It was too clean. "Thank you Holly. You have been most helpful."

Morgan did not even bother to look back. He knew they would be too busying snogging to answer him.

+++++++++

Hanna stared at Holly. It never stopped amazing her how clear Holly's skin was. She glowed with some kind of inner light. Her fluffy brown hair and huge brown eyes made Holly look like a pixie or Tinkerbelle's cousin. Aunt Holly was a mischievous sprite. Hanna had come to adore her weirdly secretive ways. No one, not even Hanna herself, understood why.

Holly watched Hanna eat a hamburger, some fries and a milkshake. She could not eat them without them coming back up. She could only tolerate baby size portions of most foods. Holly's system could only really tolerate liquids and weirdly, mozzarella sticks.

"Look," Holly smiled. "That fog is too weak to completely change anyone, though it did start the process in most people. It did feel good to me. A true fog would have knocked everyone out for a couple of days to a week, except those already converted. Look at yourself. You've already lost 20 pounds."

"So when will they try to change everyone again?" Hanna ignored Holly's comment on her weight. Holly hated answering the hard questions. Hanna wanted to become a New Lifer. She believed it would make her sexy and popular. It made everyone sexy, and a few people had even become popular. Holly sighed. She had been a Hanna all her life. Holly had brought it on herself. Hanna had not.

"So, when will I get to change? It's not fair. Everyone else gets to become a New Lifer." Hanna wanted to say become perfect, but those always-brought lectures from the adults around her. They would say you're perfect the way you are. They always say that. Aunt Holly wasn't as bad as the others were. She had sympathy for what Hanna was going through. Hanna is a minor. It tied her hands.

Holly leaned forward and inhaled the aroma of Hanna's food. It made her angry and frustrated that she could no longer eat the way she used to. Sleeping and eating had been her hobbies. Now she could only do one of them very well. She would sleep all night if they let her. It made her want to scream. "When will we go to Whitby to film?"

"So soon," Hanna's eyes widened. They were really going to do it.

"There's concern over the possible Yellowstone eruption. They want to save as many people as possible."

"What about the asteroid?"

"I think it'll miss us."

"But you don't know."

"No one knows, but they are evacuating everyone within an 1100 mile radius of Yellowstone Park." Holly sipped her tomato juice.

"It would be cruel and ironic if the asteroid hit Yellowstone just as the volcano is about to erupt." Hanna played with her food.

"You should ask the captain. If anyone knows anything about this, he would be the one."

+++++++++

Charles studied the young black man in front of him. The ultra-modern bridge of the ship suited him well. Morgan Tyler being elegant man, he has impeccable taste. Charles and the other listened as he recounted what Holly had been able to remember of the two times she had made fog.

Captain Liam Delena and junior officer Eduardo Salida were asking him questions. Eduardo would be joining any remaining land operations. He had a heavy Spanish accent, dark wavy hair and a lively personality that could easily win people over. Somehow, Morgan had gotten Holly to remember the first time she had made fog. She had been able to remember it in detail. She also remembered the second time she made fog. Charles had been there. He should have remembered the details. He was ashamed to say he had been too drunk to remember much of that night. The added element of the bacteria was completely novel to him. He could tell Tom Michaels was eager to try the new method.

The Weather Channel played in the background. Why were they reporting about a possible Yellowstone eruption and not CNN? When did eruptions become weather stories? Hanna frowned at the television. After the millionth explanation, Hanna understood that she was too young to become a New Lifer in the dramatic way everyone over the age of 25 did, though she was slowly changing into one. "Is this eruption thing something we should be worried about?"

The room went silent. They stared at the television screen. The Federal Government announced the development of evacuations routes out of the region. The only thing that could make matters worse is if that asteroid changed course and hit the earth. The reporters said that that was unlikely but admitted that computerized predictions on the asteroids path varied widely.

They all turned from the television.

"I'm sure they exaggerating, honey. We're safe here."

"But what will happen to our friends in the states? What will happen to my school? What will happen to our house? What will happen to our pets? What will happen to my grandparents and Great Grand-mamma?

"Honey, you're getting yourself all worked up. Everyone is safe."

Hanna looked at her mother, but did not believe her. "Everyone is going to die. They said so on the Science Channel. Or is it the Discovery Channel?"

Everyone gasped as an emergency broadcast came on. The dramatic music accompanying it is twice as loud as normal. The asteroid would hit the earth. Early estimates have it hitting close to Yellowstone. Evacuations in the selected areas shown on the map commence immediately. Those in other areas need to contact their local officials. Their local stations would have more information. Hanna ran from the room, screaming at the top of her lungs. The rest of the room was too stunned to stop her.

Chapter 11

Holly ran up and down the steps with Hanna and Gerry closely following her. Once she regained the top, she pointed toward the bay. "That's where the Demeter crashed and Dracula came ashore as a wolf. That's where Dracula got Lucy for the first time and where Captain Swales is murdered. Bram Stoker use to summer here. There's a bench somewhere around here with his name on it."

Gerry and Hanna laughed. Aunt Holly had already told them that about a dozen times now. She was gearing up for when they got to Romania in a couple weeks. There were parts of the city they could not go. Those were the parts were they were filming Quincy. Holly ran to the church and looked down into the bay. They were filming on the beach today near the piers.

"We had better get back to town. I have to leave for London this afternoon. I don't want to disappoint anyone."

"Oh Aunt Holly, you aren't going to disappoint anyone except the critics who are expecting a monster."

"Don't let her fool you, she is a monster."

"And you Bruce Harwood are a vrykolakas." Holly wagged her finger at him.

"A what?"

"It's a vampire. Vrykolakas is the Greek word for vampire."

"Vrykolakas, I like that. I think I'll call you Lemur Girl."

"Like the monkeys?"

"Sort of," Bruce smiled. "When Romans first saw the monkeys swinging around they didn't know what to make of them. They thought they were ghosts. They ancient Romans word for ghosts is lemures."

"Are you saying we're really dead?"

"We're dead only to our old life. I don't see how you can call me anything when you always steal my phone. Like you did tonight?" They headed back to town where transportation to London was waiting for them.

"I don't steal it. I keep it safe for you. You know how you're always loosing things."

"So how come I haven't lost you yet?"

"I'm a bad penny. You can never be rid of me."

"Ha."

"The bus is waiting to take us to the airport. We better hustle or they'll have our heads."

"Chill out. There's the bus now. Honestly you're like a mother hen lately." Holly approached the bus cautiously. Heather and Jasmine had already packed her stuff. Heather, Frank, Angel, Marlene and Bruce were going with her on this trip. Bruce was going to promote his book, A Little Night Music. Holly was going to promote her books and the movie. Heather, Frank, Angel and Marlene went to keep them out of trouble. Doug had gotten a small part in the movie and was staying behind.

The ride to the airport and the plane ride to London were uneventful. They took the Chunnel and spent several uneventful hours talking to French police who finally let them in.

"I want to visit the Eiffel Tower or the Paris Opera House. Where do we go? Disney. Is Disney making this film? Is this something someone failed to tell me? Have I been promoting the wrong studio all this time?"

"No Holly. We just thought it would be a fun place to do the next round of interviews at."

"So would the Paris Opera House or the Eiffel Tower. At least then I wouldn't have to worry about people in strange customs."

"Someone did not take their nap. Did you feed tonight?" Bruce studied her suspiciously. Holly looked pale to him, but it could just be the light in the room.

Holly huffed and walked into the next room.

"There's nothing wrong with Disney. We had fun at the one in Florida. Remember?"

"Yes, but, oh never mind. I'm hungry. How am I supposed to feed with all those reporters following us everywhere? They're not like the ones back home. These have no idea what privacy means."

Bruce nodded his head. At the airport all the reporters wanted to talk about was how Holly had managed to swipe Gregori? What did Gregori see in someone like Holly? What had happened to his last girlfriend? Why she was traveling without him? Why Gregori let her travel alone with single males? They could care less about the movie or the book.

Heather sighed. She did not want to admit it, but she already missed Kyle. The press, thank God, had not asked her any questions. She could see Holly's point when she had been reluctant to marry Gregori. The press had been the real reason behind her reluctance.

"Now Holly, you know what I always say?"

"There is no such thing as bad publicity. It's all to the good." Holly was getting tired of Frank's sayings.

"Frank, don't be a moron. Holly doesn't need the added stress at this time." Marlene stared hard at her husband. "It would do you good to remember that Holly is a pregnant woman. How are you doing baby girl? You look pale. Has Bruce fed you tonight?"

"No, not tonight I haven't."

"Gregori doesn't like it when I feed Holly." Bruce protested.

"So? Since when did it matter to you what Gregori thought?"

"Since Gregori and Holly married, that's when. I seemed to remember you being at the wedding."

Marlene stared blankly at him. She was not about to back down on her point. Holly and Bruce belonged together.

"Heather will you explain to her what I'm talking about? She doesn't seem to understand the delicate position feeding Holly would put me in."

Heather shook her head. "That never stopped you before. Go ahead, I won't tell Gregori, and I doubt anyone else will."

"The press that's hanging outside our door will. So I will politely defer to Heather for that duty."

The press kept hanging around outside their door. Mm, they would make a good meal for all of them. Heather transmitted this thought to the others, who looked toward the door in anticipation.

After that, the French press turned into a tasty diversion. They tasted the best of the European press corps. The British tasted bland. They did not transformed most of the press. They changed into followers. The followers, like the New Lifers, asked only questions about the movie and the books.

Holly enjoyed the Paris Opera House where Bruce tried to push her into the underground lake. Bruce liked the Eiffel Tower where Holly tried to push him off the top. Heather took pictures and sent them to those still in England. They took the train across Europe, stopping in major cities to do press for the movie. When not feeding on reporters, Holly snacked on Bruce. No one asked Bruce whom he was feeding on.

Wherever they went, reporters began greeting them with strands of garlic. They quickly developed a taste for garlic.

"Ah, here we are in the capital of Romania. Anyone want to guess how long it will take before someone brings us some garlic?"

"Whatever. We will get to go on the Dracula tour. I want one of those tacky tee shirts."

"As soon as we see the press or enter a restaurant we will get the old garlic treatment." Heather sighed. She hated garlic bread, garlic soup, garlic steak, garlic ice cream, garlic soft drinks, garlic chicken, garlic tea and anything else with garlic they could think of making.

"That's when I go to the restroom and puke my guts out, and every member of the press calls the studio and tells them I've been drinking, right Bruce?"

Marlene shook her head. The longer they were away from Gregori and Doug, the cuter a couple Bruce and Holly made. Why no one else saw it was beyond Marlene.

Holly really hated when they dumped the garlic on her. She had taken to ordering garlic bread with garlic butter and making a show of eating it before the main meal so the rest of her food would not be free of it. Goons viewed it as a way to poison New Lifers. It always backfired on the goons.

"I've explained what happened to Gregori and the press several times. You have morning sickness. The press is eating up the pregnancy story. They think he took advantage of you."

Holly held up the string of garlic that hung from their window. "If garlic works to off evil, why doesn't it work on the press?"

Heather laughed while brandishing a strand of garlic. "Yeah, be gone all yea evil creatures of darkness."

A cell phone rang in Bruce's pocket. "That must be Gregori with his daily updates. Here Holly, you had better answer it."

"Hi honey. How'd filming go today?"

"Lovely. The weather finally cooperated tonight. We got a lot done."

"That's wonderful."

"Yeah, we'll be joining you there to finish shooting."

"Here in Romania?"

"Yeah, we got permission to film in Bucharest and the surrounding area. Aren't you happy Babycakes?"

"Of course I am, silly. It's such a shock. I figured they shoot the whole movie on a back lot somewhere. It always amazes me when the studio shows a willingness to spend any money on it."

"Babycakes, you are such a clown. Everyone here sends their love. We'll see you in a week. Bye."

"Bye sweetie." A half an hour later Holly and Gregori finally hung up. It is their shortest call on the trip.

"The others will be coming to join us in one week, weather willing. They have permission to film in Bucharest. They're going to film the beginning of the film and the closing parts here."

"That's wonderful. Kyle had better call and say the same thing." Bruce looked at Heather out of the corner of his eye as Holly's cell phone rang again.

"Hello? Oh, hi Kyle."

"Hello Holly. Bruce doesn't have your phone?"

"I got it back from him. Silly question, but do you want to talk to Heather?"

"Yep."

"Okay, here she is." Holly laughed as she handed Heather the phone. They could talk for hours.

"Let's go to a restaurant. We need to put in an appearance." Frank nodded. "She can talk to him on the way there."

"And throughout the meal."

"And after the meal," Angel laughed as he answered his cell phone. "Hi honey. I hear filming is going well."

Holly waited a few minutes and Bruce's cell phone rang. It was Doug. Pulling out a notepad, she smiled.

"I'm going to get some writing done while you guys talk."

Two hours later, a server at a swanky restaurant was taking their order. "I'll have the cream of cheddar and broccoli soup with a side of garlic bread with garlic butter on the side. Please don't put any garlic in the soup. I have morning sickness and it won't be pretty. I trust you know what I mean." Holly said, mimicking someone throwing up in a bag when the server looked doubtful for a moment.

"Yes madam. I believe I do. Will you have anything to drink with that?"

"I'll just have some hot tea, thank you. And could you bring the garlic bread and butter out before the main meal?"

"Yes."

"Thank you, I really appreciate that."

After the others had ordered and served their drinks, Holly sat playing with her cell phone. "If I broke down and updated my phone, I could get one of the new ones with a key pad. I could store notes on my new novel on it."

"So why don't you?"

"Too cheap, and I don't want to learn a new technology. Paper and pen still work just fine."

"And you leave a mess everywhere."

"Do not. Beside I can stick the papers in my back pocket without worrying that I'll sit down on them and break them."

"Good point."

"Of course if you sit on the pen, it would give you a different kind of point."

"Very funny Heather, your pointed comments are for naught though." Holly tried to concentrate on her phone. The people around her were getting nosy. 'I think there are some goons with us tonight. They're at the table next to us, and the ones sitting behind Frank and Marlene.' Holly was developing goon detection abilities. No one said anything aloud. They searched the area until they found other New Lifers and told them of the goons. They promised to take care of them.

The rest of the week went by fast. They visited all the tourist hot spots and Holly got her Dracula tee shirt. In fact, she got one for everyone. Holly worked furiously on her new novel. The whole area gave her plenty of new ideas and plot points. Frank was pleased with her efforts. He promised to make sure a major publisher accepted her latest novel.

A quick trip to Italy proved fruitful. Holly loved the Mediterranean Sea and the beaches on it. They got back just in time to greet the movie crew as they arrived from England.

+++++++++

Dracula rose from his underground crypt. He shot from the earth and tasted the fresh air. It had been months since he had found a safe place to rest. The area around his sanctuary was beautiful and wild. It offered him complete protection from the vampire hunters and the other vampires who use to throw him into the sunlight. That little game had ended when the meeting room had also caught fire with him. They had restored sure that the meeting room. His body had taken a bit longer.

They updated the meeting room nicely with all new computers, television sets and books. Flameboy surveyed the room. There was a new book on the table. It was a hardback. He studied the title, Death Is Only the Beginning by Holly Skyhaven, an update of the classic tale of Dracula. He had already read two of her other books and liked them. He sat down to read it.

+++++++++

Holly typed furiously. She needed to get this to her publisher before they could change their minds. Everything was so uncertain. "Aren't you supposed to be getting ready to film tomorrow? You still have a couple of weeks of shooting to do."

Gregori, Kyle and Yoshi just shrugged their shoulders. Who knew? They had been preparing since New Orleans. Everyone was more than ready, yet the movie was not yet finished the movie.

"Laura says you guys need to be ready tomorrow. I wouldn't want to be the one to make her angry."

"My, someone is in a bad bossy mood."

"Cranky," Kyle shot back to Yoshi.

"Cranky part of the novel," Holly responded, stretching her fingers. All she had left to do was the final spelling and grammar check. The machine hated her. It would nitpick over every sentence fragment, even the ones she wanted badly.

"It does not hate you." Gregori rested his chin on the top of Holly's head. Her books were doing well even with the worldwide scare caused by the supervolcano and the asteroid. Nothing seemed to change that. Centers of operation had changed, but otherwise it was business as usual for the entertainment industries.

"Does too," Holly stared at the screen. She clicked the ignore button until she thought she would go crazy. The spelling was fine. It was a good program for business letters, but no one meant it for novels.

"You need a new program, Babycakes."

"Yes, but not now. I just got this one figured out."

"I'll talk to Hanna about it. She'll know which one will work for you."

She needed a new program. He was right. However, the time it would take to learn a new program would be time taken from her writing. She could not afford that right now.

Gregori slid to the corner of the room to call Hanna. Hanna being the best to ask about computer programming, just as Otto was the best one around to install programs and get them running. Gregori and Hanna talked briefly. Hanna knew of the problem, and promised to get something for Aunt Holly. It really irked Gregori when Hanna called Holly Aunt.

Sophia chuckled. "Let me read it, dear. I know a few things about grammar."

"This is American, mom, not British."

"They are the same language."

"They are not."

"We've been through this before. Let me do this so you can get some rest."

"Um, okay, but don't go slipping in any British slang while I'm not looking." Holly clicked off the spell checker as she stood up.

"Move," Sophia grinned. Holly's specialty is satiric romance novels. This is going to be good.

Holly paced the room. She would walk the walls and the ceiling if anyone would let her. They found ceiling walking just too creepy. Why was she so nervous? Gregori pulled her onto his lap where she fussed for a few minutes before settling down. Every so often

Sophia would ask a question, but those questions were rare. Four and a half hours later, it is all over and the manuscript was on its way to the publisher. Holly's new novel, Keep It Close, was on the way.

"Aunt Holly, Aunt Holly," Hanna bounced into the room. Her parents, Laura and Angel, and her younger brother, Gerry, followed her. "We have an early Easter gift for you."

"Easter's not for another month," Holly protested.

"That's why it's early."

"Open it, open it," Gerry chanted.

Holly opened it and stared. It was a new laptop. "You shouldn't have."

"It's got a special program for novelists. It'll make it so much easier for you to write the next one."

Holly propped the computer on her knees. It was like a dream machine. "How can I ever thank you for this?"

"You can't. We just want you to stop having to listen to your swearing at your old computer."

Everyone spent the rest of the evening watching Holly play with her new toy.

+++++++++

Gregori kissed Sophia on the forehead. Studying his mother's outfit, he frowned. She was wearing red shorts and a red backless top. Both of which could be described as tiny. "Mum will you put something on. You're practically naked. And what's he doing here?"

"Well hello to you too. Hey Doug," Sophia frowned at Gregori. "Are you and Holly still fighting?"

"We aren't fighting. She just gets nervous when I'm away from her for any period of time."

"Hey Mrs. C.," Doug passed Gregori and gave Sophia a kiss on the cheek. "You are looking so mighty fine. If I weren't gay and married, I'd marry you in a heartbeat just so no one else would get you. You look smashing in that little red outfit Holly picked out for you. Hey Mister C..."

"Hey Doug."

"Oh Doug, you're such a flatterer." Sophia smoothed out her shorts and blushed. "How's Bruce doing?"

"Good. He's helping Holly. He's her unofficial editor." Doug leaned closer to Sophia and whispered. "With all the writing Holly's been doing lately, Gregori is beginning to feel a little neglected. She does have a deadline to meet. And someone needs to go through the ton of manuscripts his agent keeps sending him."

Gregori glared venomously at Doug. "I have gone through every single manuscript he sent me. They all suck. What is my father doing here?"

"He's doing pushups." Sophia glanced at the full-length mirror near the entranceway. The matching shorts and top did look good on her. Holly had been the one to pick them out for her. "And the girls miss their big brother and Aunt Holly. Don't start. I can't help it if they picked up bad habits from Jasmine's children."

"They're with them now." Doug leaned over the couch so he could get a better view of Mark exercising. It was an awesome view. "I talked to Yoshi and Jamaica. They promised to work at getting the girls to stop calling her Holly Aunt. I think they just do it to aggravate Gregori."

Mark sat up and greeted Doug and Gregori. He was use to his son's hostility even though it still stung. It amused him that Gregori got so aggravated when the girls called Holly Aunt. They were just imitating Holly's nieces.

"I'm doing the same thing you're doing. I'm finishing a project."

"Which one is that?"

"The Dracula Tapes, they're making a mini-series out of the book."

"He's playing Dracula again." Sophia gave out a long sigh.

"What can I say? Dracula rocks, Right Gregori?" Mark rose from the floor and kissed Sophia on the cheek. She had never looked more beautiful.

Gregori sighed. Holly had been begging him to be civil to his father though she had a hard time remembering the word. She kept saying sibyl Mark would be the only grandfather their children would ever have. Her parents had died years earlier. He had promised to try. "Yes dad, he does." There. That had sounded almost civil. He watched his father. It shocked him to see the love in his father's eyes when he looked at his mother. His childhood memories were of them was them always fighting. Perhaps it had been the alcohol after all, just as his Mum always said it was.

"Your father just finished filming this morning. Do you have much more filming to do on Quincy?"

"Just tonight, we have to finish at the castle. We're staking Dracula tonight." Doug said brightly. It was his favorite part of the book. "Will you be staying here for the most impact? Yellowstone could go off at any time. It's not safe to return to North America at this time. Bruce thinks Holly will give birth in about a week. The impact won't be too long after that."

"How does Bruce know that Holly will give birth so soon?" Sophia and Gregori demanded. Mark had to admit to being curious as to why Bruce would know. The doctors all claimed she had another month to go.

"He says her nesting instincts are kicking in. She's looking for a place to den." Doug shrugged. "What can I say? They spend too much time together."

"Mark is going to be staying with Jasmine and me until next year. Kyle and Yoshi are planning a small film detailing the plans people are making to survive the impact.

Mark has a small part in it." Sophia smiled proudly. It made her unexpectedly happy to know her ex was fitting in with her new family.

"Hey. There's a small meadow not far from here. I say we celebrate the finish of filming by having a picnic there."

"I know just the spot. We did some filming there yesterday. Right," Gregori cheered up. "Holly could use some fresh air. It's close enough to walk there from here."

"What about the wrap parties?"

"We'll go to those too. This will just be for our family." Mark smiled. He was glad he brought up the idea. He had been sure Gregori would veto it seeing how it was coming from him.

"I'm coming in. Is everyone decent in there?"

"Oh for God's sake Holly," Bruce practically growled. "It's Gregori, Sophia, Mark and Doug in there. They aren't doing anything that would give them any reasons to be indecent. And stop giggling."

"We're all naked." Mark yelled.

Holly ran into the room giggling with Bruce trailing her. "Oh you liar," She wrapped her arms around Gregori's waist and rested her head on his chest. "Bruce and I finished our current books and sent them to Frank. Frank confirmed that he received them. We are free for a short time. Let's celebrate."

"We can go on a picnic Friday. Quincy will be done filming tonight."

"You want it after the wrap party for Quincy on Thursday?" Holly asked dubiously. "Won't that be a whole lot of hangover then?"

"The wrap party is for the crew. The picnic is for close family." Gregori rubbed his chin on the top of Holly's head.

"That sounds like fun. I can't wait."

Chapter 12

Holly peered at the man standing in front of her as if she had never seeing him for the first time. How could anyone be so ignorant? Did he really think he could outrun this thing? Tom Michaels was a complete jerk as far as Holly was concerned. "Take your hands off me. I want nothing to do with a project of yours. I want everyone to survive the coming disaster, not just some." Holly pulled away and headed along the path back to town. This was too much like one of her recent dreams. Holly reached into her pocket and pulled out Gregori's cell phone. She stared at the phone, then at the hills to her right. They had just finished filming the movie and the book tour was also over, but everyone would be in Romania until after the asteroid hit. Looking at the phone once more, she dialed her own number. Bruce answered.

"Um, Holly, this might not be the right time."

"No time for that Bruce. Get the others and meet me at the meadow above the bay. Bring everyone and hurry."

"Holly?"

"I don't have time to explain. Just do it, Bruce. Remember where we had the family picnic last week?"

"Where the caves are that fascinated you so much?"

"The cave," Gregori felt confused. "Why do you have her cell phone again?"

"Yes Holly, it would help though if you told us what this is about?"

"Good," Holly hung up before he could ask more questions. Striding over the short winding path, she spied the short windmills on the hills overlooking the bay. She did not remember seeing them the week before. "Have those been here long? I don't remember seeing them before."

"Seeing what?" Tom asked, watching her carefully. Holly was full term even though according to the calendar she was only 20 weeks gestation, not 40.

"The windmills," Holly headed toward them. There was a cave halfway up the side of the cliff with a narrow tree lined pathway leading up to it. At least there was one in her dreams, and she had seen and commented on it during the picnic. She could hear Tom talking excitedly on his cell phone. "There it is." She jumped onto the ledge and approached it cautiously. She could hear her family and the townspeople arriving just as she disappeared into the cave.

"Holly," Tom shouted. "No one knows anything about this cave. You should come out now and let the professionals handle this."

"Holly, Babycakes, what are you doing?" Gregori's voice sounded strained to Holly. She had been a bear these last few nights. She walked further into the cave. She noticed some strange things about it. The floor angled up and was grated. The grate was clearly a manufactured item. It had wide steps for easy access to the first cave chamber. If her dream were correct, a light switch would be at the top, just inside the first chamber. Gregori's cell phone rang; she used its light to see the switch plate. It was under a protective plastic wall cover. "Hi honey, just a minute." Praying silently, Holly flipped the switch. After much humming, the lights came on. "It's safe to bring everyone up. We need to explore it some more. Oh, there's a huge fountain in the center. It's beautiful."

"Huge," Tom agreed. He had followed Holly, saying that he had lived a good life. Before long, everyone was in the chamber. The all stared at the fountain. "Before we go any further, what else is in your dream?"

"Well there are corridors going off this chamber. Some of them are dead ends. The rest lead to the main chamber that is about thousand times the size of this one. There are stables, living quarters, an infirmary, and a well-stocked kitchen. I know it sounds weird, but that's what I experienced in the dream. We were all living there until the sun came back out."

"Toilets?"

"Loos?"

"Water closets?"

"Restrooms?"

"Bathrooms?"

"In the living quarters and off the kitchen and infirmary" Holly frowned. A small ripple of pain moved through her abdomen. The dream had seemed so real. But that it was real, that was just freaky. "I need to go up and turn on the interior lights. Only the stables have lights on now. There will be power to the kitchens. The refrigerator will be running. There should be animals in the stables and food in the kitchen."

"Whoa, young lady, if anyone is going up there, I am. I'm old enough to be your grandfather."

"Father, really, and you don't know where the switch is."

"Is it booby trapped?"

"No, but…."

"Hidden?"

"Sort of, it's in a room halfway up the corridor."

"Show me it with your mind."

Holly did as he asked. She nervously watched him go up the corridor. He's not going to find it, she thought as she tore herself away from Gregori. Before anyone could stop her, Holly darted down the corridor and past Tom. She ran fast and hard down the winding path until she came to an opening halfway to the end. She practically flew into the opening in the ceiling. The room was just as she remembered it from her dreams, though more detailed. It took her several minutes to find the right panel.

The whole town was out there clamoring for her to come out. This distracted her. She almost hit the wrong switch. The area above and below her became so bright she was temporarily blinded.

Gregori jumped in and grabbed her. Holly instinctively smacked him in the face and leaped out of the room onto the next level. Gregori hissed and lunged at her. He missed her by less than an inch.

"If you ever do that again you will be spending the rest of your life with your mother or some of those sluts you're always picking up in bars."

"I don't pick up sluts in bars, and you slapped me."

"You picked me up in a bar."

Gregori sputtered. How could he work through such logic?

"And don't look at me that way. You know I hate that look."

"Look at you what way? What look?"

"The look you used when you played the serial killer."

"You said you didn't watch that movie."

"I saw the commercial for it."

"Those were some really scary commercials, though the movie sucked." Bruce added, always the thoughtful one. He pulled Holly away from Gregori. "Let's explore. Won't that be fun?" Gregori hissed. Holly growled. To everyone's surprise, Bruce growled at both of them as he kept eye contact with Holly for several long minutes. Looking over her shoulder, he smiled. "Oh, look, a map, and it shows an infirmary right next to the kitchen. We should go check it out before someone gives birth here."

Holly growled much more loudly this time, and everyone tried to crowd into the small room to look at her.

Bruce shook his head and pushed Holly toward the larger chambers beyond the room. She had to get to the infirmary quickly. Bruce prayed it to be as well-equipped as Holly dreams seemed to suggest it was. "Honestly Holly, Gregori does not pick up women from bars. He never dated sluts, I would know. If he did, it would have been in all those gossip magazines I use to read." Gregori followed them closely, and everyone else followed Gregori. "And, he did not pick you up from a bar. Heather picked him up for you. Don't you remember? He just went to the bar and grill to find his mother. It is really just a restaurant not a bar and none of us had anything stronger than tea. Heather invited him over for a snack. Or, was it as a snack? I can't remember." Bruce could feel her contractions strengthen and wonder why no one else did.

Heather threw something at Bruce and Holly laughed.

Gregori smiled. The sound of Holly laughing melted his heart. He watched in concern as Holly stopped and rubbed her lower back. Bruce motioned him forward. Gregori stepped forward and placed his arm around Holly's shoulder. Bruce smiled at him, and gave him thumbs up.

Doctor Crawford from the village ran into the infirmary. He found it was as large as any found in a large city. Someone had written the word infirmary in huge letters. The lights were turned on inside. It was, if anything, far better equipped than either the village or the ship. The doctor approved of it. With Holly's labor intensifying, he was relieved that they had such a modern place for her to give birth in.

The babies were born five minutes apart and about thirty minutes after they had entered the infirmary on 23 of April 2012. It was if they had been waiting for just that moment. Strangely, Holly slept through the whole thing, waking only at the end to feed them, and calm everyone's nerves. She had little memory of what had happened or how they had come to the cave, and kept apologizing to Gregori.

Sophia pulled Bruce away from Gregori and Holly. "How did you know she was in labor?" Heather and a few others moved closer to hear what he had to say. No one else realized Holly had been in labor. Why had he?

"I could feel her discomfort. But it wasn't until she hit Gregori for trying to restrain her that I knew for certain."

"So? Why is that important?"

"Gregori is always trying to restrain her. But, this is the first time she ever hit him." Bruce shrugged. "I hear women swear and curse out their husbands during labor. I figured Holly would have to do it differently. She would definitely be a hitter."

"Oh yeah, she hit me good and hard. Didn't she?"

"You should let the doctor look at that. It's already bruising."

Gregori winced. His cheek and jaw were tender where Holly hit him. She kept apologizing to everyone. Even the film crew, though they were done filming most of the live action sequences. There might be some pick up shots, but he would heal by then.

"Yes Gregori, you had better be healed by then." Laura Sanders studied Gregori with a critical eye. He would be fine. In a night or two, it would be as if it never happened. New Lifers healed quickly. In the meantime, he would be the butt of jokes.

Holly's sense of well-being was taking a beating. She was losing her confidence. Only the babies kept her from breaking down. "The doctor gave her something to help her sleep. However, it will only last a couple of hours, until the babies wake up and demand to feed again. Have you picked out names?"

They were two beautiful babies. They had their mother's fluffy soft brown hair, and their father's huge green eyes and long dark eyelashes. "Not yet, we kept putting it off."

"What about the names Jen and Johnny? She mentioned those names before."

"What?" Sophia peered at him. Why did Bruce know more about Holly then Holly's husband did?

"Jen and Johnny," Bruce smiled broadly. "You know the cool chick Holly use to work with and her hot, sexy boyfriend."

"Jen, is she the one who kept taking her picture and annoying her?"

"That's the one."

"She mentioned them once or twice," Gregori mused. "I think you're right."

"She said Jen and Johnny when I brought it up last week." Heather volunteered. "I thought the two of you had agreed to those names?"

"That's what she told Doctor Crawford when he asked her." Hanna was perplexed as to why there would be any questions about this. "Holly said it is the names the two of you had agreed to months ago."

When Holly woke up, Gregori presented Jen and Johnny to her. "Oh, Gregori, you remembered that we agreed to those names. You really do listen to me, sometimes."

Gregori wisely did not try to correct her as she leaned over and kissed him.

Doctor Samuel Crawford, Tom Michaels, Eduardo Salida, Mircea and Radu Vambery, Laura and Angel Sanders conferred together for over three hours after the birth of the twins. Mircea and Radu Vambery were brothers from the nearby village. They had been doctors in their youth and were now helping spread the New Life to unconverted populations. There were still a few of those left.

"I don't want to move her. Frankly, there is no reason too. When the asteroid hits, we could hold up here for months, if not years."

"I think that is why she led us here. We should move our families here as soon as possible. What do we have? Thirteen weeks?"

"It will hit the earth in twenty eight weeks four days and a few hours, providing it does not pick up speed as it approaches earth. It's going to hit on November 6. It's a Tuesday." Radu Vambery was just packed full of information, some of which was even useful.

"We need to bring everyone in on this. A town meeting so everyone can have a say." Eduardo waved his arm in the general direction of the kitchen. Everyone was in awe of its size, the appliances and cookware it contained, and the food that filled the refrigerators. The living quarters also had a few small appliances, and were quite generous in size.

The meeting took a short time to convene. They could move their important stuff in quickly. If they had enough time, they could get to everything else. The living quarters would be more than enough for ten towns.

It is with great reluctance, and a CNN report of increased activity at Yellowstone National Park that made them agree to start evacuating to the caverns at once.

Chapter 13

Holly gently patted Johnny on his bottom, attempting to coax a burp out
of him while cooing at his sister, Jen. "What good little babies you are. Yes, you
are. Give Mommy a burp. It's not paying rent in there. So let it go."
Gregori shook his head. Baby talk made no sense to him. "Maybe Daddy
should burp him so Mommy can feed Jen? Yes, you think that's a good idea."
Gregori reluctantly reached for Johnny. He could get Johnny to burp, but then
he would always throw up on him. For some odd reason, the babies would then
both laugh and coo as if it were some big joke. They were only five weeks old.
Holly frowned as she started to hand Johnny to Gregori. Some instinct
made her hold him over a wastebasket instead. Johnny burped loudly and
puked into the wastebasket. "Um, maybe having Daddy burp you is a mistake.
Why do you always throw up on Daddy?" Johnny cooed and laughed. Jen
joined him. "That's more than a little creepy." Holly fed Jen while Gregori
cleaned up Johnny.
"The others will be here shortly. Won't they?"
"They'll be here in about an hour." Holly burped Jen and put her into the
crib next to Johnny. Gliding over to Gregori, she pushed up his tee shirt.
"It's time to feed Mommy."
"Oh yeah," Gregori pulled Holly closer as she licked his chest. He
moaned loudly as her teeth pierced his skin. To Gregori it was the most erotic
sensation he had ever experienced. It got better every time she did it. Pressing
his nose into her hair, he smiled. He loved the smell of her, and the way her
body felt against his when she fed. "More
Babycakes feed some more, drain me." He closed his eyes in ecstasy.
Holly pulled away, closing the wound on his chest.
Gregori pulled her to the couch, his lips devouring hers as his hand
explored her body. He would never get enough of her. Never, he could live for
the rest of eternity and it wouldn't be enough. Holly would always be the only
one for him.
"Someone's at the door."
"Let them wait."
"Okay," Holly wrapped her legs around his hips, moaning loudly as he
nipped at the base of her throat. The knocking grew more insistent, forcing
them to separate. When Gregori opened the door, Otto snarled at him.
"Are we interrupting something?" His tone dripped with sarcasm.
"Yes," Gregori replied, closing the door on Otto's face. They could hear
Nicole and the others laughing.
"Gregori," Holly adjusted her shirt, and slipped a sweater on. She shook
her head. Since when did Otto show up early for anything? "You missed a
spot." Holly pointed to a drop of blood on her throat.
Gregori sucked on the spot as she pulled his tee shirt down. "There, we're

presentable. We can let them in. Preferably you'll do it before Otto knocks the door down."

Holly leaned forward and listened before Gregori opened the door.

"Really Nicole, Bruce and I make wonderful baby-sitters. Holly uses our services all the time as does Mark, Jamaica and Wendy. The twins never throw up on us the way they do on Gregori." Doug proclaimed loudly, and with great enthusiasm. He loved children.

"No," Holly threw the door open. "You can't have my baby-sitters. Get your own."

"About time you opened the door. Are you deaf or something?"

"Or something, hi everyone, come in and make yourselves comfortable. Do you know how many more are coming?"

"About a dozen more," Bruce said cheerfully. "We brought snacks."

"Mozzarella sticks?"

"And chicken strips," Bruce smiled. He knew the way to Holly's heart.

"Okay, you can stay. The rest of you can go home."

Gregori laughed, scooping Holly into his arms. He led everyone into the central living area. The guest continued to show up.

"You two make me sick." Otto complained as he helped Nicole with their triplets. Nicole laughed as she punched him on the arm.

"Oh, look, little Jen and Johnny are awake this time. Hi babies, say hi to the babies Otto."

"Hi babies. Damn, they're getting big. What are you feeding them? Fertilizer?"

"Seriously, they're huge. What are you feeding them?"

"Just me, it's the breast milk. They won't take formula, though I keep trying." Holly hunched down and looked at the sleeping triplets. They were so tiny compared to Jen and Johnny even though they were two months older.

"Doesn't it make you want to have more Jamaica?"

"No Aunt Holly, it does not."

"Yes, it does." Yoshi corrected, "Just not right now."

"Who are we waiting for?" People were pouring through the doorway.

"Wendy and Colin," Jasmine answered while trying to get Hugo to calm down. "Elijah and Bobby Joe returned home. His mother's having trouble with vampire hunters."

"I've got him." Mark scooped Hugo up and gave him a dirty look. Hugo had been running around and falling over things. "Are you going to calm down or am I going to have to tickle you into submission?"

"No."

"I'm sorry we're late. Did you start without us?"

"No," several people replied while jumping up to help them.

Once all the children settled down, Gregori pulled Holly unto his lap. "Okay, does everyone know why we're here? Good."

"Hey Aunt Holly, don't damage anything you might need later."

Holly smiled at Otto and gave him the one finger salute. This caused hoots of laughter throughout the room.

"Are there anymore smart asses in the room? Good, this is what I've asked you here to discuss. Does everyone remember the nightmare I had? Is that nightmare where I went insane and left Gregori for a life in the wild?" Holly pulled Gregori's arms around her. She needed the comfort of his touch. Every adult in the room was watching her closely. "I thought it is only a nightmare. But now I'm not so certain."

"Why is that?" Hanna asked while placing a plate of hot mozzarella sticks and chicken strips in front of Holly. She and Gerry were helping with the food. "Is it because you found this place through a dream?" People were staring at the food. "There's more food in the kitchen. Everyone feel free to help yourselves."

Holly nodded yes. She felt foolish, but there you were. A dream had brought them all together, would a dream tear them apart?

Bruce grabbed one of the chicken strips and dipped it into some hot sauce. Everyone else headed for the kitchen in search of the promised food. "That's an excellent question Hanna. You and Gerry did a good job with the food. Doug has something on his computer that he wants everyone to see." Bruce waved a mozzarella stick under Holly's nose. It and chicken strips were her one weakness. The other one is Gregori.

"Okay, I think we're ready now. Can everyone see the screen? Good," Doug sat next to the television and out of everyone's way. There was a 62-inch wide flat screen HDTV in the living room Doug and Bruce shared with Holly and Gregori.

"I want to thank all of you for coming. Now, I believe most of us remember Holly's dream, though it seemed like a lifetime ago that she had it. Now if you will look at the television set, you'll see pictures of the first place seen in the dream."

"Where the hells were these pictures taken?" Laura demanded. These were the exactly as she remembered them from the dream.

"Mom, you promised to clean up your language, especially in front of the young children. Dad, will you talk to her?"

"She's right honey, you did promise." Angel Sanders smiled at his wife, and winked at his daughter.

"Now back to the topic, here's another view of the same location. Everyone from Northern Ohio should be able to recognize where these pictures are from, anyone?"

"The Cleveland Metroparks," several people shouted at once.

"All of the places in the dream can be found in the Cleveland Metroparks. The only places not there are my house, the windmills and Holly's underground lair."

"But the house could be located where the haunted castle is now. I remember going there when I was younger and being scared nearly to death by creepy lights and loud banging noises." Heather shoved the mozzarella sticks at Kyle who just laughed.

"Me too," Bruce said. It was such a delight to be able share the memories. These memories are important reminders of the world they were leaving behind. God bless the internet. "I should also point out that my house could be located somewhere in Southern France."

"The place where the windmills are reminds me of my favorite place not far from where I grew up in Indiana. Bruce and I went there shortly after we became a couple."

"Doug is so romantic. How come you're not romantic, honey?" Kyle nudged Heather.

"But wouldn't all of these places be under ice during an ice age?" Gerry came out of the kitchen to look at the pictures.

"That's a good point Gerry."

"They should be at the leading edge of the glacier.

That would make then tundra with no forested areas during an ice age."

Soon people were watching the television and chatting back and forth. Bruce pulled up a chair for Holly. She got off Gregori's lap so he could eat.

"I know we haven't really touched on the real issue. But let's let them eat first."

"Okay."

"Bruce," Gregori leaned forward. "Are those pictures real?"

"Absolutely," Heather confirmed before Bruce could reply. "I can't tell you how many happy hours I spent there."

"Remember when Otto saved my life there?" Holly sniffed at a chicken strip to hide her smile as she pointed to one of the earlier pictures.

"You tried to take my life you mean." Otto mentally sent everyone in the room a picture of Holly careening down the stream on her backside, her arms and legs flailing as she slammed into Otto.

Holly added the image of Otto standing on one leg with Holly clinging to it. His other leg was up in the air, and his arms were waving around as he tried to keep his balance. This was too much for several people who fell off their chairs laughing.

"It's funny now, but it wasn't then." Holly stuck a piece of mozzarella stick into Gregori's mouth.

"It had just rained," Heather explained. "The currents were running very fast. Then poof, there goes Holly down the stream. That was one of the funniest thing I had ever seen."

Holly smiled. "Let's not forget the important thing here. We all lived to tell about it." Holly took a bite of a hard taco and tried to keep the pieces from going everywhere.

"There's more food in the kitchen everyone. You will have to serve yourselves. I'm not your server. Not you Hugo, you ask your Mommy to serve you." Hanna had had enough of Hugo for the month.

"But you served Aunt Holly?"

"Are you Aunt Holly?"

"No, but ...."

"So why should I serve you?"

Holly sighed and looked at Bruce. "I know. This keeps getting off track. As soon as everyone gets something to eat, we can start, again."

"Maybe just the three of us should talk about this? The others weren't really involved in the dream." Bruce nodded and moved closer to Holly. He glanced at Gregori and cleared his throat. "It's hard to tell from the dream, but I believe the stress caused by not being able to go home affected all of us. That's why so many joined the Wild People movement."

"But this animal thing, The Wild People thing, I mean, I turn into a polar bear and run away?"

"And now you're turning into a nervous eater." Gregori added.

"I've always been a nervous eater. You just didn't want to see it."

"It's a way of dealing with stress that Holly and I both share. Turning into an animal would also serve that purpose. When I'm an animal, I don't feel emotions as sharply, and my worries seem to disappear." Bruce frowned at Gregori. He didn't like the way he said the last thing. If he didn't approve of Holly's eating habits, he should have said something before they got married.

"I don't get it."

"I do." Holly pushed her food away. She had already eaten more than her stomach could handle. She loved being a dog, and an owl, but not a cow or a pig.

"What's your take on this Gregori? You've been awfully quiet."

"You're just repeating what Holly said in the dream. Why don't you say what you really believe happened?"

Bruce studied the ceiling, giving the others in the room only an occasional glance. He needed to find a way to say what needed to. He decided to be blunt. It would be painful, but they had little time left. "I believe the cause of your rift and that of many other couples rifts, is that the children and infants were not protected during the impact. The aftershocks from it caused a section of the roof to collapse. It's above the chamber where they are now planning to house the children. I lost Doug in it."

Everyone in the room grew quiet. The parents all felt sharp pains in their hearts. Their babies could be lost in such an event.

"How is Doug lost?"

"He went in to calm them. He could feel their fear." Holly hugged herself and rocked back and forth. She could not bear the thought of losing Jen and Johnny. "I'm sorry."

"Babycakes," Gregori pulled Holly back onto his lap. "We will prevent this tragedy from happening. I promise you this."

"But I remember Doug being there. He was alive in the dream."

"It is a different Doug. That one will be my son." Jasmine said softly. "But don't ask me who the father is, I don't know. I wouldn't tell even if I did. Which, I don't. So there."

Doug coughed loudly to get everyone's attention. "I'm not dead yet. I have no plans on dying anytime soon. I do plan on living for many, many more years. And someone will not hook up with Jasmine's son Doug if something does happen to me." Clapping his hands, he strode around the room, making a point of looking into the eyes of every parent there. "We will not lose any of the children. We will work through what went wrong and find a way to prevent it from happening. In fact, we should find several ways, and then we can pick the ones that will work the best. Is that understood?"

Positive murmuring filled the room. "Good, let's break into small groups and come up with some solutions. We'll have a group discussion in one hour. This is too important for anyone not to partake in this discussion. Is everyone okay? Let's get started."

"Does that include me?" Gerry wanted to know. He had just turned ten, but he felt this was important. He wanted to help too.

"Yes it does and your sister too. Why don't you form a group with some of the other kids?"

"Okay," Gerry and Hanna formed a group with Hugo, Nymphea, and Angeline. A couple of teenagers from the village joined them.

"I remember what happened. There was a deep rumbling from deep in the ground and the walls. A few minutes after that a large thudding noise came from the closed air duct near where we were. It vibrated the whole room until the ceiling came down. A huge chunk came straight at me. I don't remember anything after that."

"It came from the air duct? Are you certain?"

"Yes, it sounded like some huge fist hitting the vent. It was a huge. As soon as it hit, I was knocked down by the shockwave."

"And the vent was closed? You're sure about that?"

"Yep, everyone made a big fuss about closing them. They said the temperature outside would get so hot it would bake us like we were meatloaf if we didn't close them."

"Do you remember anything else, Gerry? Anything you can remember could be important."

Gerry shook his head. It was hard remembering one's own death.

"Can you remember what happened before you went into the chamber? Try Gerry, this is important."

"We ate our last meal about an hour before the impact. The local government sent people around to close the vents. Holly, Bruce and a few others went to do it. I heard Holly found a new cave system and some people wanted to investigate it, but there was not any time. It got real hot and stuffy. I went in and stayed with some of the babies who were crying." Gerry gestured to the infants who were sleeping in the room with them.

"Go on, what else happened?"

"I tried to get in touch with their parents. Doug is the only one who came in. The others might have been coming, but that's when the vent blew. I was looking toward one of them when it happened. I don't remember anything after that."

Other members of the wider community let themselves into the apartment. Tom Michaels, Eduardo Salida, Mircea and Radu Vambery and Samuel Crawford were some of the ones who joined them.

"We are planning on closing the vents. But if what he says is true, we are going to have to rethink our plans."

Doctor Samuel Crawford had a vivid memory from his own dream. He was holding the body of young Gerry Sanders in his arms. The boy's lifeless eyes stared at what had once been a vent. The bodies of the other children scattered everywhere. He could hear the dying crying out in pain. The others in the room picked up his emotions.

"Perhaps we should have a structural engineer look at it. There is a retired couple from a village not far from here. They taught it before they retired. Dorothy and Joseph Morris," Mircea said.

"I'll look into it," Radu said leaving the room.

"There has to be others nearby we can contact about this. I'll let the other communities know of our concerns."

"I hope so. We have only 23 weeks to sort this out." Samuel looked at all the children in the room, and made a vow to keep them safe.

"Do you know where these other caves are Gerry?" Angel asked. "Can you show us the entrance to them?"

"Yes to both questions. But Aunt Holly could show you, she's the one who found them."

No one complained. They simply formed into groups and began coming up with solutions. The vents seemed to be the key. Perhaps the new caves Gerry had mentioned.

"I'll try to remember," Holly closed her eyes to think. "Doug and I were closing the vents. We had just closed the first three vents when I went down the wrong passageway. I remember because we had a fight about it. He kept saying I was going in the wrong direction and I kept telling him he was full of it."

"The first vents?"

"The ones in the parts of the caverns that is furthest from here. They're about a mile from the stables. The vents are about halfway up the cavern wall there. I think they're the oldest of them. The new caverns would be to the right of them. The pathway goes up. There is a secret room in the ceiling, four different passageways from there. It leads to a main area. It has lighting. I can show you what I remember from that dream."

"Please Babycakes, just do it."

"Okay," Holly focused on the way into the cave until everyone in the room knew the way. She leaned against Gregori as he hugged her in relief. Gerry reached out to hold Aunt Holly's hand.

Tom took 30 minutes to find the room. He studied it carefully. It was a small room, maybe two yards long and wide, and three at its highest point. The Roman arches, which dominated the entire underground complex, were here.

When he reached the far end of the room, he pushed a spot in the center of the archway. It opened with a loud grinding noise. Tom held his breath as he stepped into the next room. Just inside the archway, on the right wall he found the fuse box. He had the power up in less than a minute.

Samuel Crawford joined him. They studied the four passageways that lead deeper into the cave system. Two contained stairways and two had ramps. There was one stairway and one ramp leading up, and one stairway and one ramp leading down.

"We can help." Joseph and Dorothy Morris, a married couple with 8 children, 20 grandchildren and 50 great grandchildren appeared. They had also been structural engineers in their youth and had taught it at the local college. That was how they met. She being from Romania and having been visiting his home state of West Virginia. It was love at first sight for both of them.

"Joseph, Dorothy," Tom held out his hands in greeting. They came to examine the first set of caves that Holly had located five weeks earlier. "It is very nice of you to join us. Was your journey long?"

"Not really, the weather has been very good. We brought the family along with us. That won't be a problem. Will it?"

"Of course not, we have more than enough room for everyone. Are they being settled in?"

"Yes, they're doing it now. Is this what you wanted us to study?"

"The original cavern is our main concern. We have some concerns about a possible collapse during even a major earthquake. We are going to give this new one a quick once over."

"You do manage to find the most interesting things." Joseph thoughtfully as he studied the passageways leading from the room. "Which way do you want to go, up or down, the stairs or the ramp?"

"I'll take the down ramp." Sam smiled. "It is my show after all."

"I'll take the stairs up." Tom laughed. "Sam is such a wimp."

"Then I'll take the up ramp." Dorothy sighed. "You men are all a bunch of babies."

"I guess that leaves down the stairs. Anyone want to trade?"

"No," Dorothy kissed her husband on the lips and headed toward her passageway. It had a long, gentle upward slope. Dorothy bent down to touch the floor. It was just rough enough to give traction to anyone walking on it. The passageway was two yards across and four yards high. She sent the image to those waiting below. After looking over her shoulder one last time, she turned into a fox and ran.

Joseph watched his wife of 85 years head up the ramp for several minutes before heading down the stairs. The steps were a foot deep and yard across with three inches from one level to the next. It would make for easy walking.

The passage was the same dimensions as the one Dorothy took. He sent this information back to the other. Without bothering to see what anyone else was doing, he turned into a wolf and bolted down the stairs.

Sam turned into a coyote and headed down his ramp. He took extra care to watch for any sign of other secret passages. The walls were clean with no ornamentation. They formed the basic Roman arch. The Romans had built miles and miles of such structures. They built structures to last. Strings of lights were the only illumination though they were bright enough to his old eyes. He sent this information on to the others.

Tom watched them leave. He took in their reports and smiled. When he was sure they were well on their way, he turned into a baboon and took to the stairs. As the agile monkey, he made good time.

Whoever built the passageways had made them well lit, but plain. Every so often, he would touch the minds of the others in his group. As leader, he had to make sure everything and everyone stayed safe. He could feel the anxiety of those waiting behind. He sent reassurances to them.

Dorothy darted around a column. She had passed only three of them on her journey, all within a hundred feet of each other. Rounding the last one, she came to a broad patio. Reverting to her human form, she reported this to the others.

The patio wrapped around a large section of an even larger cavern. She detected the familiar Roman arches that made the huge space. Scattered around the patio where open stairways leading up and down to more levels. Passageways honeycombed away from the main chamber. Dorothy looked over the rail at what seemed like a bottomless abyss. She reported this to the others.

Sam touched her mind and reported that the view from the bottom as being equally spectacular. There were several more stories below him. What appeared to be a large lake was at the bottom.

Joseph, who came out a story below Sam and on the other side of the cavern, agreed. It was a lake. An area near the lake was suitable for raising livestock. There were several goats feeding on the slopes below where he was. He could make out the arches used to give the walls of the cavern extra support. He did not think a whole team of engineers could study it adequately in the time given. Dorothy agreed with him.

Tom was the last to reach his destination. He found it funny that there were telescopes on his side. They were similar to the ones found on tall building to view the cityscape. When he used them to look down, he could see a lake with a huge indoor pasture. In the pasture, he could just make out cows. On the surrounding hill, there were goats and rams. There was medicine and other supplies stored on his side. He could just make out the passageways that would lead him across to where Dorothy was. He followed them easily, and told the others what to look for.

Soon they had all regrouped at Tom's side. They found the area well stocked. In several of the rooms, they found computers with layouts of the entire network. The layout included undiscovered caverns. They reported this back to the others before returning to them.

Holly paced back and forth in her rooms. She had returned with Nicole and Wendy in order to feed the babies. Once they had returned, they found that Hanna had already fed them. She had used the breast milk Holly had stored in her refrigerator.

"There are so many caverns in this area. It's like Swiss cheese." She was producing enough breast milk to feed an army of babies. She had to use the breast pump again but only Gregori could get it to work comfortably.

"The others are coming back now. They can study the other caverns in detail from the computer records they uncovered."

"Really Aunt Holly, you just keep discovering places. It's so weird."

"Yes, it's very weird."

"It's frightening and I'm not going to tell that little snitch anything ever again." She wished someone else would find something.

Doug laughed. It was so like Holly to overreact, especially to something that had drawn attention to her. Holly took little notice, she grabbed Gregori's hand and led him to the bathroom, and handed him the breast pump. "Get this damn thing to work before I explode."

"Say please."

"Please gets this thing working so I don't have to kill you."

"Yes master, anything else master."

"Mmm, I could use a new husband. The one I have isn't very responsive to my needs lately."

"Show me this person so I can kill him."

Holly laughed and kissed him.

Flameboy surveyed the room. It took him several minutes to realize that the people in the room could not see him. It was an oddly comforting sensation. It was like he being behind a two-way mirror looking in. He would have to relate this to the others. As he listened to their conversations, he recognized the woman he was watching as being the author of the book he had just finished, Quincy. She had also come to him in several dreams in which she offered him advice and a selection of books to read. Facts he relayed to Erik and Mina when they joined him. He had met her before in his dreams, in her dreams. This he did not give Erik and Mina the details of those dreams. They watched the people on the other side for several minutes. No one knew what to make of it.

Flameboy had enjoyed the books. The character of Dracula as written in the book had delighted him. He wondered if she based the character on him. It was true that the Dracula in the book did not burst into flames in sunlight nor was he caused pain by silver. There was a certain physical similarity between them. Flameboy had to admit it, if only to himself, he wanted to be the Dracula from Quincy. He was cool.

After about three hours, they returned to report on their findings. They had the Historical Group to deal with. They wanted only solid facts to base their next move on.

Chapter 14

"Holly, come to me. Come to me now. Come to me and join with me, believe in me for I am the way to eternity." The man beckoned her closer. He looked like Gregori, except he was short, and far too chunky. He had long curly hair that went below his shoulders, and a super long curly mustache. He looked like someone with a bad temper. He looked familiar. Holly refused to get any closer to him.

Bruce shook Gregori awake even as he continued to take baby Jen away from Holly. "She keeps tossing and turning and calling out in some foreign tongue. Help me get Jen away from her before she hurts the baby."

"What?"

"I can't wake her up." Bruce gasped as he pulled Jen from Holly's arms. He handed the baby to Heather as he continued to try to wake her.

Gregori grabbed Holly, pulling her up unto her feet as he rose. "Babycakes, speak to me."

Holly's eyes flew open. She was not awake. "What do you mean by that? I don't know what that means. Don't touch me. The babies don't let him get the babies." Holly babbled incoherently. Tears streamed down her face.

"Babycakes," Gregori pleaded. The twins, trips, and little Mina began to wail. This finally brought Holly out of her trance.

"Let who get the babies?" Several people asked at once.

"I don't know. He rather looked like Gregori. Except, he was short and fat and had a really long mustache and long girlie hair." Holly peered up at Gregori. "He's definitely not a macho man like Gregori. He's just a little taller than me."

"A midget," Otto cracked.

"An evil one," Holly shuddered.

Gregori gazed at Holly's tear streaked face. Something had really frightened her. A man with long hair, Gregori pulled her close and stroked her hair.

"Holly, can you share with us what he looked like?"

"Yes," Holly closed her eyes tightly and projected the remembered image from the dream of the man who in some ways threatened her and her family. She could not stop shaking. The babies stopped crying as soon as Holly tried to remember the dream. The room became eerily silent.

"We've seen him before." Gerry volunteered. Hanna nudged him, and shook her head.

"Where?"

"Everywhere, he looks like the historical Dracula. Well, like the statues and paintings of him that is all over Romania. He's a national hero here. Hanna will you stop hitting me? It's getting annoying."

"Hanna? Why are you hitting your brother?"

"Because, he's telling what happened in the dream. The man from the dream said he would find us and kill us for telling anyone about the dream."

"Honey, what man? When did he threaten you?" Laura ran over to her daughter. Hanna had been acting strangely since moving to the caves.

"The man from the dream," Hanna wrung the edge of her shirt in her hands. Her was breathe was coming hard, and was wide eyed with fear. "Please don't make me tell. He said he'd hurt mom and dad if I told. Please?"

Angel wrapped his arms around Hanna. "No one is going to hurt anyone. Just let Mommy and me touch your mind."

Hanna shivered, but let her parents comfort her. The man had been angry. She did not want to make him angrier.

"He tried to bite me," Holly whispered to Gregori.

"But I didn't let him. That's when he threatened me, the babies and you."

"He bit Hanna. I saw him do it." Every eye turned to Hugo as he said this. "He wasn't interested in me. He only wanted girls."

"Where did he bit you?"

"On the neck, right here," Hugo jabbed himself in the back of the neck with two fingers.

Angel found the large, angry looking bite marks just where Hugo said they would be on Hanna's neck. There is a stunned silence. No one could believe something this terrible could happen to Hanna. Doug called the leaders of their community to report what had happened.

Tom Michaels came to the apartment with Samuel Crawford. They examined Hanna's wound and questioned her about it. Hugo blabbed out everything before Hanna could even form an answer.

Mircea Vambery arrived shortly after. He denied that a Romanian national hero could be responsible for the attacks, and most people agreed with him.

Radu Vambery showed up with a medical kit. After sniffing the wound and taking some swabs, he let her parents heal it.

"Now Hanna, I know this is traumatic, but we're here for you. Okay?"

"Okay," Hanna said in a voice that sounded small and frightened.

"I'd like to examine her at the infirmary. The electricity's not up in most of the caverns, but they are in the infirmary and kitchens. Much of the equipment is up and running."

"We'll bring her down. You might want to check Holly. We couldn't wake her earlier. And when we did wake her, she kept going on about someone trying to get the babies."

"It is the same man who bit Hanna." Hugo volunteered. He hated being out of the spotlight.

"I'm fine. Take care of Hanna," Holly pushed away from Gregori. What she needed more than anything at that moment is to hug and kiss her babies.

Doctor Mircea Vambery watched Holly wobble over to the babies. She was unsteady on her feet, but otherwise seemed okay. He would have Gregori bring her in. "Let's go young lady. If we delay much longer, your parents are going to worry themselves half to death. Now your mom tells me you are going to be 15 in a couple of weeks. Is that right?" The corridors were dimly light, with torches every few feet. It gave everything a medieval feeling. The power had mysteriously gone out 17 hours before. It might be another 15 hours before they got them back on. They had yet to determine the cause. Although some thought, it might have something to do with the opening of the new caverns.

"Yes," Hanna clutched each parent by the hands. It was somewhat scary with the lights out. "I'll be 15 on June second. Will Aunt Holly be okay? Bruce and Gregori really freaked when they couldn't wake her right away."

"I'm sure she'll be fine. Heather assures me Holly has always been a heavy sleeper and that she frequently tosses and turns in her sleep."

"And talks," Angel added. Holly had explained that to him. Though she claimed, she no longer did so.

"Are you sure?"

"I'd have to check her out to be 100% certain. However, I think she will be fine. Gregori's bringing her in now." The lights were on in the infirmary making them look modern and inviting if not warm.

A nurse led Hanna through a series of test.

Another nurse tested Holly as she protested that she was fine.

"Well Sam, what's the diagnosis?" Tom inclined his head toward the patients as Sam went over the tests.

"You had best not say I'm pregnant."

Ignoring Holly's outburst, Sam shook his head. "Hanna's blood count is down, but not enough for her to require a blood transfusion."

"We'll keep an eye on her."

"I am not pregnant."

"I can't say that Holly's not pregnant, but she'll kill me if I say she is. So I let Doctor Vambery say it."

Radu shook his head. They had such fear of a short little pregnant woman. Maybe he did not know her as well as the others. "Yes, Holly is pregnant. Tests indicate she's at least five and a half weeks along."

"That would be 11 weeks gestation?" Hanna asked.

"That would be correct."

"You see why I don't like doctors? They never tell you what you want to hear." Holly sighed as she pulled Gregori closer. It was too soon for her to be pregnant again. How would her cubs survive? Holly frowned. Why had she just called her babies cubs? "I am not."

"Yes you are. Deal with it."

"Cause they're unbearably cute like their mother." Bruce shook his head. He did not want to remember Holly's last pregnancy.

Holly pulled Gregori closer. "Do you remember the party we had to celebrate the announcement I was pregnant with the twins? And how I locked myself into the restroom?"

"Babycakes, everyone remembers that." Was that fear in his voice?

"And then afterward I spent the whole evening drinking tomato juice and feeding you mozzarella sticks?"

"Yes."

"Good. Let's cut to the fun part. Let's go somewhere crowded so I can feed you something fattening." Holly rubbed Gregori's lower back, and propped her chin upon his chest. She stared doe eyed into his eyes. Gregori let out a breath he did not even know he was holding. "Anything you want Babycakes."

Radu leaned toward Tom and whispered. "We have to find out who this man is. We can't let him just go on attacking our women and children."

"Do you have any idea who this person could be? I'm not even sure if he's really a male."

"What do you mean?"

"Some months ago, some guy kept picking up men at a bar. He was disguising himself as Holly. We wouldn't have even known except some of his victims tried to kill Holly. It took a while to track him down and deal with him."

"But that is in the physical world, this is happening in dreams." Sam watched Holly as her family surrounded her. "We'll have to remain alert. I'll contact the others and see if they had any similar incidents."

On a different continent, Frank woke up and rubbed his neck. "I dreamed George Washington bit me on the neck. It's somewhat funny in a sad, sick kind of way. His dentures got stuck and pulled out of his mouth when I pushed him away."

"Um, dad, you have someone's dentures sticking out of the back of your neck." Chet stared at the dental work attached to the back of his father's throat. They looked very old fashioned. They were the kind that George Washington might have worn.

Marlene pulled the dentures off Frank and examined them. "Look, they have little fangs, but otherwise they look just like a set I saw in a museum. It was an exhibit of George Washington's personal effects."

Keyshia cleaned and closed Frank's wound. She winced. Telepathy gave her a headache. "Captain Liam tells me that he has received word of a similar attack on Hanna and Holly. Several of the children witnessed it in their dreams."

"George Washington bit Holly?"

"No, Vlad Dracula bit Hanna. Holly would not let him near her. He's a national hero in Romania. Like, George Washington is here."

"National heroes are coming back and biting people? I hope George gets new dentures." Chet held up the dentures Marlene had pulled out of Frank's neck.

Everyone laughed at that. Several toothless vampire jokes made their rounds.

"I promise to look into this. Who is with me?"

"I am." Chet volunteered immediately. This person had attacked his father.

"We are too," volunteered Michol who is speaking for her brothers, Kim, Fran and Jan.

Frank reached out with his mind to check on Holly. He needed to know if his best client was okay. Holly shared with him of the attack on Hanna and herself, and that she was pregnant. Frank shared with her the attack on himself. They could come to no immediate answer, but promised to look into it. There was silence a moment as he relayed this to the others.

'Thanks Frank, you just got me into trouble.'

'How?'

'I broke out laughing at the sight of George Washington's teeth stuck to your throat just as Radu is having a serious discussion on his national hero.'

'I'm sorry. How's Bruce?'

'He's fine. Now let me tell everyone why I'm laughing.' Holly gazed at Radu and turned red, but could not stop giggling. "I really do have an explanation. It's all Frank's fault. He connected with me to see how I am. A national hero attacked him too. Does everyone here know that George Washington wore dentures?"

"Yes."

"No. They had dentures back then?" Radu looked confused. He could not remember if they really had dentures back then.

"Yes, they did. Oh, just let me show you what Frank showed me." Holly gave up trying to explain. The sight of George Washington's teeth stuck to Frank's throat, and the now toothless George trying to get them back caused several people to stifle their laughter. The Romanians did not find it as amusing as everyone else did. However, they had to admit to the toothless part being funny in a strange and horrifying way.

+++++++++

"It's the work of the Wild People." Otto asserted as he worked on Holly's computer. After the meeting, everyone broke into discussion groups and returned to their rooms.

"No, this has to be the work of a new group. No one turned into animals, just into national heroes." Gregori covered Holly with an extra blanket. She had been complaining of being cold lately. Some polar bear she would make.

"It's the same thing. Some of them were animals."

Otto glared at the computer, as if doing so would make it more cooperative.

"You can speak for yourself. My nation has only heroes of the highest caliber." Gregori checked on the sleeping babies. Jen and Johnny had just turned 18 weeks. They would be 28 weeks when the asteroid hit. Seven months, how had the time passed so quickly?

"Oh, that's a good one. Next thing you're going to tell me is they can cook. Everyone knows they have the worst cuisine in all of Europe if not the world."

"We do not. You apologize right this minute."

"Or what, are you going to try singing again?"

"Holly likes my singing."

"Aunt Holly is tone deaf. I can't believe you got her pregnant again. Don't you two believe in birth control?"

"And what's it to you? You got Nicole pregnant again, too."

"Okay guys. Let's change the subject before we wake Aunt Holly or any of the babies." Jamaica was as far along in her pregnancy as Holly. She did not want to hear any more of that birth control crap. She had definitely used birth control, but she still got pregnant. Heather and Bobby Joe had also used birth control, and they were pregnant. Of their group, only Sophia and Jasmine were not pregnant.

"Besides, the doctors have already explained that birth control does not work for New Lifers. I don't want to hear any more about it. Okay?"

"Okay," Otto grumbled. "Say Gregori, do you have a hero? And why do you think Dracula showed up for Aunt Holly?"

"Personally no, I don't know. Holly probably got Dracula because she did so much research on him. It's just something that stuck in her mind." Jamaica smiled as she fed Johnny. They were getting so big.

"Man, she did watch a shit load of vampire movies. Frankly most of them sucked, and I do not mean that in a good way. She told me in one of them they couldn't afford wolves so they used German shepherds." Otto shut down the computer. It was okay for now. He could no longer put off helping Nicole with feeding the trips.

"She told me about that one. She said that they admitted it would be too much trouble to train wolves on the DVD. They used police dogs instead."

"Then, there were the ones from Mexico. She said those were all strange and bloody, and filled with half naked women with too much prosthetics on the actors playing the vampires."

"She complained to me about them. She did like a couple of vampire films, but not the ones from Mexico. I can't remember any of the ones she liked. I think they were English."

"Cough, cough, we are supposed to be discussing who might be behind these nightmares that everyone is having. Is that garlic above Aunt Holly's head?"

"I can't believe you just noticed that. There are some at the foot of the bed also. She says she doesn't have nightmares since she put them up." Gregori shook his head. Nevertheless, it was true. She hadn't wakened him in the middle of the day with nightmares since she put them up.

"I've got to try that."

"I don't think it's the Wild People. I think it's a new group. But frankly, I only dream about Holly." Gregori burped baby Jen. She was starting to burp on her own. Otto tried not to roll his eyes. Those two were just too lovey dovey for him. "But this is the historical Dracula, not one of the movie ones. I know she studied him too, but the one she really liked is from a series of detective novels. Why didn't he show up?"

"The real question is how did he leave real bite marks on Hanna if he is only a dream? How could George Washington's teeth wind up in Frank's throat? Into the real world, are we bringing fictional characters to life? If we are, how are we doing it? This would explain how they were able to modernize so quickly."

"Since we have to call them something, how about the Mock Ancestral People?"

Otto rolled his eyes again, but said nothing. It was Nicole's suggestion and he did not want to argue with her about it.

"Let's take a vote on it."

"I like it." Nicole said while changing Katherine's diaper. "It's got a weird quality about it."

"I don't think we're bringing fictional characters to life. They all seem to be real historical figures. They seem to be modernizing their clothing because they're getting ideas about modern life by reading our minds."

"Or, they could just be modern people trying to fool everyone by pretending to be national heroes."

Holly shook off the blanket and sat up. "Did I miss feeding the twins again? You people should just wake me. I get enough sleep. Really," Holly yawned. "I dreamed about Dracula again. There were two of them this time. One was the historical and the new one who I didn't recognize. The new man didn't say anything. He just watched. Perhaps we're creating these dream figures from our unconscious minds. What do you think?"

"You dreamed of him again?"

"Yes, this time he was wearing a suit and a tie instead of the medieval clothing he had on before. He sat in a large chair, reading a book by the fireplace. It looked like the kind they have in old movies. It was very rich and expensive with paintings on the walls. He motioned me forward and told me that he and his kind had the right to live too. He wanted me to pass on that message. The new one stood closer to the fireplace. He just watched."

"He is real." Gregori didn't like the sound of that.

"He seemed very real to me. He apologized for trying to bite me. George Washington is getting dental implants."

"What?" Otto snickered.

"Vlad said George is tired of losing his dentures and is getting dental implants. George said too many people were laughing at him. It was embarrassing to the others. They demanded he go ahead with the procedure. He's getting rid of the powered wig and the colonial clothing too."

"Since, when are you on a first name basis with him?"

"He asked me to call him that. We can't even be sure their real people yet."

"She has a point. How do we know for sure?"

"Invite them over for lunch?" Jamaica volunteered. Everyone looked at her as if she is crazy. These people attacked several people in their dreams. They could be dangerous.

"She has a point. In our dreams, they can get us alone. In the real world, we probably out number them. We have the advantage here." Nicole finished changing James's diaper and handed him to Otto.

"I don't know. They appeared in dreams but influence things that are happening in the real world. Wouldn't that make them more powerful than us?"

"We can argue this for the rest of eternity, but it won't get us anywhere. Let's take this to the council and let them decide." Holly rubbed her back and paced the room.

"Frank tells me the same thing. George appeared to him in an elegant setting and apologized for biting him. He seemed quite contrite according to Frank. And younger than George had been in the first dream."

"Someone should find out if Hanna had the same dream. Any volunteers Otto?"

"No, I'm not volunteering. So don't even think of volunteering me, oh wifey of mine."

Hanna and her family walked into the door at that time. "Someone needed me here? I had a dream about him again. He apologized and asked me to bring a message. It's or everyone."

"Wait, write it down. I'll write mine down and then we can compare them." Holly handed Hanna a pen and a piece of paper. They wrote for over an hour. When they examined the papers, their accounts were almost identical.

+++++++++

Frank packed along the coast not far from where he would be staying during the impact. They had moved into it 15 weeks earlier. It was hard finding and keeping space. People from all over the country were appearing at various sites with all their worldly belongings. Who could turn them back? He and his family were new comers to this place. Most of the world had taken to hiding in caverns that had appeared out of nowhere and had always seemed to have just what everyone needed to survive. It was a New Life power. There were so many of unknown New Lifers had undiscovered powers. Were these dreams of historical figure also a New Lifer power? Did George really mean it when he apologized?

People were sleeping during the day, and staying up during the night. The night was beautiful even when it was storming as it was now. Frank wondered why he had never noticed it before. He wished he were alone. However, his son Chet followed from a distance.

Chet was more careful of his footing. He didn't want to trip and fall into the ocean. Chet could not swim. He watched his father scan the horizon, but he could not see anything. "Dad, why are you out here?"

"I need to think about something."

"What?"

"How the dentures got into my throat if it is only a dream. How Hanna got wounds in her throat if it is only a dream."

"Are you saying it's not only a dream? It's real?"

"Do you have any other explanation?"

"No, but…"

"Then it has to be someone who is already around us. But how can we tell with people arriving every day?"

"Holly's, Hanna's and your dreams occurred while there were people all around. No one saw anyone approach."

"Sigh, I give up. Let's get back to the caverns before someone takes our place. This will just have to wait until after the impact.

Chapter 15

Holly watched the enfolding disaster on two large screen televisions. One had reports from CNN, the other from the Weather Channel. Well, she thought bitterly as she fed Jen, the weather would at least allow for a good view. The satellites would have a good view of Day Zero, as they were calling it now. The weather outside their new home was a constant blizzard with heavy, blowing snow.

Though Yellowstone was not the site of the asteroid's impending impact, the government had everyone in a 1000-mile radius of it evacuated. The supervolcano continued to put out ash, mudflows, and lava. Many people who had to be convinced to leave their homes were still unhappy about this but understood the necessity. Those outside that zone had taken to living in underground cities. They had mysteriously appeared in every area they were needed. No one could explain it, though some thought it is an exotic New Life power that no one had ever noticed before.

The new site of the impact was Beijing, China. That was just as bad. No, it is worse. Far more people lived in the target zone. They had been given only weeks to evacuate. Less than ten percent of the population had converted to New Lifers. It was chaos over there.

The asteroid, soon to become a meteoroid, was traveling through space at 20 kilometers per second. That would be 72,000 kilometers an hour. Which would translate into roughly 44,740.8 miles an hour? With ten hours to go, the asteroid is still 447,408 miles or 720,000 kilometers from the earth.

The double cloud of debris from both events would plunge the planet into a deep ice age. Nothing could stop that now. The asteroid was less than a quarter of the size as the one that finished off the dinosaurs, but that was little comfort to those in the impact zone.

Holly wished she could go home, but everyone she cared about was here. Her entire family had come on the book tour, even the family pets. Well, she did miss her fellow co-workers, and hoped they would come out of this okay.

"Hand me Jen, so you can feed Johnny," Bruce smiled. He liked being Jen's godfather. It was almost like having his own children.

Holly nodded and handed him Jen. Doug handed her Johnny, who was his godchild.

"They say it will hit during the night over there. Another ten hours, do you think we'll lose electricity when it happens?"

"No."

"I saw a television movie about an asteroid hit. It was on the Science Channel or maybe the Discovery Channel, I can't remember. They said an electromagnetic pulse from the impact would wipe out all the computers on the planet."

Gregori snorted as he walked in. He never watched the educational channels. "That's silly."

Mark smiled to himself. Gregori was beginning to except his continued presence. Angeline and Little Nymphea enjoyed staying with Jasmine and Sophia. They loved playing with Jasmine's grandchildren. Despite the seriousness of the situation, he found joy in the way his family was coming back together. He loved his little grandchildren. "I saw that movie. They also said that a rain of fire would raise the temperature of the planet to 500 degrees Fahrenheit. And that the rains would be so acidy that it would be the equivalent of battery acid raining down on us."

"Of course I saw a program that counters that," Holly adjusted Johnny so he could feed. She couldn't wait to wean them. "Groups of scientist pointed out that a rain of fire, and acid bath would have killed many species who we know today are sensitive to the acid rain of the weak kind we have now."

"Not to mention that 500 degree temperatures for even half a day would cook everything on the surface of the planet." Bruce smirked. "It would be like being dry roasted."

"I don't like dry roasting. It makes meat taste like leather." Holly snorted. "Can you imagine dry roasted elephant? Gross."

Gregori moved closer to Holly. The giant wave thing had him freaked out. He did not want to admit that in front of the others though. "They've secured all but one entrance now. But everyone had everything they needed secured here nights ago." He ran his fingers delicately over the baby's brow as he nursed. Things had settled down since the tense and strange delivery. Holly was back to being her normal sweet self.

"I don't think there will be a wave if it hits so far inland." Holly added. "The movie had it hitting the Yucatan peninsula the same way the one that killed the dinosaurs did. This is entirely different."

Doug nodded. "They'll be closing the kitchens in a little while. Do you want me to get you anything?"

"They still have some vegetable beef soup. Bring a whole pot for us, I'm starving."

"Does anyone else want anything?"

"Noodles."

"Does anyone else want anything?"

"They won't be closing it for five hours. Bring me some of those deep fried snickers bars from the refrigerator. We have a deep fryer in our kitchen."

"Anything else?"

"Some more of Heather and Kyle's wedding cake, with lots of frosting this time." Doug loved cake.

"Okay, am I the only one being sensible here?" When everyone just looked at her, she sighed. "Fine, you can bring me some of the mozzarella sticks and extra frosting too. And bring me some of Wendy's birthday cake, it's better than the wedding cake anyway, and it'll be fresher, and some of Elijah and Bobby Joe's chili."

Bruce laughed. "Heather and Kyle have been on a honeymoon ever since they met. Why do they have to have another one?"

"You're just jealous because now you and Doug aren't the cutest married couple in our group any longer."

Holly laughed, handed Johnny to his father, and adjusted her top. She had lost most of the weight she had gained with the pregnancy. The rest of it made her look healthy, not anemic the way she had before. She was feeding well thanks to the boys.

Sophia and Hanna entered carrying a pot of soup, some noodles, mozzarella sticks, and some frozen snicker bars for deep-frying. "The kitchen is closing early and everyone else has what they want from it. I sensed that this would be your choices. Do you know you have real food in the small kitchen refrigerator?"

"Hey, beef vegetable soup and noodles is real food. Don't lump me completely with these guys." Holly looked at the CNN countdown to disaster clock in the right hand corner of the television. They had only Eight hours and fifty-eight minutes to impact. The Weather Channel was playing on the other television. She hoped they weren't going to be putting some poor weather person too close to the sight of impact. It was bad enough watching them blown away during hurricanes, but to have them blown up would be way over the top.

"I'm glad were keeping the babies with us. I never liked the idea of separating them from us. Did anyone bring any extra frosting?"

"Sorry, but someone get it all before we got to the kitchen."

"Ah, hah," Gerry called out. He held out a large cottage cheese container. "I grabbed some earlier. I got some cake too; it's hidden in the back of your refrigerator."

"I love you," Holly smiled as she took the container. "Do you want to share?"

"Sure do."

"Absolutely not," Laura shouted from across the room. "You can't have that much frosting."

"He's not. I'm going to eat some of it. Doug's going to eat most of it. Isn't that right Doug?"

"Hey, I like frosting too. You had best have brought enough for everyone." Bruce looked at the television, only eight hours fifty-five minutes and some seconds left until impact.

The asteroid was just approaching the moon's orbit. Observatories from around the world were sending live images of it, while politicians bemoaned the fact that nothing they did had any impact on the asteroids trajectory. They had in fact tried several things, but they had all failed to deflect the asteroid. They may in fact have made it worse.

Meanwhile satellite images of Yellowstone showed the supervolcano continuing to erupt. A thick cloud of volcanic ash kept spreading across the West at an alarming rate. Earthquakes and aftershocks registered on seismographs as away as Northern Canada and Southern Mexico.

"I saw a movie on the Discovery Channel that said we would lose all our computers when the asteroid hits. Some sort of electromagnetic pulse will wipe out all of the circuitry." Gerry said knowingly.

Hanna shrugged. "Sure, they know that because they found the dinosaurs electronics and none of it worked."

+++++++++

Erik Dracula gazed over the back of the chair at his fellow prisoners, well-kept prisoners though they were. It was a mile high above ground and a mile and a half below ground. Their prison was pyramid shaped. It was really two cites connected by an underground tunnel. Regular people lived in the upper levels, if you could count cave dwellers and space aliens as normal. A huge lake just outside their meeting room was part of the systems water filtration system.

It was a dissimilar group with nine of them claiming to be Dracula, including Erik himself. They therefore chose to use nicknames. They could not all be Dracula, yet all believed themselves to be the real Prince of Wallachia. Were they really the product of someone's overactive imagination? Thomas Jefferson and Carl Jung seemed to think so. Of course, they thought themselves to be real.

However, that raised more questions. How had George Washington lost his dentures? How had they come to be in Frank TeCruzada's throat if he was in the real world and George was in a dream world? It should not have happened. How did real bite marks come to be on Hanna Sander's neck?

"We are a dream being made to manifest in the world." Mina Harker came around and tapped one of the males on the head. He claimed to be the third eldest Dracula at 2012, but most of the time he acted as if his age was anywhere between 12 and 18. All he ever thought about was feeding, sex and television. "It doesn't matter where we came from. All that matters is where we are going. I want us out of this dream and into the nightmare of the real world. Who's with me?"

"Does this mean Flameboy here will keep going up in flames? Or will we be able to find a way to stop it?" Gil Dracula was the second oldest. The oldest was also a Gilgamesh, though he called himself Radu Dracula. He was 8000. He claimed to be 1000 years older than Gil. Gil was Flameboy's guardian. It was his job to keep Flameboy from any direct sunlight and therefore setting the place on fire. Flameboy, as his name suggested, went up in flames when exposed to sunlight. The boy had no sense. Of course, Simon, Brad and Couch Potato also went up in flames when in direct sunlight. Flameboy slammed his hands on the table.

"Damn it. I am sick of people treating me like an asshole. Do not call me that. You know I hate it when you do that. Call me by my real name."

"You mean your real birth name? We could use your real name." Tom Dracula asked while flirting with his wife, Katrina.

"No, I'd rather be called Flameboy then that."

"Will you use your birth name? Or the name Mina chose for you?"

"The name I chose for myself. Why is that so hard?"

"There are nine Draculas. So, we will call you Flameboy Dracula." Several people in the room shouted back at him.

"The name I chose for myself."

"Do we need to watch the DVD's again? I don't care what you think, we're not real." Mina walked back to Flameboy, stroked the back of Flameboy's head. The DVDs showed them just to be movie characters. This had left them in a state of confusion. She smiled at his confusion. She liked being unpredictable. "Fine, I think we should call you Zeus. It is Zeus Dracula or Flameboy Dracula. Your birth name is still available, if you want. Is that acceptable?"

Flameboy scrawled at Mina for several long minutes. "Fine, yes," Flameboy said after thinking for a moment. "I accept it. I'm Zeus Dracula from now on. Okay?"

"That's wonderful Zeus. I want you to promise to top pushing Couch Potato Dracula into the sunlight. He keeps setting the furniture on fire. And yes, we'll find a way to stop you from bursting into flames."

Zeus stuck out his bottom lip, and then thought better of it. Mina had a bad temper. "Yes, of course, if that's what you want."

"That is what I want. Now where were we?"

"How George's teeth wound up in Frank's neck if we aren't real and he is."

"Maybe we're real and Frank's the dream." Brad Dracula grinned like a little boy. He was always trying to hit on Mina though he had a steady girlfriend. She ignored him. Brad was, for wont of a better name, Zeus's twin brother. They called Couch Potato their illegitimate father. They were really all the same person. They knew that from watching the DVD's.

"Anyone else have any ideas?"

"What's wrong with my idea?" Brad, like Simon, Zeus and Couch Potato, weren't the sharpest tool in the shed.

"Well for one thing, there are nine Draculas. That is eight too many. There are four of you. The only difference is your hair color and one of you looking like a child molester. There are four each of Mina and Lucy."

"I do not molester children."

"Yes, but you do look like someone who would." Everyone in the room shouted before Couch Potato could continue his protest.

"It's the blonde hair. You're too old for it." Katrina said helpfully. "It makes you look like an old pervert."

"There can't be nine. I think you counted wrong." Gil broke in before the fight could intensify. "We need to take a count."

"Let's see, there are Vlad, Erik, Matt, Richard, Simon, Zeus, Brad, Couch Potato, Gil, Mark, Radu, James and Tom."

"That's 13."

"Yes, but Simon, Zeus, Brad and Couch Potato count as only one. So there is still only nine."

"They should count as four, not one. They don't always behave the same way. Brad is much more romantic then either Zeus or Couch Potato. Moreover, Brad, Simon and Zeus aren't as scary looking as Couch Potato is. Simon doesn't even look like he's hit puberty yet. Let's take a vote."

"Can I be called something besides Couch Potato?" Couch Potato interjected before they could take a vote. He felt sick of the nickname everyone gave him just because he liked to lay around watching television.

"How do you feel about the name Jonathan?"

"Um, it's okay." Couch Potato sat down next to Lucy Harker and smirked. She smacked him in the face and walked away.

"Now Brad," Mina tried to sound reasonable. She gestured to a group in the corner that everyone considered purely fantasy characters and not real people. They were just too perfect. "Do you real think any of this is real?"

"No but, it is so beautiful. Just look at everything around us. We're living in such splendor that even the Romans could not have imagined it. And we have Romans running around upstairs." He ran his hand over Minnie's and she slapped it away. She was the younger Mina, and deferred to the older Mina's judgment. No one had to tell her to stay away from that idiot. She moved across the room to sit with another Mina called Mara and a young girl named Katrina.

Everyone looked around. They had to agree with him. This might be their prison, but it was a very beautiful one. It was a huge city set in what everyone described as an alien landscape. It was not earth, and everyone missed their homes on earth.

"Okay, let's get back to the issue. These gentlemen, the Historical people, think they are real, and not one of us."

"We are real. We belong in the Historical Group." They were from the group that had not come from movies. Everyone called them the Romantic Group. They came mostly from romance novels. Their leader is Alfred Singleton.

Mina answer was to pick up a romance novel and begin to read. Giggles erupted through the room as the passage she was reading dealt with Arthur having sex with his wife, Aimee, for the first time. By the fifth book, they got the message, by the twentieth everyone was getting embarrassed by the graphic sexual content. They were no more real than anyone else in the room. They just had better sex lives than most. Several of their women broke into tears. Others were just embarrassed.

Mina walked up to Aimee with a box of facial tissue. "What has changed? Nothing. The dentures and bite mark are a clue. We may not have started out real, but we can become real. We are as real as we believe ourselves to be." Mina circled the room, making eye contact with everyone. "We are as real as we want to be. It does not matter where we came from, only where we are going. And we are going wherever we please." She eyed some of the more depressed member of her little group. "We are going to work this out. We outnumber the Historical Group; the numbers are on our side. That's something of which to be proud. There are numbers on our side. Now where were we?"

"I think we're trying to enter their world. They need us for some reason. With the supervolcanoes erupting and the asteroid hitting the earth, a vacuum has opened that only we can fill." Luce sat down by Richard Dracula. They were holding hands. Her bright green eyes surveyed the room, threatening anyone who dared to contradict her. "We need to learn to control our powers and how to combine them. What we need to learn most of all is how to combine ours powers and eliminate our weaknesses."

"And how do you suppose we do that?" Matt Dracula demanded. It was like one big extended family, one with quadruplets in it and huge age differences.

"I believe Mister Carver has a few ideas. We should let him tell you." The Historical Group entered quietly. With everyone seated, Mister Carver explained his theory. Everyone wanted to know what needed to be done to test it.

+++++++++

Holly sat on the sofa. Doug and Bruce were on her left and Gregori on her right. She held baby Jen in her arms. Doug had Johnny. After having fed the twins, both babies were sleeping soundly. The asteroid would hit any minute now. It could be occurring now. There is no way to tell with all the power off. Holly wondered if they would feel the ground shake. No one would feel anything for several hours, if at all.

The only heat and light in the room came from a fireplace. The local government deemed it safe for just that purpose. The six of them huddled under blankets. The others had long returned to their rooms. A blizzard continued to blow outside with subfreezing temperatures and high winds.

"Do you think they'll tell us like they said they would?"

"No, I think it's already hit."

"How can you know?"

"I don't, but according to my wristwatch, it's past the time they said it would make impact."

"Let me see. Damn you're right."

"So when will we have full power again?" They had been able to shut power down to everything except refrigeration units.

"Somewhere between 11 and 25 hours after impact, they want to be certain about the electromagnetic pulse doesn't destroy all the electrical systems and computers."

"I hate waiting."

"Heather, Kyle, Nicole and Otto are at the door. Someone should let them in."

Bruce got up and went to the door. "Hi, I thought you were going to stay in your room. What happened?"

"They wouldn't rate our fireplace for use. I think yours is the only one working."

"Don't close the door. We're coming." The rest of the family poured through the open door and made themselves comfortable. Someone set up a makeshift crib for the trips and Lucy.

+++++++++

Frank TeCruzada huddled in a well-stocked cavern in Northern Maine. It was well lit and warm. He was as far away from the supervolcano as one could be and still be in the lower 48 states. Well-secured kerosene lanterns hung along all of the walls in the room at nine-foot intervals.

Frank kept everyone distracted from the coming disaster by reading from Holly Skyhaven's latest novel, For the Dead Travel Fast, to a group of tired New Yorkers, and other friends who had followed him up north. The novel was only one of a few paper copies of the novel Holly had finished just weeks before. It a marvel that she could finish a novel so soon after giving birth to twins. He had Bruce Harwood's new novel, Primero Los Pies, to read to them when he finished Holly's novel. Frank felt a deep satisfaction to be the literary agent for both of them. Taking them on as clients was one of the smartest moves Frank had ever made.

Frank had just finished a chapter when they felt the earth lift and a moment later to fall. It was a gentle, but noticeable motion. It was not the fierce shaking feared by many. That was just the initial eruption. There would be more aftershock to come.

Marlene leaned into her oldest son, Chet as the ground continued to shake. It was only a few seconds, but it seemed like an eternity to her. A quick look around showed that only the quaking earth had disturbed their nerves.

Marlene hated appearing weak. However, she had a deathly fear of enclosed spaces. It was killing her to be underground. However, it would also kill her to be above ground at this time. The only thing keeping her from freaking out was the size of the place. Each room was at least 18 feet high, while larger chambers were 30 or more feet. The rooms were 24 feet wide by 36 feet long, making them feel huge. Unlit chandeliers hung from three points in the ceiling. Everything was so beautiful. It was like a Home and Garden display instead of a cave.

Frank cleared his throat. "Does anyone want me to continue at this time?" Several people murmured yes.

Marlene listened as Frank continued to read. She had met Holly and Bruce and their significant others. She had been the one to calm Gregori down when Frank had set Myles up. She had reamed Frank good when she had learned he got Myles to try to steal Gregori from Holly. She had not accepted his explanation. She had had to remind him of how her parents had pulled a similar stunt on them. He was lucky they had decided to keep him as their agent.

The room swayed occasionally, but it was so gentle that no one really noticed. Marlene hugged herself as Frank continued to read. She remembered the first time she had met Holly. Bruce had been with her. It had been in Cleveland, before they went to New York, before they had met Doug and Gregori. Holly and Bruce had made such a lovely couple. They looked so lovely together. How they finished each other's sentences. It's true about Bruce being gay, but they had a way of looking at each other that spoke volumes. Marlene had never seen Bruce and Doug look at each other that way. Nor for that matter did Gregori and Holly ever do so.

She looked up at a chandelier in the center of the room. It quivered gently for a few moments and stopped. Marlene sighed. The next time she saw Bruce and Holly was on the cruise ship, the Princess Ayala. It was at Holly and Gregori's wedding. Though she had known it was coming, it was a crushing blow to her hopes for Holly and Bruce. They were different too. It was hard for her to pin it down. Something had definitely come between her, and it was Gregori's fear of humiliation by another woman being that something. Marlene was positive. They say he went through woman the way other men change their pants. That something being truth was women just got tired of him and dumped him. Only gold diggers like Vanessa Lee could stand him, and she had only stuck around for his money. Marlene hated seeing Holly stuck with such a jerk.

Frank stopped reading. He stared at his wife until she realized that he was looking at her. As he suspected, she did not even look embarrassed. She had never failed to tell everyone who would listen exactly what she thought of Gregori Cornridge. Frank sighed. Marlene would not take the time to get to know the real Gregori. She always viewed him from the perspective of the roles he had played. She had only seen him play a serial killer, and a lawyer. They were not two of his most flattering roles. Gregori made Holly happy. Doug made Bruce happy. Even Holly's Gregori hating nephew, Otto, was getting along with Gregori. Otto still thought Gregori's acting sucked. Why couldn't Marlene let go of her prejudices?

"You can continue. I promise to behave myself."

Everyone's attention shifted back to Frank. He continued to read. Frank was halfway through with the chapter he was reading, when he mentally reached out to Myles on the cruise ship. He could never think of him as Charles. In truth, Myles was now using his real name. With so much of the world's population turned to the New Life, he no longer hid behind a pseudonym.

Myles was studying one of three monitors in his cabin when he felt Frank touch his mind. Like everyone else in hiding, Frank wanted to know if the meteoroid had hit yet. It had. The impact had been spectacular. It would be as if a giant had thrown Mount Everest into the earth. Ash and debris is spreading from the impact site and spreading across the ocean. Soon it would join the debris cloud from the Yellowstone Supervolcano eruption. The earth would continue shaking as aftershocks continued to rock the planet. They were strong enough to create a as a gently rocking in the Mediterranean Sea. This continued for the next 72 hours and then tapered off.

Chapter 16

Heather watched Holly sleep with one twin on her legs and the other sprawled over her chest. She looked so innocent when she was sleeping. Heather glanced at Gregori. He was also watching Holly sleep. No one could deny his devotion to her. This gave Heather a good feeling. Her baby sister deserved to be happy.

This pregnancy crap was overrated though. She had had her one child and had not wanted anymore. Thank you. All of them had become pregnant at the same time.

Heather, Holly, Wendy, Jamaica, Bobby Joe and Nicole had all discovered their pregnancies at the same time. All Heather wanted to do was sleep, have sex and feed, and in that order. It is no wonder Holly had been so grumpy during her first pregnancy. Gregori hadn't been having enough sex with her. This made Heather smile. Kyle stirred next to her. He was very sensitive to her moods. Heather leaned into his embrace. He was warm and cozy. The room itself felt like ice.

Doug got up and tended to the fire. It had been over 12 hours since impact and there was still no word as to when the power would be back on. He soon had the fire crackling. The room began to fill with warmth.

'Ohm,' Heather thought, snuggling up to Kyle,

'Sex sounds good right now.'

'There are people here,' he thought back.

'So what,' she thought right back to him.

'You are insatiable,' he thought back.

Doug coughed loudly. He knew they would ignore him, but he had to try. He had been exposed to sex that is more heterosexual in the last eight hours then he had been in his whole life. It was disturbing, yet strangely exciting. Not that he would admit that to Bruce. Doug did not want to upset him. Truth was the cornerstone of their relationship to use the old cliché He supposed he would have to tell Bruce eventually.

Bruce snuck up behind Doug and goosed him. He loved grabbing Doug's ass. He loved it when Doug squealed and jumped. Especially when he knew, Doug was thinking of girls. They both shared a particular fascination with a particular married girl. Bruce leaned closer to Doug. 'Let's find ourselves a warm spot and have some fun. Come on, how often do you get to survive a meteoroid hitting the earth?' He thought to Doug. No one talked anymore. They just used telepathy or thinking it to someone. It was a faster and much more comprehensive way of communicating information. It was also quieter which is a good thing when everyone was sleeping.

'You've got a point there. Okay, but you have to help me check the fireplace vents first. I don't want to suffocate anyone.'

'Okay.' They took a little over a half hour to check and clean the vents before retiring to some warm cozy blankets. Slipping under the covers, and out of their clothing, they made love passionately.

Jamaica woke up and checked on the children. They were all sleeping soundly. She moved closer to the fire and tried to clear her thoughts that were in chaos. How could she be pregnant again and yet be so happy? She had never been so happy in her life. She had no idea of how to handle being happy. Everyone else seemed to take it in stride. How did they manage it? She looked at Gregori who had Holly tucked under his chin. He even looked happy in his sleep.

'Sweetheart, you think too much. You've just got to accept the happiness you feel now, and stop second guessing it.'

'I try. But it's hard after so many years.'

'I know.' Yoshi kissed Jamaica's forehead. 'But we've got years to work it out.'

'But, I want it now.'

'Patience little flower, all will come to you in time.'

Holly moved closer to Gregori and snorted in her sleep causing Jamaica and Yoshi to break out laughing.

'Let's move the twins off of her so she can sleep.'

'Okay.' Yoshi bent over Holly and picked Johnny off Holly's legs. He handed him to Jamaica before picking Jen up. They transferred them to a nearby crib. 'We need to pick out names. What about Joanne?'

'It would be a tough name for a boy.'

'Yes, but our daughter might like it.'

'Are we having a girl? Then yes.'

'We only have five weeks to decide honey. The doctor said you were having a girl.'

'No, he told me I am having a boy.' They stared at each other for several long minutes. They could not both be right, unless Jamaica was having twins. The doctor would have told them. Wouldn't they have?

Holly got up and waddled over to check the babies. Seeing that they were fine, she returned to Gregori's side. 'She's having quads,' Holly thought frivolously as she passed the couple. She sat next to Gregori and pulled his head down onto her lap.

'That's not funny, Aunt Holly.'

'Do you know what you're having?' Yoshi inquired.

'Yes,'

'What?'

'A baby,' Gregori stirred in his sleep and Holly pulled a blanket around him and stroked his hair. She had not realized how much physical contact had come to mean to her. 'I want to be surprised this time.'

'Oh, you weren't surprised the last time.'

'No, I wasn't. The doctor told me right away, what I was having. The hard part is coming up with the names.'

Mark got up and checked on the girls. He could just make out his daughters sleeping on the cots not four feet from the fireplace. He tucked them in and made sure they were warm and comfortable. It was warm now, but he could have sworn it had been like ice in there just a few minutes before. Someone had probably worked on the fireplace, he thought as he rearranged the girls' blankets. The fire gave everything a rosy color.

Mark pulled Jasmine and Sophia closer to himself. He watched them sleep for some time before sleep overcame him.

Mina and Erik stood in a small grotto set against the far wall of the living room. They had just learned to build the grotto a month earlier. They had to rebuild them every time they visited. They watched everyone sleep, have sex and talk about the meteoroid impact and the supervolcano. Only the fireplace lighted the room. Mina reached over and took a blank sheet of paper. Erik took paper clips. They needed to bring them back with them.

"This is silly. We're clearly in their world at this moment." Mina folded the piece of paper into quarters.

"I know, but we have to do this precisely. If we are in their world why can't they hear us?"

"They're too busy doing other things."

Erik linked his paper clips together to form a chain. "We should grab that computer CD while we're at it. It might come in handy." Erik reached in and pulled it from the desk. He read the label. It was Holly's latest novel, For the Dead Travel Fast. After pocketing it, he returned to Mina's side. "We can protect this for them."

"I think you just want to be the first to read it. Let's get out of here."

After they left, the grotto remained though invisible to those inside the room.

Chapter 17

Erik and Mina watched Holly play with the twins while Gregori talked to Laura about how Quincy was doing. Nicole fed her newborn, who they had named Jonathan. Little Jean-Luc slept by her side. They were going to celebrate Lucy Franklin's first birthday. It is on Christmas Eve, which is on a Tuesday this year. It was four weeks after the supervolcano and the impact. They would celebrate Christmas as a group the next night. It was a chance to celebrate just being alive.

"Why do members of the Historical Group only attack people while they're sleeping? Are they cowards?" Erik grasped his lover's hand and gazed into her eyes. He hated cowards.

She squeezed his hand back as she thought this over. People called them the Wild People, but its Historical Group are the ones who act like wild animals. Mina rested her forehead on Erik's arm. They could communicate without words but preferred not to. "I don't know."

A small tugging drew Mina's attention. James Skyhaven waved a chubby fist at her and cooed.

Erik and Mina exchanged startled glances. Everyone was awake, but contact is happening. How had the baby crossed the invisible barrier separating them from the rest of the world? Is their hidden grotto no longer a hidden grotto?

Thinking quickly, Mina hunched down and gave James a quick hug. "Here Sweetie, take the pretty ball and go show Mommy and Daddy. That's a good boy, go show Mommy and Daddy."

James cooed and toddled back with his new toy to show his parents.

"Where did you get that honey?" Nicole took the small, clear plastic ball from James, who quickly voiced his protest, and waved his arm toward where Mina and Erik where hiding.

Mina panicking pushed herself and Erik back into their dream world. Mina watched them from the other side of the new barrier. She could see them but they could not see her. An idea came to her. Grabbing Erik's hand, she dragged him back to the others.

Gregori and Otto examined the small grotto set into the wall. It had not been there that morning. They could come to no conclusion. With the birth of the babies just two weeks earlier, everyone was nervous.

"We had better block this off or the kids will want to play in it." Otto took a picture with his camera phone and sent it to the others.

"What kind of barrier should we construct?"

"It's not wide. Let's get some plywood and just board it over."

"What if they just make another grotto in a different part of the apartment?" Holly fed her newborn baby. She had a bad feeling about this. The strange dreams had ended three months ago. Was this a sign that they were returning? "What about putting up about a half wall? We just need to keep the babies from going into them. Right?"

"She has a point." Gregori sighed. "We don't need more grottoes popping up."

Otto shrugged. "A half wall it is then. The other's will be over soon. We can get them to help."

Sophia and Jasmine arrived with the birthday cake. They made Mark carry it. Angeline and Little Nymphea carried the presents. Everyone else arrived with their respective brood. Wendy and Colin brought Mina, Lucy, Paul and Dorothy. Jamaica and Yoshi brought Joanne and Andrew. Heather and Kyle came with Bobby, Joey and Dorothy. Elijah and Bobby Joe came with Matthew, Mark, Luke and John.

Kyle and Yoshi went to get the plywood, after a long discussion on the size, thickness and quality of the plywood that they needed. They went with a 1/2 inch birch wood 4x8. Holly followed them to the door, reminding them to get nails, screws, hammers, screwdrivers, molding, paint and maybe some screening for the open area. A nice color of paint, she did not want any pastels.

Holly gave George to Heather and picked up his twin. George and Janis, this twin thing was getting tiring. Holly found herself gazing into the grotto as she fed Janis. If you looked into it hard enough, you could almost see another world. It was a world that was warm, sunny. It was far away from the dusty gloom caused by the meteoroid and the supervolcano.

"Hey. Is that my CD? The one I lost during the impact. The one I used to hold the back-up copy of my new novel on it."

"UM, it says For the Dead Travel Fast. So it must have been here all along." Otto frowned. That could not be right. He had just worked on the computer that morning, and it had not been there. "Okay. Who had this all this time? We can get the fingerprints checked on this if we have to. I mean it."

Holly walked into the grotto and put her hand through the rear wall. He hand tingled going in and it is warm on the other side. After hesitating just a moment, she handed Janis to Nicole and stepped partway through the gateway. She had a brief glance of a walled patio and a small lake that ran under it and beyond before Gregori pulled her back.

"Remember when Jamaica suggested that we invite them for dinner? Well, I have an idea. We need to talk about it." Holly blurted before Gregori could vent on her for endangering her life.

"It was four weeks ago, during the first nightmare," Hanna promoted. "The one where Vlad Dracula bit me, tried to bite Aunt Holly, and George Washington's dentures got stuck on Frank's throat."

Tom and Radu showed up a few minutes later. They examined the grotto and agreed with Holly. There could be more of them out there. They promised to find the underlying cause of the thief of Holly's CD and called in experts to finger print it.

Holly fixed her eyes on Tom. It was a simply plan, but Holly was sure it would work. She needed Tom and Radu to agree to it before it could move forward.

Several others had joined the group, including Herb White, Steven Grams and Julie Hermine. She hadn't seen them since England, though she knew they had come with the cast. They were waiting for Samuel, Mircea, Vlad, Mary and Joseph to join them. They were on their way.

"There's drinks and food in the dining room." Hanna announced. "The others are at the door. Let them in Hugo."

Once everyone was in the room, Holly motioned them to seat themselves near the grotto. "There is a gateway at the back of this grotto. It leads to another place. I can show it to you. There is a large lake, and I think a body is floating in it. I could see people on the far shore waving their arms. I could hear people nearby talking about how they could get to him. The currents were too strong and they needed stronger boats. They had to wait for someone to wake up. The boat builders, I think."

"Okay, we can enter their world. We'll build stronger barriers so children don't get through the gateway." Radu frowned. There was something compelling about the grottoes.

"I think we can convert these people the way Myles converted much of North America."

"What do you suggest we do?"

"They can't get the body until they build stronger boats. If we can dump our special formula into the water, it should produce a spectacularly strong fog. The sooner we do it, the better."

"Okay, so we have someone throw up over the railing."

"No. We prepare set amounts and dump it into the water. We can use babies' diapers to prepare it." Holly explained how she had accidentally created fog when she emptied a diaper into the toilet after someone had thrown up in it. The toilet that is, not the diaper. "So we take the dirty diaper, listen to make sure no one is near the gateway then have someone throw up in it and heave it over the railing into the water, instant fog."

"That's brilliant Holly. Mind you, it's also sick and twisted." They got to work on it immediately. It took only a sort time to realize they could hit the lake from several different gateways that appeared in various apartments around the world. They created the strongest fog ever. It was even stronger than Myles's first fog.

+++++++++

Zeus sat the table reading the stolen copy of Holly's unpublished novel, For the Dead Travel Fast. He felt strangely drawn to the character of Zoë. He wanted to get to know her better. He felt as if he had met her before. He was glad Mina had named him Zeus. How did she know about the character in the novel? Turning to Gil, he smiled wickedly. "Three things, first this is crap.

Second, do you think this Zoë character would date me? Third, is it me or do you think the character of Zeus and Dracula from Quincy are similar?"

"If it's crap, then why do you keep reading it?" Gil asked as he pondered Zeus's lack of good taste in anything.

"I haven't read Quincy yet. So I don't know. Why would a fictional character want to date you? There are plenty of real women around here for you to hit on."

"I'm sick of all the women around here slapping me in the face. I can't even say hello to them anymore. Besides, we were fictional at one time, and we're here. Look at how many more people are claiming to be Dracula now. There must be thousands of them."

"Women do seem to enjoy smacking you in the face, although some prefer the back of your head. I think I'll talk to Erik about getting them to stop doing that. It might be damaging what few brain cells you have."

Zeus bared his teeth at Gil, but refrained from joining him in the little game. It was belittling and petty. "I like it that Mina changed my name to Zeus. I'm just like Zoë's love interest in the book. I'll bet Holly watched my movies and based Zeus on me. What do you think?"

"Did you work on that project Mister Carver gave you? Or have you been just rereading that book?" Mina and Erik had borrowed Holly's CD of her book. They had returned it two months after they had downloaded copies, which was just that morning. Zeus kept reading the paperback edition. They produced it for the computer illiterate. Zeus liked computers, but Gil hated them. It was Gil's copy.

"I did my assignment." He reread the description of Zoë and pictured her naked, her voluptuous body rubbing against his. A young woman walked through the hall and smacked him on the back of the head.

"On the other hand, maybe you deserve to be smacked in the head. Quite picturing them naked and I'll bet they'll stop smacking you."

"Perhaps you're right. I doubt it. Do you think Holly based Zoë on herself? They both look alike." He had no sexual interest in Holly but Zoë was hot.

"Perhaps, I can see the similarities. Here they come. Oh look, another new one. And she looks just like you imagined Zoë except with clothes on."

Zeus stared at Zoë for several minutes. He felt strangely happy. She is a newborn character for him to play with. A woman, who would, perhaps, not hit him.

Gil smacked him on the head. "We don't play with characters unless we're writing a novel or doing a play. How many times do I have to tell you that?"

Mina introduced Zoë Dulcet and several others before the meeting could begin. The Historical Group was up to 100 members. The Wild People could now claim over 9000 members. It is a cause of disagreement between the two groups.

Zoë stared at everything. It was hard to believe she was a character from a third rate novel. She felt so alive. She listened quietly to Mina's plan for some of them to take residence in the unused caverns that Holly Skyhaven had discovered in Romania. There were undiscovered caverns elsewhere, but this would be the test case. No one knew if anyone could survive for long in the real world. Only a small group would go, and no pregnant women would be included in the test sample. It sounded dangerous.

This immediately caught Zeus's attention. He quickly volunteered. They turned him down because of his personality. This only lead to him protesting and causing delays. The romance novel group wanted to go, but they had too many pregnant women. The Historical Group believed that they should be the ones to go. The group as a whole vetoed the idea. They had spent too much time biting people as it was.

Mister Carver promised to come to some kind of compromise on the issue. They moved on to talking about the grottoes where the New Lifers had seen several of them.

"They keep boarding them up. They know we're there. They keep getting freaked out by us." Radu commented. He was trying to make brownie points with the new girls.

"Wouldn't you if you thought someone's spying on you? We're lucky that no one has been hurt so far." Luce shook her head. It was so obvious to her. Why could not anyone else see it?

"Simon is hurt. In fact someone killed him." Brad pointed out. "Zeus's, Jonathan's and my life are in danger from those fanatics." They had cut Simon's head off and left his body and head to rot in the middle of the lake that feeds the city's water reserves. They did not have any boats that could handle the currents, yet. They were working to correct that problem. It was strange and very disturbing time.

"That wasn't the New Lifers fault. We let the people who were hunting him in the movie get him. We're keeping a much better eye on those people now." George Washington said as he studied the group. He could tell this latest turn of events had left them shaken. He needed to build up their confidence. He looked across the table at Thomas Jefferson, and shook his head. "Vlad Dracula is heading up a group to study the problem. Anyone who wants to volunteer can see Vlad after the meeting. I need a list of people who would like to test the caverns theory. I'm assigning Carl Jung to evaluate the candidates. If you are interested, you will need to see him about it after the meeting. I urge everyone who wants to volunteer that it could be dangerous, if not fatal. We don't have enough information at this time. And yes, we are working on the boats." When no one had anything to add, he adjourned the meeting.

Several of the single men went over to talk to new arrivals. Zeus quietly made it known that Zoë was his. Zeus moved closer to Zoë. He was going to get lucky tonight. It was a clear warm night. He looked his best. Nothing was going to stop him.

"Is it always this foggy?" Zoë peered out the window. The whole area outside and around the lake is blanketed in a thick white fog. She rubbed her arm, suddenly chilled despite the warmth of the night. "And the fog is so white here. I've never seen such a brilliant white fog. Have you?"

"It is a thick fog." Zeus commented, moving closer to Zoë. He put his arm around her shoulder as she opened a window and let the fog in. It rolled in and completely blanketed the room in moments.

Zoë quivered and pulled away from Zeus. Raising her arms, she ran out into the fog. Mina ran out after her. Once Zoë reached high ground, she looked up. Fog poured down from the upper levels of their city prison and from the lake.

Chapter 18

Zoë woke up with something heavy on top of her. It took her several minutes to realize it was Zeus. What Zeus was doing or how he came to be there was a difficult matter for Zoë fog addled mind to take in. Fishing around in her mind, she remembered the fog pouring through every vent and from the lake. It had made her dizzy. Zeus had promised to escort her home. She knew she should have refused, but the fog kept getting thicker. By the time they got to her apartment, the fog was so thick she could not see her hand in front of her face. Zoë had become so sick by then that Zeus had had to carry her into her apartment. The fog had made him ill too, and he had lain down beside her.

So why was he on top of her? Did he toss and turn in his sleep? Zoë attempted to shove him off. He was unmovable. It was nearly impossible to breathe with him in this position. Hoping to dislodge him with pain, Zoë bit him on the chest. He tasted so good. She drank long and hard from him. She felt him wake up, but to her dismay she felt him get a hard on. It was just her luck that he became sexually aroused when someone bit him. This stumped Zoë. She had no idea what to do next. Maybe, she thought, if I bite him again I'll drain him enough so he'll pass out. There was something wrong with her logic, but she could not figure it out. She sank her teeth into him again and drank.

She learned the hard way what Holly had learned more than a year before. Once you had bitten a person, it was nearly impossible to get rid of that person. He moaned in ecstasy, pulling Zoë closer. He rolled over onto his back. Zoë breathed a sigh of relief. His dead weigh was off her chest.

Zeus pulled her up into his arms and fiercely kissed her. He quickly stripped their clothing off. The feeling of her skin against his almost more than he could handle. He was sure Holly based the character of Zeus on him and that meant Holly made Zoë for him. He was certain that Holly had seen the Dracula movie he had been. He rolled Zoë over and pinned her to the bed as he kissed her.

Zoë pushed at his arms. Before she could protest, he sank his teeth into her neck and drank deeply. She felt her body go up in flames. The world around them dissolved as he drank of her essence. She dug her fingers into his arms as his throbbing manhood entered her moist canal, and cried out loudly.

Zeus gasped. She was so tight, yet he knew she was not a virgin. He swirled his tongue over the bite mark on her throat closing it, a part of him wondering about that. He had never been able to do that. He did not wonder about the new ability for long. He had more interesting things to wonder about. Pulling Zoë's hips to his, he entered her repeatedly, savoring her cries of pleasure and her moans of despair at every withdrawal. The sounds of her pleasure increasing his own. She was driving him half-mad by her hands caressing him.

Zoë woke up hours later with Zeus wrapped around her like a blanket. She wanted to scream. The fog was as strong as ever yet it no longer frightened Zoë. She welcomed its embrace the way a lover welcomes the embrace of her beloved. It comforted her and calmed her the way nothing else could. She drifted off into a dreamless sleep.

Zeus woke several hours later to find Zoë glaring at him. "You took advantage of me. I was sick. What you did is rape. I mean it Zeus. I'm taking this to the council. You violated my rights. You violated my body."

"I did not. Everything I did, I did with your consent."

"Liar, I never said that I wanted you inside me."

"I know you wanted me. You could have just turned to mist and left if you wanted to. It was in your mind." Zeus pulled her closer and sniffed her hair.

Zoë frowned. She had thought about leaving that way and had chosen not to. Did that mean she had wanted to have sex with him? "Perhaps you are right, but don't do it again, and get off me. Is the fog getting thicker, or is it me?"

++++++++++

Holly gazed at the snow-covered landscape. Though it was noon, the sky was as dark as night during a power outage. Fine particles of ash and soot blanketed the sky. Sulfates continued to cloud the upper atmosphere and would continue to do so for years to come. Fierce snowstorms blanketed both the Northern and Southern hemispheres.

Blizzards had blanketed the area with snow giving the area a uniform color in which everything blended into one swirling mass. Nothing moved in this desert of snow. It is depressing in a beautiful sort of way.

Bruce sidled up to her. He enjoyed the view as much as she did. It was a pristine paradise. It was an escape from the confines of the apartment. Raging cabin fever kept threatening everyone's sanity. He drew a deep lungful of air careful to breathe through his scarf. The temperature had hovered around 40 below zero since the week after Day Zero.

Holly sensed Bruce coming closer to her. That meant that Doug was watching the babies. It was New Year's Eve. Holly did not want to be inside for it. She was beginning to understand why she had turned into a polar bear and ran away. The need to stay in the caverns had finally driven her insane. 'Hi Bruce?'

'Hi to you' he thought back. 'We should get back inside before Gregori comes looking for us. Besides, it's cold out here.'

'I need just a little longer. I can't breathe in there. I need a little more fresh air. I'll be right in. I promise.'

'Babycakes, what are you doing out here?' 'She's getting fresh air. Let me pass you. I'll go back in so you two can have some privacy. We need a bigger walkway here.'

'Thanks Bruce,' Gregori thought as he let Bruce pass. He moved closer to Holly.

'I just needed some fresh air, honey. I'll be right in. Why don't you and Bruce go check in on the babies?' Holly hugged herself. Something was going to happen out here tonight.

'Babycakes, you're freezing. Come on in and tell me what's really the matter.'

Holly hesitated. Nodding her head, she took Gregori's hand and let him lead her back to their home. Holly told him about the dream of meeting him out in the stables in the new section. It is the man from the dream. He isn't Vlad. He's the man who stood by the fireplace and said nothing. She told this to Tom, Radu, Sam, Eduardo, and they had promised to look into it.

Gregori paced the room while Holly gazed into the fireplace. He ran his fingers through his hair. How could he keep her safe when she didn't always confide in him?

She had felt safe out on the walkway. Bruce and Doug were taking care of the infants. "I'm sorry. I admit I haven't been as open as I should be. You get so worried and take everything out of context. I told the people in authority and they said not to tell anyone."

"I know Babycakes. I'm not mad at you. I just wished I'd known."

"And what are you doing in here young man?" Holly bent down and picked Johnny up. He was supposed to be with Bruce and Doug. "I had better take you back."

Holly frowned and reached out telepathically to Bruce. 'Do you guys know that Johnny isn't with you anymore?'

'Dang, sorry Holly, he escaped when Jen created a diversion for him. She started crying, and when we turned around, he was gone. I'll come and get him.'

'We'll come to you. I have something to tell everyone.' Johnny waved his arms and sucked on his mother's cheek. "I think we need to tell everyone about my recent dream. Let's start with Bruce and Doug and work our way around."

Gregori pulled Holly off the couch and into his arms. Johnny laughed as his parents' kissed. They moved quickly to Bruce and Doug's side of the apartment. "I'm glad we're going over there for a change. Everyone always seems to come to our place. We never get to visit anyone."

Doug greeted them warmly, taking Johnny from Holly's arms and gesturing for them to make themselves comfortable. Since the impact, Doug made a small living as a baby-sitter. He started a nursery and watched everyone's children so they could get some down time. "I know this sounds crazy, but I'm telling you baby Jen made a diversion so Johnny could escape. He's been trying to get back to your apartment since he woke up from his nap this afternoon."

"That's okay. It's not like he got far." Holly bent over and kissed baby Jen on the cheek, and ruffled Johnny's hair. "Are you two going to be good for Uncle Bruce and Uncle Doug? Or do I have to get Aunt Heather to watch you?" Jen cooed and clapped her hands. Clapping her hands was something her Daddy had taught her. After checking on George and Janis, Holly heard a knock on the door. Soon the rest of her family had joined them.

Holly sat on Gregori's lap and faced her family. "I want to tell everyone about a dream I had recently. I know. This is beginning to feel like therapy. Look, Holly had another dream, oh boy. I know. However, I really only bother you about serious dreams. Dreams sometimes have something to say about our future."

"Get on with it already. You can't help it if you keep having weird dreams." Otto helped Nicole check on the trips. They were quietly playing with some blocks and chatting with their older cousins.

"It went like this; I was alone in the stables playing with MareMoo when I heard a man's voice behind me. I didn't pay any attention to him at first. Then MareMoo went over to him and I realized he was talking to me. He was the man from the dream. The one in which Vlad apologized for trying to bite me. He was taller than Vlad, and considerably better built. He spoke with a cultured voice. There was a hint of an accent, but it wasn't I could recognize. MareMoo seemed to trust him, but she thinks everyone just wants to play with her. I asked him what he wanted." Holly began showing them what happened with her mind.

In her mind, the man approached her again. "I want what everyone wants. We have the right to live freely. Without the help of people like you I'll never be able to do that."

"How can I help you? What do you want from me?"

"Some of my people will be coming through on December 31st. I want to know that they will not be harmed."

"I have no authority here. I'm just a writer."

"You have no idea how much power you yield. Talk to the authorities and tell them what I said. We will be coming through the gateway on December 31. We will enter the stables in the new section where no one lives. We wish to join your world. Will that be acceptable?"

Holly barely nodded her head. She had no idea why he thought she had power, but he did. "How many of you will be coming through?"

"Just ten, there will be five married couples." He watched her intently, seeming to memorize her every move. After a few moments, he hunched down and scratched MareMoo's belly. "I hope you can convey our wishes and our hope that our two people can learn to live together in peace. We want to help you."

"We don't need any help."

"Don't you?"

Holly said nothing. She watched him carefully. "I woke up at that time.

Tom and Radu where still studying the grotto. I told them right away."

"So you had the dream on Christmas Eve?"

"Yes, it is while they were building the partition. I just closed my eyes for a few minutes and that's when it happened. It was right after I made the suggestion about the fog. I hope they don't hold it against me."

"Why would they do that?"

"Not everyone is as found of the fog as I am. They may take it as a threat or even as an attack on them. Do you see what I mean?"

"No."

"She's right. They may view it as some form of attack."

"Hey everyone" Hanna ran breathlessly into the meeting. "Did you hear? Ten people from the other side came over in the new section. The committee is bringing them to the infirmary for everyone to meet." Everyone looked at Holly who merely closed her eyes.

"Come on everyone. Don't you want to meet them? They're going to be our new neighbors." Holly got up and nodded her head. "Lead on, I just need to gather up the babies. I'll be right there." Less than eighteen minutes later, everyone was in the infirmary greeting their new neighbors.

+++++++++

Mina had watched the fog engulf the entire city. It bubbled out of sinks, tubs, toilets, swimming pools, spas, water fountains, the lake, the water parks and even puddles. She took a deep breath and looked at Erik. "How long do you think this will continue? It's already gone on for over a week."

Erik took Mina's hand into his own and kissed her knuckles. He had no way of knowing if the fog would ever end. Not the answer Mina wanted to hear. "It will probably linger for another month. The one in the city of New Orleans lasted that long. They made this one stronger than they expected it to be. The ten couples we sent over there all report the same thing. It's passed through the gateway and has re-infected them."

"It serves them right, but they enjoy the fog. Don't they?"

"They do according to Bruce's autobiography. The paperback edition has new photos and an expanded section of the fog and its effects. I wonder, how much do you suppose he got for it?" Erik examined the new boots he had purchased. He purchased them from a specialty store on the upper levels.

Mina gazed at Erik's boots. Sometimes she wondered if she would ever fit into the modern world. Erik took to it like a fish to water.

"It'll come to you. You just have to give yourself time."

"By then everything will be different again."

"That's how life works, my love."

"Why can't we find Simon's body? Do you think they've taken it?" Mina bit her bottom lip, a sign of anxiety she could not control.

"No, the Romantic Group reported that they knew nothing about it. Most of them hadn't even seen the movie he's from."

"Why don't you write a book about this? You've written six or seven books. They've always done well." Mina sat on his lap, playing with his tie. They had already been over poor Simon's disappearance enough times. There is nothing to be gained by drudging it up.

Erik wrapped his arms around her waist and regarded her thoughtfully. "A book would be a good idea. But what period should I set it in?"

"This one, you should write about us. The world needs to learn about the Wild People. You can think of it as giving our movement a voice."

Erik smiled. He would have to talk to the others. He would need their permission if he were going to write a book about them. It was definitely doable. "Excellent, I'll start it tonight. Do you want to help me get everyone's permission? I'll need to put most of them into the book to get the proper perspective on what's happened."

"I'd love to."

+++++++++

Bruce screwed up his face. 'Yes Frank' he thought tartly. 'Holly and I are working on our next books. You have heard of burnout. Haven't you?'

'Of course I have' Frank thought back. 'But we have a deadline. Quincy is coming out soon. You'll get nothing done while you're on tour with Holly.'

'Why will I be on tour with Holly?'

'Because you said you would.'

'Fine, then let me finish For the Dead Travel Fast first. Okay?'

'Zoë dies at the end.'

'No. How could you do that Frank? How could Holly do that? She never killed one of her characters before. This is unacceptable.'

'She did now. Get over it already.'

'What if I get Holly to write a sequel? She could bring Zoë back. Zoë and Zeus make the perfect couple as Marlene would say.'

"Can you convince her to write another one? If you can, then I'm fine with it. When will you find the time to finish your book?'

'We can write it together. Let me talk to her about it. I'll get back to you as soon as I know anything. Now let me finish this book.'

'Okay. But hurry.'

Bruce slammed the book shut and cursed Frank and Holly. How could she kill sweet little Zoë? It was as if she killed herself. Zeus needed to be more grief stricken. The other characters needed to be of more help to Zoë against the nasty piece of work, Deirdre, who called herself Zoë's sister.

Doug glared at Bruce. If he kept it up, he would wake the babies. 'Didn't like it?'

Bruce reached out and mentally slapped the back of Holly's head. 'She killed Zoë '

'I could have told you that. Now quit slamming things around. I have babies sleeping here.'

'Damn it Bruce. What'd you do that for?'

'You killed Zoë'

'And your point is? You killed Mary and Todd in your last book. You kill many characters I like in your books. Do you see me crying about it?'

'I need to talk to you. All of this telepathy is giving me a headache. I'll be right over. Doug just got the babies to sleep.'

'Okay' Holly waited for Bruce to enter her apartment. 'She died killing her evil older sister. Her death prevented others from dying. She died heroically for the good of many people.'

"But not for the good of her babies. Don't give me any lip about them being adults. The youngest is only 18. She had grand-babies that needed her."

"They were old enough to get married. You're just a romantic."

"Bring her back and fix her up with Zeus. I want a happy ending."

They were still working out their differences when Gregori returned for lunch. The beginning of an outline had taken shape.

Chapter 19

Erik and Gil watched George Washington pace back and forth. The auditorium slowly filled up. No one knew why George had called the meeting. He just kept pacing.

George barely noticed the others entering the auditorium. His mind preoccupied. They had yet to decide what to do with Simon Dracula's murders. They would punish someone for those murders. Everyone agreed to that much. The question was how.

They had also to think about the Romantic Group, a subset of the Wild People, who had entered the New World. They claimed to be doing well. The New Lifers had received them well. The fog was a part of everyday life over there. Their leader, Julian Reed, sent back reports every day. The others did so once a week. The Don of the Group, Alfred Singleton spoke to them constantly. He was here tonight to confirm their latest report that all was well and that all of their women in the group had become pregnant. They were all due in late May. They had acquired the New Lifer's shortened pregnancies. Everyone was very happy for the couples. Zeus had organized baby showers for them.

Alfred walked across the stage to George. "The Romanian Group has sent word. The weather has worsened. They are talking about heading south in spring or maybe late summer. Some of their air vents lead to the Mediterranean Coast. They're sending an expedition to explore that route."

"Did they say how long it would take?"

"It's hard to say. Some of the vents are slick with ice. They also have steep angles and sudden drops that travelers had to avoid. I doubt they can make the round trip in less than a month."

"Very well, please keep me advised on this matter." Alfred nodded his head, and went to stand besides Erik and Gil. Mina and Zeus joined them. "I think you should have an idea of why we are here," George continued. "We have the problem of Simon Dracula's killers to deal with. Although I have to admit that making them watch the Dracula movies they were in is driving them crazy. The making of features is particularly unwatchable. A suitable punishment has yet to be devised."

"Let's make them watch some of the other crummy Dracula movies." Several people shouted at once.

"The ones from Mexico and Italy" someone else added. The group liked using creative ways to punish them.

"No one wants them executed?" George asked dubiously. They had been calling for their heads when the crime had first been committed. The fog had mellowed all of them.

"No, we all make mistakes. We just need to keep them from making any more costly mistakes." Everyone stared at Zeus. He was being unusually gracious. He usually just wanted to impale the offenders no matter how forgiving the crime. Since the fog, he had become the most forgiving of all the people in any of the groups. "Let's take a vote. Who wants to keep them watching those horrible movies? Let's have a show of hands here."

Jonathan sighed. He felt like the Count from Sesame Street. He gave them the number of hands he saw held up. Then he did the same for those who wanted a harsher sentence. The ones who wanted them to continue to watch the movie won. "The vote is 72% for, and 28% against."

"Now what should we do in response to the fog?" Alfred demanded.

"Nothing" Erik responded. "You have ten of our people over there. We should do nothing that would jeopardize their lives."

"I have to agree with him, but for a different reason. The New Life people do not believe they have done anything wrong. The fog that we hate so much is the same fog that saved so many of their lives. Let us look at Holly Skyhaven Cornridge. Before the fog came, she was an overweight, middle-aged woman dying of cancer. She had only months, maybe days left to live. Now she has a husband and children. She would not have had those without the fog. Bruce Harwood weighed 650 pounds before Holly converted him. He probably would have lived only a few more days if not hours before Holly converted him. Gregori Cornridge had lung cancer. How long do you think he would have lived?" Zeus stood up and leaned his palms on the table. "We probably would not even be here if it is not for some strange New Lifer power. They can bring dreams to life. We are their dreams." He looked over the auditorium, daring anyone to disagree with him.

Everyone in the auditorium stared at Zeus. He had never been so reasonable. It was so unlike him that many wondered if he was sick. As if, someone had stolen the real Zeus and replaced him without anyone noticing until now.

"Am I the only one to read the books? It's right here in Bruce's autobiography, The Sleeper Has Awaken. The new paperback edition has more pictures and an expanded section on the fog and its effects. Come on people, it's only three new chapters for you to read."

"What about Holly Skyhaven's betrayal of us? Should we just sweep that under the rug?"

"He's right. What about her betrayal?"

"What betrayal? She was never one of us. She never joined our cause. What she did, she did to protect her own people. We were spying on her, her husband and her children. We were watching them have sex. As far as she was concerned, she had to protect her family. Look at their pictures in this book. She went from this, to looking like this." Zeus showed them the pictures he had copied from the book. The older ones showed an unhappy woman who looked like someone's bald Aunt. The newer ones showed a happy married woman with children and a doting husband.

"We threatened her life and the life of her family. She did what any of us would have done. She moved against us to protect her family. It's what any of us would have done. Tell me I'm wrong. What you people need to do is read this book. Then we can argue about motives."

George shook his head. He hadn't even known that Zeus could read let alone be so reasonable. He thought he had only been looking at the pictures. He did not trust him. Someone would have to keep an eye on him. Gil needed to work harder at it and maybe he could use some help. "All right everyone, we cannot discuss this properly until we take Zeus's suggestion and read the book. Let's reconvene this meeting in two weeks."

+++++++++

Gregori tapped his feet. He had less than patience with the media every time he had to deal with them. He put on his happy face and marched out with Laura and the others to greet them. The film version of Quincy was coming out on 24th of June 2013, and Laura Sanders wanted everything to be perfect. They had spent hours coaching Holly and Bruce on what everyone expected of them.

Holly expressed her faith in Laura Sanders. She nodded her head and told the press how much she liked what she had seen of the movie so far. She had not seen any of Quincy so far, but she did not mention that. Moreover, she did like the cast and crew.

Holly and Bruce were writing a sequel too For the Dead Travel Fast. It's tentative title being The Darkness of the Path. She let Bruce discuss this. It was his baby. He was more than happy to do so.

Gregori announced that he, Steven Grams, and Julie Hermine were going in on a movie together. It was a comedy about love and losses at a toy store during the Christmas season. It had the tentative title of Serious Injury. Angel Sanders would produce it. It would be Julie Hermine's directorial debut. The film company planned for a tentative summer of 2014 release date. The same crew that had worked on Quincy would be working on this new movie. They would be filming in Southern Romania.

Simon Dracula watched the proceedings from offstage. It amused him that no one knew who he was. Everyone he knew thought he was dead. Moreover, the New Lifers just took him for one of their own. He was a bit reluctant to return to his people with his killers running lose, but he would have to return soon. He could not avoid the inevitable forever. Nevertheless, he wanted to get close to Holly first. She had something important that he needed.

Chapter 20

Gregori rocked back and forth on the balls of his feet. They had found a way to travel south. They were going to film Serious Injury in Southern Romania. He could not wait to get out of those caverns. The rest of his family would follow in June. He hated being away from them, but it felt good to be working again.

Holly had watched Gregori pack the vans. She watched him staring at the vans in anticipation. They had fought the night before about his leaving so close to the twins' birthday. Jen and Johnny would be one in just ten nights.

Sighing to herself, she went back into their apartment. The pain of his leaving was almost more than she could handle. It was as if he twisted a knife into her stomach.

"Holly" Gregori called. He was ready to leave. He had said goodbye to everyone except Holly. Holly came over to Gregori. She hugged him fiercely. It was as if she would never be able to hug him again. She did not want to let go. She had the oddest feeling that she would not be seeing him again. Her dreams had been fuzzy later, she was sure it was just her insecurities talking to her. She knew she should tell him about the dreams, but he didn't take them seriously.

"Travel safely and call everyday so our babies can hear your voice. You don't want them to forget you." Holly's body trembled with suppressed emotion. "I'm sorry about last night. However, you've known how I've felt about this for a long time. Someone the children know should take care of them if something happens to me while you're away filming." They had fought the night before because Holly had insisted on giving custody of their children to Bruce and Doug in the event anything happened to her while Gregori was away filming or promoting a film. Gregori had insisted a family member could take care of their children if, God forbid, anything happened to Holly. He had only relented to stop her from crying. It tore him in two when she cried. Feeling her trembling body up against his, he wondered if she was going to start crying again.

"Babycakes, nothing is going to happen to you."

"I don't know that. The roof could cave in." Holly stretched up and kissed his chin. "You've got to work. It's in your blood." Holly pulled away from Gregori and took a deep breath. "You best say goodbye to the babies before you leave. You have to leave now before I do something stupid like lock you in a closet." She took in the sight and smell of him for this would be the last time she would see him until he completed filming. He would be working on two or three films in a row. One would be Serious Injury and the other a made for television special and the last one Holly knew nothing about. Holly had no idea of when they would be finished. The thought of not having Gregori by her side for so long frightened her. God, it was just as she feared. She was becoming needy.

"I'll visit as often as I can. I promise to call every evening so we can talk. Don't cry Babycakes. You know I love you."

"I know." Holly picked up Jen and smiled. "Give Daddy a kiss."

Gregori pulled Holly close and kissed her fully on the lips. Jen played with her father's hair and cooed. "If only we had more time." Gregori kissed their children before kissing Holly again. He headed for the vehicle as his family waved goodbye.

Kyle stepped in front of Gregori as he got to the passenger side door. He understood Gregori's need to work. It was the reason that he and Yoshi had started a community theater for their little group. "Holly looks mighty unhappy. Are you sure you're doing the right thing?"

"Yes Kyle, I am. Not that it's any of your business."

"You forget Gregori. I married Holly's sister. That makes her my sister-in-law. When she's unhappy, I'm unhappy." Kyle clapped his hands on Gregori's shoulders.

"Look, she's just getting paranoid that something going to happen while you're away. We'll keep an eye on her and the kids for you. She'll be okay."

"Thanks, I appreciate that."

"Of course if we hear any unseemly rumors that, say, you're cheating on her."

"Kyle, I would never cheat on Holly."

"That's good, because I'd hate to have to hold your mother down while Heather beats the shit out of you. And she'd do it too."

"She sure would." Gregori smirked then frowned.

Heather was hard to get angry, but it was not safe to be on her bad side when she did.

"I mean it. No affairs while out from under our watchful eyes."

"Did I cheat while we were filming in Whitby?"

"I was there. Laura didn't give us any time to think let alone cheat." Kyle gave Gregori a great big kiss on the lips and sprinted away laughing. "No, you were always faithful to me sweetie." They could hear Heather, Holly and the others laughing behind them as Gregori wiped his lips off in disgust. They all piled into the vehicle and left.

Simon watched Heather throw her arms around Holly and pull her into the house. He had been looking for this opening. She would be unprotected tonight. He would slip into her room tonight and drink her blood. He could picture it. He would slip naked under the covers next to her. She protest and he would tell her that she had invited him in. It would be perfect. They would blame any tiredness or weakness she exhibited on her depression over Gregori leaving. It had been easy for him to get Hanna to invite him into Holly's apartment. She thought of him as a good friend. He is the kind of vampire who needs an invitation to enter a home. Everything was going the way he wanted it to.

+++++++++

Bruce smiled as little Johnny ripped open his birthday presents, tossing the papers around in glee. His sister, the much more thoughtful, fingered the paper and cooed over the gifts. She didn't really seem to want to open them. "Come on Jen. Rip the wrapping open so we can see your present. Come on babies, Uncle Bruce wants to send Daddy some nice videos of you two. Ahhh, there's Mommy flirting with Uncle Doug. Stop that Mommy."

Holly threw a pillow at Bruce and laughed. They had been working hard on The Darkness of the Path. Bruce called Gregori every night. Gregori called Holly every night. It worked out well. Holly seemed to be getting over her fears.

Everyone had been worried about her increased appetite for blood. Doctor Crawford had done a complete evaluation of her and determined that she was becoming anemic. He suggested that she feed more. They had been unable to determine the cause of her anemia, which worried everyone. Bruce and Doug were contemplating watching over her at night to make sure no one was using her as a food supply.

Erik and Mina watched the party from their new spy spot on the far wall. They had no idea why they kept coming to this place. It was just as Zeus had said. The Cornridges were just one big happy family. End of story. They had beautiful babies. They had enough babies to populate a small village.

They had dropped all plans to punish anyone for the fog. They had moved on to getting more people to join the Romanian Group. The original members were claiming that all of their women had gotten pregnant. All had successfully delivered. The babies were all thriving. It was the highest rate of pregnancy ever for them. Ten more couples had joined them just the week before. Things were going well.

Mina was worried. She did not want to admit it to anyone, but on the night of the fog, she had had sex with Brad. It was a stupid thing to do. She feared she would regret it forever. She had just learned that she was pregnant with his child. Erik had been very forgiving. He admitted to having sex with another woman also. He did not know if she was pregnant. He did not think so. To make matters worse, she had been one of the people accused of killing Simon. Erik needed to be choosier about the women he choice to sleep with.

Bruce swung the camcorder around as he grabbed Katrina under the arm as she ran toward the door. At the time, he did not notice the odd couple watching them from the vent in the far wall. Gregori would notice them nights later when he watched the birthday party footage. No one could explain why they were there.

Chapter 21

Gregori rubbed his stomach. It is an embarrassing situation. In his dream earlier in the night, Holly had accused him of being with another girl and had savagely bitten him on his stomach. It had left a nasty mark and he had been almost unable to film a sex scene that night.

Fortunately, the makeup department had come through and the last night of filming saved the day. He had apologized to the crew. Holly had apologized immediately. It had been as if she had been in a trance, which had only been broken when he screamed in pain. He would have a long talk with her when he called her later.

"So Gregori" Angel asked while sipping on his drink. They were in a chic restaurant celebrating both the end of filming Serious Injury, and the release of Quincy into theaters Holly should be here, Angel thought wishfully. It was her night as well as the rest of the cast and crews. "Are you sure you don't want that part in the made for television movie?"

"Positive. Holly has been very sick since I left her. If she could be by my side, it would be different."

"Have they determined what's wrong with her? I heard she's anemic?" Yoshi asked casually.

"No, they haven't been able to pinpoint a cause for her anemia yet. Bruce and Doug are convinced that someone has been feeding on her. They have yet to catch anyone." There were gasps of horror at this. No one should be able to feed on someone else without that someone's permission. It was just wrong. "The others aren't so sure. That's why I'm anxious to get back to her."

"I'm sorry to hear you'll miss the part, but sorrier to hear Holly's so sick. I understand, but family comes first." Angel had thought it strange that Gregori had passed up the part when he had seemed so anxious to get it before they had left the caverns. Holly being sick brought everything into perspective. "Your cell phone is buzzing."

Gregori stared at his phone. It was Bruce calling. Bruce never called this early. "Hi Bruce, what's going on?"

"Oh, my God Gregori I am so sorry. We said we'd take care of Holly but he got to her anyway. I'm so sorry. Doctor Crawford says she'll be okay. The babies weren't hurt. They didn't catch the bastard but they're working on it." Bruce babbled. He had been the one to catch Simon in the act of feeding on Holly.

"Bruce calm down and tell me again. This time do it slowly." Angel reached over and put the speakerphone on.

Bruce took a deep breath and explained the situation again. After the third attempt, everyone understood what Bruce had been trying to say. They just did not want to believe it.

After Bruce hung, Gregori stared at his cell phone.

Bruce had been in an incoherent panic. Hanna's friend Simon had attacked Holly. He had escaped. Holly had needed several transfusions. He needed to get back to her right away. She needed him. She needed him now. Angel gazed at Gregori as he talked into his cell phone. He closed his phone and shook his head. "It's all cleared Gregori. There's a transport back tonight. I want you on it. Yoshi and Laura can go with you. I don't think you should be traveling alone."

"I have to pack."

"No you don't. You have clothes back in the caverns. And once Holly is able to travel, you should bring her and the babies over here."

"There's a more creative atmosphere over here. It'll help her with her writing." Yoshi nodded his head. "I think she'll love it here."

Gregori nodded just as his cell phone rang. "Hello Mum. Yes, Bruce told me what happened. I'll be on my way back tonight. Good I'll see you then. Take care of my Babycakes, and Jen and Johnny and George and Janis too."

Laura grabbed Gregori's arm and started pulling him toward the transport depot.

+++++++++

Bruce handed his cell phone to Doug and stared at Holly. They had her connected to several different tubes and strapped down to prevent her from pulling them out. There were feeding tubes, tubes for blood transfusion and tubes for oxygen. Holly kept pulling the tubes for blood transfusions out and sucking them like a straw. She would suck them dry and look around confused and bewildered until the nurse would come back and hook her up again.

She wasn't breathing on her own, though her oxygen levels remained above normal. No one had any reasonable explanation for this abnormality. There were bruises on her forehead and cheek. Simon had thrown her to the ground when they caught him sucking on Holly's neck. The coward had escaped. The trauma had nearly caused Holly to miscarry. Only the doctors and Gregori had known she was pregnant. It was a very sad situation.

MareMoo came up to his knee and whimpered. They had forgotten her in all the commotion. Bruce slid down to the floor and held her in his arms. "You can't be in here girl. What will the doctor say?"

"Dogs are good for a patient's moral. Now get off the floor, and go and feed her." Samuel Crawford stared down at Bruce and MareMoo. The young man could not take the blame for what happened to Holly. He had been the one claiming just such a thing was happening. He had done everything in his power to prevent this from happening. If it weren't for him, Simon would have most likely killed Holly. Simon was a ruthless bastard. "Now go on, and get yourself something to eat too. I promise not to leave her until you come back."

Bruce nodded his head. Doug and Otto came in with PahGoo and Trouble. He smiled. "We brought food. Heather and Kyle are watching the babies."

"Sophia told me Gregori is on his way back. The made a special transport just for him. Angel arranged it." Heather reported. She followed Otto and Doug in with some more food. Mark and his girls followed in with a tray of food. They brought enough to feed the doctors and the nursing staff too. "They'll be here in less than four hours."

"That's good to hear. Has her condition changed any?"

"The Romance Guys were in tonight. Their doctor believes she'll be up and around in a week, possible less. Of course, Doctor Crawford begs to differ. The Romance Group promised to track this Simon person down and makes sure he pays one way or another for what he did to Holly and the others. Did you bring MareMoo any food?"

"Yeah, I brought you dog food and MareMoo, Trouble and PahGoo people food." Otto thought himself the funniest person around. Everyone else knew better. PahGoo pranced around his legs.

"Bruce? Bruce? Why am I tied down?" Holly sat up, somehow ridding herself of the restraints and the tubing at the same time. "This packet of blood is empty. Can you get me another one?" She stared sadly at the empty tube that she used to suck the packet dry.

Bruce walked over to where Holly sat on the bed. She was staring forlornly at the empty packet. Her color was just starting to come back. When he had her, she was a bloodless waxen white color like one of those victims in wax museum movies. Bruce had thought her dead. "Hi Babycakes, do you want some solid foods? Otto brought you some mozzarella sticks."

Holly shook her head. The thought of eating solid foods made her sick. All she wanted to do was feed, see her babies and get some more sleep. Gregori was away filming. He would not be back for another month or so.

"You need to eat something if you want to heal for Gregori and the babies. Don't you?" Otto laughed as MareMoo tried to get on the bed with Holly.

Holly resisted the urge to bite Otto somewhere sensitive and drain him dry. Families being important, even cocky nephews were family. "I'm not hungry for solid foods. Why don't you let me take a chunk out of you and suck you dry so you can know how it feels?" Holly bared her teeth and leaned expectantly toward Otto. One of the Romance Guys, Paul Duenna, came in with another three blood packets for Holly. His wife, Rose followed him in with three more. They set Holly up with the packets. She drained them immediately and curled up to sleep.

Rose stopped her. She insisted that Holly eat some solid foods. "You don't want to disappoint your family. Do you?"

"When they keep pushing solid food on me I do." Holly frowned. Why was everyone staring at her? Was she wearing her hospital gown backwards? No. Did she spill blood or something on herself? Again no, "all right, if it will get everyone off my back, I'll try some of the mozzarella sticks. But don't blame me when they come right back up."

Everyone watched Holly eat. They could not help to notice that she only seemed to breathe when she was talking. It had to be an illusion. She had to be breathing.

When she ate three mozzarella sticks without the predicted vomiting, everyone breathed a sigh of relief Holly rubbed her eyes and yawned. Everything was staying down. She felt so tired.

"It's natural to feel tired after what you've been through. Isn't that right doctors?" Bruce squeezed Holly's hand. Gregori would be back in little over three hours. He hoped Holly would be awake when he returned.

"I will be Bruce. Why will Gregori be back in three hours? He still has another movie to film. I'm sure he'll be gone for another month." Holly smiled, tilting her head. She frowned just as quickly. He'll be upset that they didn't cast him for the part. He really wanted the part.

"He chose not to accept the part. Gregori won't be that upset about it. He'll be upset about you getting hurt again."

Rose watched the conversation with some amusement. Holly and Bruce communicated telepathically without even realizing they were doing so. She touched Paul's mind and shared this with him. He agreed with her. They would bear watching.

"Now get some sleep. I'll wake you when Gregori gets here. I promise. Here, I brought your favorite purple comforter." Holly nodded once more as Bruce tucked her in. He watched her sleep like a doting father.

Rose and Paul pulled the others aside to discuss the precautions everyone would need to take to protect themselves against Simon. There were special silver screens to place over all air ducts. Silver burnt Simon. They kept a constant over the most vulnerable women. He was unpredictable and vengeful. Not part of their group, but of a separate group who came from movies. In fact, he was from a horribly bad Dracula series shot in the 1970's. There were many claiming to be Dracula on the other side. Simon was, so far, the only bad one.

Holly listened to this quietly. Her mind clung to Bruce's mind for comfort and security he provided. It was unconscious on her part. It was just something that Bruce and Holly shared. They simply took it for granted that they understood each other better than anyone else possible could. Holly drifted off to sleep, blissfully unaware of how strong her connection to Bruce had become.

Gregori reached out and touched Holly's mind. He could tell whether she was sleeping or awake. She was asleep now. He was just learning to share her thoughts and memories the way Bruce could. He was sure he would get better at it with time. He desperately needed time.

Laura touched Gregori's arm. "Are you all right? You seem awfully quiet."

"I don't know. I'm terribly worried about Holly. She has been horribly cranky lately. She's been better these last few weeks. Then she goes and bites me this morning. Now this attack on her, I just don't understand any of it. She's pregnant you know? Already seven weeks, it must have happened on one of our first weekend visits together in early May."

"I've heard. It's the only thing Hanna wants to talk about. You'd think Holly had never been pregnant before. She bit you about the time Simon attacked her. Isn't that right?"

"I think so." Gregori studied Laura as she played with her phone.

"And Hanna introduced her to him? That must have been some time before we left."

"I suppose so."

"According to the Romance Group he was killed early the day we did the fog and his body disappeared shortly after that time. That was early January."

"It was New Year's night. We met him on February 2. Hanna introduced him to us right after the press conference about Serious Injury and The Darkness of the Path."

"And everyone went back to your apartment after that. Didn't they?" Laura remembered the night well. It excited everyone that the new movies and books were on the way. "That's when he snuck in. He could have been feeding on her since that night, or on any of us for that matter and we'd never know."

"How could I have not seen it? Why didn't anyone see it?"

"Why didn't any of us know? Maybe we did. You said she's been very cranky lately. Maybe we just misinterpreted the signs as her usual plain old cranky, clingy, pregnancy troubles, when in fact Simon was feeding on her. I don't know. But I'm going to find out for both of you."

"Look, we're coming to the terminal now."

Gregori smiled. He did not want to discuss how cranky Holly got when she was pregnant. How could you blame anyone for being cranky when she kept popping out babies as if they were popcorn?

Sophia paced back and forth at the terminal. She could not bring herself to stay in the infirmary. When Holly slept all of her body functions shut down. It was as if she was dead. Then someone would wake her and she would appear almost normal. It was freaky, scary and just plain abnormal. No one could explain why it was happening.

They had decided to keep this from Holly. It would only frighten her. However, someone would have to tell Gregori so he would know what to expect.

Nicole sighed. Sophia's constant pacing was getting on Nicole's nerves. It was hard seeing Holly sick again. This was why she had agreed to accompany Sophia down to the terminal to greet Gregori and the others. She really did hate hospitals.

"Your cell phone is buzzing."

"Hello Otto. What's new? She did. That's great. Only three, well that's a start. She's sleeping now. MareMoo is on the bed with her. What did Doctor Crawford say about that? That it is good for her. Okay. Love ya' and I'll talk to you later." Nicole pocketed her cell phone and turned to Sophia. "Rose got Holly to eat three mozzarella sticks without throwing them up. She's sleeping now. Bruce had her favorite comforter brought in so she would feel more comfortable. MareMoo is sleeping with her."

"I do wish she would eat something besides mozzarella sticks. You'd think her cholesterol would be sky high with the kind of food she eats."

"I think that's Gregori's transport now." Nicole injected before Sophia could continue on her favorite rant. What and whom Holly ate was none of her business.

Gregori peered out the window as the transport approached the terminal. He could see his mother and Nicole waiting for him. Doug would be watching the babies with Heather and Kyle's help. They moved closer to the infirmary so they could stay close to Holly. It was good to be back. He missed Holly and the babies.

Nicole and Sophia greeted Gregori, Laura and Yoshi warmly. They spent the rest of the trip back trying to prepare them for Holly and the other's condition. It was a long trip back for Gregori who only wished to see Holly and hold her in his arms. He had a hard time concentrating on what they said.

Gregori watched Holly sleep. Nicole had been correct. It was a scary thing watching Holly sleep. If it were not for the life support machines, he would have thought her to be only sleeping. The machines told a different story. They were flat lining. Hot wet tears escaped his eyes and flowed down his face. He was in agony.

Bruce sighed. Gregori had been told what to expect, but seeing it was far different than simply being told about it. Bruce reached over and turned on the sound for her heart monitor. It immediately set off klaxons.

Holly jerked awake. "Bruce, please go for the doctor. Someone died again. What's wrong with the doctors in this place?" The klaxons went silent as Holly's heart started working again. She felt Gregori scoop her into his arms. "You know, my husband is the jealous type. He won't like to have a strange man kissing me." Holly smiled at Gregori as she said this.

"Babycakes, I'm so frightened. I don't want you to leave my side for a moment from now on."

Holly wrapped her arms around Gregori's neck and buried her face in his hair. There was no place she felt safer than in Gregori's arms. She could point out the small fact that they both had to work for a living to him later. Why spoil his special moment with reality now?

Erik watched the scene unfold in front of him. He was painfully aware of Zeus's quiet presence just a few feet behind him. Zeus stood brooding next to Mina. They were trying to track Simon. Simon is a loose cannon and a crazy person. They had to stop him before he killed someone.

"He's hiding in the vents on the far wall. The silver screens they put up are restricting his movements." Zeus rubbed his hands together. He wished Zoë would react to him the way Holly did to Gregori. He felt certain that with time Zoë would warm to him. "Gregori's standing a few feet in from the vent."

"I see him. I don't think he sees us yet." Mina smiled as she sent the exact location to the members of the Romanian Group. They were in charge of capturing Simon.

A series of loud pounding sounds and screams came from the vent behind Gregori who jumped at the sound. He attempted to put Holly down, but she just clung to him. Everyone in the room just stared at the vent. The sounds went on for several minutes. They stopped as abruptly as they started.

Rose and Paul entered the room to check on everyone. They were three other women in the infirmary who claimed to be Simon's victims. They all had the same symptoms as Holly. Rose inclined her head to the vent.

"You'll be happy to know that we've captured the person who attacked Holly and the others. And Holly should still be in bed."

Gregori frowned at Rose, and then smiled slyly. Placing Holly on the far side of the bed, he quickly took off his clothes and slipped under the covers with her. Everyone in the room saw the evidence of his desire for her clearly.

"That is not what I meant and you know it." Rose frowned while trying to look stern. A job made difficult by the laughter of the others in the room.

Holly pulled the thick comforter around herself and Gregori. She stroked the length of him with both her fingertips and her palms. Gregori moaned loudly as Holly fingers sought out that special spot that always drove Gregori wild.

Gregori found Holly's special spot at the same moment. She moaned loudly, inviting Gregori into her depths. An offer he readily accepted, plunging deeply into her warm tight cavity. Holly moaned loudly, clinging to his back and leaving deep scratch marks. With no place to grab for support, Holly sank her teeth deeply into his chest just below the left nipple. A few minutes later, Gregori returned the favor, biting her just below her right ear.

Gregori was truly amazed. She was so tight even after giving birth twice. Every penetration was like slipping on a velvet glove made just for him. She always knew where he liked to be touched. He was in his own personal heaven and never wanted to leave. With Holly, it got better every time.

Erik watched Mina avert her eyes. It surprised him that she had watched as much as she had. Turning to Zeus, he coughed loudly. "What are you doing Zeus?"

"I'm taking notes. Zoë say I have no imagination and need to learn some new positions. She says I'm boring."

"But taking notes? Boring, what's the matter with you?"

"I'm inexperienced."

Erik broke out laughing. That had to be the funniest thing he had ever heard. Zeus was inexperienced the way Erik himself was. Together they could write a how to manual on sex and seduction. Still, if it made Zoë happy, he was all for it. Zoë was a skittish as a deer catching the scent of a predator nearby. Zeus was definitely a large predator.

"What the hell do you think you're doing?" Alfred demanded of Zeus when he approached the group.

"I'm taking notes. They're using positions I'm not familiar. Do you suppose we can get them to give up on the comforter? I can't see everything the way I'd like to."

Alfred opened his mouth to say something and thought better of it. Some things were better left unsaid. This being especially true when it came to Zeus.

"I understand that your people have captured Simon. Please tell me this is true." Mina inquired, distracting Alfred from Zeus's strange hobbies.

"It is. He put up quite a fight but they wrapped him in silver and he quieted right down. But I'm sure Zeus must know this, Brad and Jonathan claimed they could feel his pain as if it is their own."

"I didn't feel a thing. Ahhh look, the comforter just fell off. Oh, that looks to be great fun. Ahhh, where's a camera when you need one?"

"Are you certain?"

"Oh yeah, that looks like a great fun position. I've got to get Zoë to try it."

"I mean about the pain."

"What pain?" Zeus look confused for a moment. Gregori and Holly didn't look to be in pain to him. They were exhausted from all the acrobatic maneuvering maybe, but definitely not in pain. "They don't seem to be in any pain to me. They look real happy if you ask me."

"Yes, you're quite correct. They look quite happy." Alfred studied Zeus carefully. He remembered Jonathan withering in pain when they wrapped Simon in silver. Brad, as usual these days, was nowhere to be found. Leaning toward Erik and Mina, he whispered. "He's not joking. Is he? He really didn't feel anything. The others did."

"We didn't notice anything different about him. They others were really in pain?"

"Withering on the floor and moaning, we couldn't get them to quiet down. In fact, we had to drug them. Fortunately they react to drugs the way regular humans do." Alfred nodded his head as he watched Zeus pack his notebook. The man kept getting stranger; maybe his devotion to Zoë was changing him. They would have to keep a close watch on him.

Gregori pulled Holly close. The feel of her bare skin as she cuddled close was a temptation all of its own. Still, he watched the area of the far wall where he had seen those people watching. It had alarmed him when he had first seen them. Two of them were the same pair he had seen in Jen and Johnny's birthday DVD. Gregori felt certain that Paul and Rose knew who they were. They could identify them and put an end to their voyeurism

Rose had come and checked on Holly several times. There was something wrong with her pregnancy, but no one would say what. Sometimes he wondered if he is even the father. If Simon could slip in and feed on her without anyone noticing, how hard would it have been for him to rape Holly or any of the other women? Looking at Holly's innocent face, he wondered why it even mattered to him. He caught Rose's eyes and gestured her closer. "I've got to know." He whispered. "Am I the baby's father?"

Rose hesitated. It was such an explosive issue. What made it explosive was that they did not know for sure. They knew Simon was definitely the father of the other babies, but not of Holly's. Did that automatically make Gregori the father? That was the question. There being an 85.1% chance that Gregori is the father of Holly's unborn children. This compared to the 97.8% certainty that Gregori is the father of the four infants Holly had given birth. It is a good chance he was the father. It just wasn't a certainty. Rose explained this to him.

Gregori took this in quietly. As hard as it is for him to hear, he knew Holly would take it harder. She took a certain amount of pride in Gregori being her only man. The knowledge that he might not be the father, and that she might be carrying another man's children would kill her. "Look at this innocent little face Rose. Would you break her heart by actually telling her that? I think there's enough chance that I'm the father that we should just tell everyone that. Anyone asks that's what I want you to tell them. Gregori is the father. Okay?"

Rose thought his generosity and love for his wife was amazing. She passed on his request to Paul and the others in the Romanian Group. "Of course we'll honor your wishes on this matter."

"On what matter," Bruce inquired. He had just returned with the DVD and a portable DVD player.

"On how often Holly should be fed. Did you bring it?"

"Aw, okay" Bruce gazed into Gregori's eyes as if trying to read his mind. "I brought the DVD. Do you want to look at it now?"

"Yes, that would be a good idea. Rose, I'd like you to look at this and see if you can tell us who these people are."

Rose sucked in her breath as she watched the DVD image of Erik, Mina, Alfred, Zoë and Zeus. They had called it the Birthday DVD but it was really a compilation of footage taken over a period of several months.

There was no way for them to get around this. Lying now would only backfire on them and destroy whatever trust they had built up with the community. "Yes, I know them. They weren't responsible for the attack on Holly or anyone else. I can vouch for them."

"But who are they?"

"And how can you be so certain? This one looks like Simon to me. Bruce had beaten Simon up when he had been caught attacking Holly. They also had taken numerous clear photos of Simon in the months since Gregori left to film

Serious Injury.

"He looks like Dad to me." Holly studied the photo through half-closed eyes. "You know, my father-in-law, Mark Cornridge."

"Yes. It does look like Dad."

"No way, you're getting as senile as Otto. We've gotten off the point. What is someone going to do about them constantly watching us?" Bruce made a point of looking at Rose.

"I'll express your concern to everyone. I'm certain that once they know how uncomfortable it makes you, they'll stop doing it." Rose watched Gregori. Gregori was the son of Zeus, or more correctly, the son of the actor who played him. That would explain the genetic closeness of the babies.

'Only if Zeus is the father,' Paul shot back. 'But not if Simon is. A completely different actor plays Simon. We need to do more genetic testing to know for certain.'

'I'll ask Zeus. But let's do Zoë too.'

'Okay.'

"That would be a good beginning," Holly said. She had the feeling that an unheard conversation was taking place. She became determined to learn it contents. She wrapped her arms around Gregori and rested her head on his shoulders. "When we go south, I want to go to a water park or maybe even a beach. The babies would love it. I know I would. What do you think?"

"That would be a terrific idea and lots of fun."

+++++++++

Zoë smiled broadly. She knew a water park would be great fun. The children would love it. It even had an adult's only section where adults could have fun and not worry about the children catching them doing something that they shouldn't see. They needed some playtime too. The teens had a section of their own.

Not everyone wanted to leave their prison or as Zoë liked to call it, their own little piece of Cloud Nine. She kept working at getting everyone to call it that. In any case, Cloud Nine sounded better than prison. It certainly had to be better than living through an ice age. The earth was experiencing the worst one in 23,000 years.

"Aunt Zoë" one of the dozens of children milling around her tugged at her dress, "cut the ribbon so we can get this show on the road." They were all dressed in their bathing suits and clutching their rafts.

"Does everyone want me to cut it? Let's hear you say it loudly."

"Cut it now."

"I can't hear you. What did you say?"

"Cut it now Aunt Zoë."

Zoë laughed as she cut the ribbon. She had not believed grand openings could be so fun. "I declare the Fool's Gold officially opened." The children rushed forward with their rafts, flying down the slides as soon as Zoë cut the ribbon. This was the second grand opening she was officiating tonight. She had done the one for the teen section earlier. The teens had tried to act cool about it, but she could tell that they had been excited too.

The adults on the other hand needed some encouragement to try out the rides. Their grand opening would be in three hours. Zeus insisted on holding a pre-grand opening ceremony for the adults without children. There would be food there. The werewolves were the biggest eaters of the group followed by the cave dwellers and everyone else who didn't drink blood. Zoë loved the werewolves and cave dwellers. They had the best sense of humor of any of the groups. Zeus loved hosting parties. It was not something anyone would expect of him.

Zoë joined the party. She talked to as many of the people there as she could. Everyone expected her to be a social butterfly. She hated that. She had met her three sisters who didn't want her dead. They had had nothing in common to talk. They just wanted to have babies and pretend nothing had happened between their eldest and youngest sisters. It had been a big disappointment for Zoë

Alfred and Aimee approached Zoë. Everyone knew it was difficult for Alfred. He hated the smell of cooked meat. However, he hated to disappoint his wife. She was the only one who could put up with him. The meat was for the cave dwellers and the werewolves. The spacemen called the cave dwellers and werewolves perverts for eating meat.

"Will you be coming to the ribbon cutting ceremony? I'd like to see you two be the first ones to go down the Lover's Lane slide." Zoë crossed her fingers behind her back.

"I think we'll pass."

"We'll be there. Won't we honey?"

"Yes dear" Alfred kissed his wife's fingers and sighed.

"Excellent" Zeus came up behind Zoë and wrapped his arms around her. "Have you heard anything from the Romanian Group? I hear they want Zoë and I tested genetically. Do you know why they want the genetic testing? Because I don't and it's really starting to tick me off."

"They're trying to find out who the father of Holly's unborn babies are. The genetic match is close to Gregori's but not as close as the match between him and their older children."

"What are the percentages?" Zoë liked hard numbers.

"For their older children, it's a 97.8% certainty that Gregori is the father. For the unborn ones, it's 85.1%. The probability that Simon fathered Holly's unborn babies is only 23.5%. He is a good match for the other three who claimed Simon raped them. They have a 94.7, 95.2, and 96.3% certainty."

"So you think it might be me? I have not touched other women since Zoë and I started dating. I don't care if Mark Cornridge played me in a crappy Dracula television series. Maybe they should ask him instead."

"Is he even alive? He must be in his late 70's by now." Zoë puzzled. "I heard he fell into booze and drugs when the series was canceled after only four seasons."

"The last we could find out is that he is living in Mexico with someone young enough to be his granddaughter. I heard she thinks he has money." Aimee shook her head. Alfred is right. She did spend too much time on gossip sites.

"This does not change anything. We will still need a genetic sample from both of you."

"Besides, Mark Cornridge got back together with his ex-wife. They're living together with his daughters from his affair with Jasmine Homestead. They're making a threesome of it. I think he favors Jasmine. Sophia was briefly dating Liam Bliskowski." Zeus frowned. Liam Bliskowski's wife had died in childbirth just five months before the first fog. "They've been staying close to Holly and the children. That way they can help her with the children when Gregori's away filming."

"Are you sure?"

"Positive." Zeus frowned.

"But that doesn't mean you're not the father."

"Okay, but I'm telling you Zoë has been my only sexual partner. I even dream about having sex with her. Isn't that right dear?"

"It's true. We dream about having sex with each other. In fact, I'm pregnant right now. Zeus is planning to have a baby shower for me. I hope you can come. Your celebrity gossip always makes those things go faster."

"Are you sure it was him?" Alfred wanted to keep the conversation on track. He knew it was bound to fail. Still, he had to try. "It's always with each other?"

"Zeus and I always talk it over when we wake up. We always have the same dream."

"Of course I'll come. Have you picked a date for it yet?" Aimee was thrilled. At least someone appreciated her skills. They seemed to be failing her when it came to Mark Cornridge.

"Not yet, but I'll let you know within the week. On the other hand, maybe you can pick one for us. You seem to have no problem booking places."

Max came up and took a swab of the inside of Zoë and Zeus's mouth. "I'll get back to you with the results in a couple of nights, if not sooner. They're developing some new test from a science fiction series. I can't tell you if it is a book series or a movie series. I find them to be all too confusing to follow."

"Then we'll meet you and your charming wife at the ribbon cutting ceremony?"

"Wouldn't miss it, we'll be there as soon as I drop these samples off at the lab."

"It's time for us to go too. The ceremony's going to begin in half an hour." Zoë nodded. She doubted with the way most of them were dressed that any of them would be going into the water. It was likely to be the most disappointing part of the night. After making some parting conversation, she headed to the last ceremony. Zeus followed her closely. When the appointed time came, it was quite crowded.

The gathering pleased Zoë, but it disappointed her that so few were wearing swimsuits. Of course, it would have helped matters if Zoë herself had been wearing one. She had on a clingy blue dress. It showed off her curves, but was definitely not a swimsuit.

Zeus watched Zoë cut the ribbon. He promptly scooped her up and dropped both of them onto a waiting raft. The raft reacted to their combined weight and just as promptly shot them down the slide. Water washed over their heads as they headed down the slide toward a secluded area. It would not be a lover's lane without a make out spot.

They could hear the other couples hooting and laughing as they moved rapidly away from them. Zoë was soaked to the bone. She felt Zeus flip her over and cover her with his body. The water in her eyes prevented her from seeing much. She was aware of the exact moment Zeus started to remove her dress.

'Don't. I don't want to lose it. I'm not going to be running around the park naked.' They couldn't talk with the water washing over them without swallowing a great deal of it.

'Okay, how about half naked?' Zeus pushed the dress aside at the same time he worked on his pants. He could feel Zoë's thighs against his hips as he worked to find the right position to enter her. She was so tight and delicious. It drove Zeus crazy with lust.

Zoë moaned. She was beginning to think she was becoming easy. Everything Zeus did drove her crazy with pleasure. The ride took a sharp turn and drenched them with water. Zoë buried her face into his chest, her pelvic region grinding against his. She could not get enough of him. He was so long and hard. He fit so perfectly. Zoë just wanted to scream, which she did. She screamed his name repeatedly as he brought her to one climax after another. He felt the same way about her and purred her name with each thrust.

They soon came to a secluded area. It is the last part of the ride, and the only quiet part. With only the quietly lapping water to support them, they expressed their love for each other in the most physical way possible.

The others had laughed when Zeus had grabbed Zoë, but soon other males were imitating him and dragging their wives onto the ride. It hadn't taken long for occupants to fill all the secluded areas. In the coming weeks, they had to expand the area four times.

+++++++++

Mark cursed vehemently and covered his daughters' eyes. No one had told him there would be full frontal male nudity in Quincy. Damn, Gregori's well hung.

"Poppa, I can't see. Did Van Helsing kill her?"

"Is she going to be a vampire? Are they going to stake her?"

Mark sighed and dropped his hands. What were they thinking? "Let's watch and find out."

On the screen, Mina screamed and went through the motions of being horrified. On the other hand, maybe she really was horrified. They had just found her in a compromising position with a naked man who was not her husband while her husband slept next to them.

"Did I miss anything?" Zag had finally returned with popcorn.

"Dracula was naked and Mina screamed like a baby when the guys broke down the door." Little Nymphea declared. "And Poppa covered our eyes, but I saw Dracula naked anyway."

Zag eyes went wide. He had never seen Mark turn that shade of red. Hell, he didn't even know Mark was capable of blushing, let alone becoming so embarrassed.

"Nymphea."

Nymphea and Angeline giggled like the little children they were. "Dracula has a hairy chest." Nymphea added. "It is very, very hairy like an ape."

"Zag laughed. "I've got to text message that to Sophia. She'll get such a kick out of it.

"And let her know I let the girls watch an R-rated movie, over my dead body. It's bad enough that Jasmine will kill me over this."

"Poppa," Angeline protested. "Dracula was naked in the coffin earlier and you didn't cover our eyes then."

"Was he? I don't remember."

"That's when you went to get popcorn. I'd have covered their eyes if I knew you are so squeamish. Veronica and Nymphea use to take them to nudist and clothing optional beaches all the time. Those two hated clothing."

"When did this happen?" He could barely squeak it out.

"When you were drunk or working on a film or both, they were big on nudity as a positive thing."

"Poppa, when is the Dracula movie you made coming out?" Nymphea asked hopefully. For some reason she was in love with Dracula.

"Next week. Do you want to go to the premiere?"

"Yes," they shouted in unison.

"No," Mark shouted back.

"Good. I'll arrange it. Come on Poppa. There isn't any nudity in your version. Is there?"

"Yes. There is. Strangely they are in the same places."

Zag did not know how to respond to this. They watched Quincy die in Harker's arms. Mina wept. His death lifted the curse.

"You know what; this is a pretty sweet ship. Gregori and Holly were

174

married on it by the Captain." Zag observed as Quincy returned to London nine years later.

"It was on this ship? Really?"

"That's right. They were married on the Princess Ayala. It was just before they sailed to England to film Quincy." Angeline said proudly. They had both attended the wedding three years before. Nymphea had been too young to remember it. Angeline could just barely remember it. "We're going to Romania to film a movie." Dracula slipped into bed with Mina just as the credits began to run.

+++++++++

Gregori watched Holly bounce Jen in the water as Johnny cooed and clapped his hands. Hand clapping was their new big thing. George and Janis slept by Gregori's side. Doug and Bruce had the night off from their baby-sitting chores.

He was glad Holly had wanted to go to a water park. They were so relaxed now that they were out in the moonlight, fresh air and water. What with filming, writing, producing a new movie and Holly and Bruce working on three books at once, the last couple of months had been intense. It was little wonder that everyone was tired and cranky. They needed to pace things better.

"Uncle Gregori? Will you go swimming with me? Uncle Otto said no." Katrina tugged on Gregori's arm.

"Your mom said no swimming tonight. You bit Hugo. Remember?"

"But he deserved it. He said Auntie Holly looked like she ate a medicine ball. It's more like a softball."

"Auntie Holly won't like hearing you say that." Years of being fat had made Holly overly sensitive about her weight. She was as thin as a rail with breasts and a tiny pregnancy bump.

"Auntie Holly won't like who saying what?" Jamaica asked. She was happy to be out of the caverns if only for a little while. It had been over a year since they had first moved into them.

"That I said she looked like she ate a softball. Hugo said she looked like she ate a medicine ball. That's why I bit him. He's a very bad boy but he tasted very good." Katrina was really beginning to chatter.

"Katrina. Auntie Holly doesn't even look pregnant. Uncle Gregori is right. You shouldn't be talking about people like that." Jamaica frowned. Auntie Holly was wearing a skimpy two-piece bathing suit that left nothing to the imagination. It covered what it had to cover, and nothing more. Auntie Holly had become very muscular since the fog. From where did these children get the idea she was fat? "And I'm going to talk to Hugo about this. Medicine balls my butt."

"I'm sorry. Can I go swimming now?" Katrina tried to peer around Jamaica to see if her butt really looked like a medicine ball. She didn't think so, but if Mommy said it, it must be true.

"Maybe after dinner Uncle Elijah will take you.
Okay?"

"What about Aunt Bobby?"

"If you behave yourself she may join you." Elijah and Bobby had been talking about taking the older children swimming tonight, so at least that much was true.

"Aunt Bobby's going to what?" Bobby Joe asked. She was due the next month and it showed.

"Take us swimming." Katrina volunteered. "We can go, can't we?"

"You'll have to ask Uncle Elijah. He's over by the food court eating."

"Okay, I'll be careful." Katrina ran to the food court calling out Uncle Elijah's name.

.Holly placed Jen in her life raft and picked up Johnny. She tried to take turns with each of the babies, but knew one of them would still accuse her of favoritism when they grew up. Sometimes she tried imaging the book that one of them would write. "Oh" Holly fretted. "You need some more sunscreen. You're starting to turn pink." Holly lavished the extra strong lotion on them as they squirmed and giggled.

"I heard you lost your book again. Do you need help finding it?"

"Doug found it under the crib this morning. I have no idea how it got there. He thought maybe one of the older kids was playing with it and forgot about it. In any case, Bruce sent his copy to Frank. Frank loved it. He's hoping we can get more money for it."

"Which one do you think took it?" Jamaica asked, studying her fingernails. She was sure it had to be one of hers. They were always taking things that didn't belong to them.

"Does it really matter? The CD was found with its data intact. That's all that matters to me. Can someone help me get this sunroof up before Jen and Johnny turn into lobsters?"

Jamaica and Gregori jumped up to help her at once. It took a while to get the babies out of the water and into their well-covered playpen. They expressed their unhappiness at leaving the water. They calmed down once they were drinking from their bottles. George and Janis slept though the ruckus. Holly thanked the Gods that they had finally developed a formula that Jen and Johnny would drink. She hoped they would soon graduate to cow milk. It would be such a blessing when George and Janis also started taking the formula.

Holly dunked herself into the water. She wasn't used to being out in the moon. She had forgotten how hot it could make her feel. Wriggling into one of Gregori's tee shirts, she joined them on the lounge chairs.

"Does Frank really think he can get more money for this one?"

"He says For the Dead Travel Fast out sold Quincy by four to one. Based on that, the publisher offered twice as much for the sequel. Of course, Bruce is getting a cut this time. He wrote most of the book." Holly curled up under on one of the shaded lounge chairs and studied her toenails. She loved wearing Gregori's old tee shirt. They were so baggy and comfortable on her. She knew he secretly found it sexy. It made his mother insane, though Holly had no idea why. "Frank wants me to start another novel soon. But I haven't the slightest idea what to write about."

"What about a sequel to Quincy? You could have the count and Quincy going to New York or New Orleans."

"I'm not sure. It would almost have to be a historical novel. I'm not very good with those kinds of details. Bruce is much better at that then I am. Perhaps he could help me with it?" Holly shook her head. She had had it with writing for a while. She wanted to play doting wife and devoted mother for a while. The babies needed her, and so did Gregori.

"You could just set it in modern times."

"You mean just before the asteroid and the supervolcano? I'm not sure I know that much about them from that period either."

"I can help you with that. I lived there for years." Gregori smiled. Attempting to write a novel had never occurred to him before. Why couldn't he help Holly write a novel? "I want to try. What do you think honey?"

"That doing so could put our marriage in a lot of trouble. But I'm willing to give it a shot." Holly hopped off the lounge chair and dove into the pool. She needed to cool off and do some thinking.

Gregori watched Holly do laps. She wasn't a strong swimmer, but she certainly enjoyed the pool. Holly stuck her head out of the water and splashed Gregori. She laughed as she drenched him with water. She laughed even harder when Gregori jumped into the water and tried to dunk her.

Chapter 22

Zeus gazed steadily at the computer screen. He thanked the Gods that he was able to get an early copy of The Darkness of the Path. The other may laugh, but he knew that he was the inspiration for the male lead. When he touched Holly's mind, as he had on numerous occasions leading up to Simon's capture, he found only confirmation of this. Holly had loved the Dracula series he had done, not all of the series mind you, and just the parts he did.

The viewing room was large. Twice as long as it was wide, it held a large screen television, bookcases, couch, a sunken area in front of the television, a bar, and a table and chairs for reading and relaxing. They held their group meetings there. In fact, he expected the others to join him shortly. Zeus returned to the novel after making a copy for himself. Bruce had helped Holly write this one and it showed. Bruce had made some of the minor characters more flamboyant then Holly would have. He was glad Holly had brought Zoë back. He was deliriously happy that Zeus and Zoë got together before the end of the novel. He wasn't so sure about her having quadruplets though. Who would want to have that many babies at one time? Especially if there is, a chance of having more babies later. One at a time was how he liked it. He hoped his Zoë was only having one baby. The doctors had not told him yet.

There were other things to consider. He had accidentally walked into some sunshine the day before. The last time he had exposed himself to sunshine he had earned the nickname Flameboy by setting himself and an entire room on fire. His reflection in the mirror distracted him. He had never seen his reflection before and had had a hard time recognizing it. He had stared at it for several minutes before realizing he was standing in direct sunlight. He still did not know what to make of the event. He hoped to talk to Max about it after the meeting. Perhaps Max could shed some light on the strange occurrence.

Max was coming in tonight. He had news about the results of the genetic testing. Something about this made Zeus nervous. He began reading the Darkness of the Path again.

Erik watched Zeus sitting at the computer. Zeus was in a particularly thoughtful mood. Erik had noticed that about him. When he thought no one was watching him, Erik would lapse into a thoughtful silence while gazing into space as if he could see something the rest of them couldn't.

They had all the results from the genetic tests that their medical community had deemed necessary. They had decided to test everyone just to be fair. Max would be announcing the results in about a half hour. Their meeting never managed to start on time, so it could be even later than that. Erik had chosen to come early to set up. It is likely to be a big meeting. Everyone wanted to know the test results.

Mina slipped her hand into Erik's hand. She had seen Zeus in this kind of mood before. It happened rarely and only when Zeus thought himself to be alone. Pulling Erik's hand, they fully entered the room. Zeus immediately looked up at them.

"We got to get the place set up for the meeting. Are you going to help us?" Mina studied the room. She still had a few things to get the room ready for the meeting.

"What do you want me to do?" Zeus asked, shutting down his computer and putting it away. He followed Mina around the room as she pointed out things that still needed to be down. The work went quickly with three people doing it.

The meeting started promptly one hour late.

Max stared at his victims. They had in their hands folders, which contained copies of everything the government knew about them. Several would find out that they weren't who they thought they were. Some of course would have their worst fears confirmed. The ones from movies tended to share DNA of the actors who played them. The ones from novels were a looser bunch with the novels, which coming from movies having the actors DNA. The rest were more creative.

Zeus stared at the folder. The results pretty much confirmed what he had expected. They had some weird revelations too. There was a 98.4% chance that he was Gregori's father. Well duh, Gregori's father played him in the movie. There was an 85.2% chance he was the father of Zoë's baby but a 97.5% chance that he was the father of Holly's unborn baby. There was a 97.6% Gregori was the father of Zoë's baby. That was impossible. They had never had sex. They knew that Simon was not the father. There was only a 23.5% chance of that.

Zoë reread her report three times. Zoë shared 98.1% of her genetic material with Holly. That was fine with Zoë. How could Gregori be the father of her unborn child? When had she had sex with him? Could the dream sex she thought she was having with Zeus really have been with Gregori? Was Zeus having dream sex with Holly but thinking it was Zoë. This whole thing gave her a headache. She whispered to Zeus what she thought might have happened.

"It's not important Babycakes. What's important is that we provide them with a good home and plenty of love." They kissed while everyone else grumbled about the test results and asked to have tests redone.

"Gentlemen, Ladies, let us have some quiet now." The room quieted down, though some people were startled to see Zoë and Zeus kissing. "We need to go over these test results. Mister Carver, Carl Jung and I will answer any questions you have."

"I will ask each of you if you have any question. Please wait your turn. Will start with Zeus and Zoë, you two seem happy with your test results."

"No, we're not. Nevertheless, we can live with them. It's not like we have a choice or anything." Zoë felt herself to be practical. "There is a question of Dream sex. Can someone get pregnant doing it? I think that's what happened to me and Holly."

"I've never heard of it, but it is something new. Can I look at your folders?" The room grew quiet. They had all engaged in dream sex. Everyone considered it the safest form of sex since it is widely believed one could not get pregnant that way or get sexual transmitted diseases. The doctors talked amongst themselves for several minutes as Mister Carver examined Zoë and Zeus's medical folders. "It looks like you're right. We need to discuss this further."

"I say we save this until the end of the meeting when we'll have more time to go over the ramifications of this find." Mister Carver was getting a headache.

"Okay. I think Erik should be next. Are you satisfied with your findings?" Max had a bad feeling about this, but they had to talk to everyone. Someone had to be happy with his or her results.

"No, I'm not." It was a very long meeting.

+++++++++

Erik peered into the mirror. Damn if Zeus wasn't correct for a change. He could see himself. It had been over 500 years since he had seen himself. He had aged well. All the members of his group could see themselves in the mirror. The transformations that had taken place since the fog had come into their lives pleased him. If Zeus hadn't brought it up, no one would have ever noticed. Mina wrapped her arms around Erik's waist, her belly pressing against his back, the babies kicking in protest.

"You look absolutely fabulous. Now let's go to that meeting before the others have us dragged there."

"This is going to be a difficult meeting. You know that don't you?" Erik adjusted his tie. It went well with the suit he chose to wear. "The cavemen and werewolves kept pushing us to try to eat human food. They've convinced the spacemen to join them on their quest. The Romance Group will fake eating it then go throw up."

"So they really are the cause of the last four fogs?"

Erik shook his head. "We can't pin it on anyone, but they seem to be the only ones who could have done it. It's common knowledge that they fake eating and then throw up when they do. The spacemen caught them doing it at the last meeting. They were quite angry about it."

"I remember them accusing them of lying. Is that what it was about?" Mina tugged at Erik's hand as they headed for the doorway.

"Yes" Erik glided after her. "They were very agitated by this and kept yelling that if they could not trust them in this one little thing, how could they trust them with something truly important."

"Then they are going to expect us to eat something this week?"

"Without a doubt" Erik opened the door for Mina. Zeus and Zoë waved them down. They wanted them to sit at their table.

"Erik" Zeus waved him over. "We want to know when your book is going to be published. You promised it months ago."

"I sent it to the publisher to be proof read yesterday. It shouldn't be long now." Erik slipped into the seat next to Zeus and Mina slipped in next to Zoë

"So Erik, tell us when your book is coming out?" One of the spacemen with the ironic name of Guy Organic asked as he strutted up to the table. He kept popping cashews into his mouth as if he was starving to death.

"It's going quite well. Thank you Guy."

"Are you going to eat anything this time? With the fog, solid food should not be a problem for you anymore."

"They say the fog does a great many things. They have yet to be proven." Erik never hid his feelings on the issue. Guy and his ilk knew this and were always pushing it.

"How about eating one little bite of stew or chili to prove me wrong? What about it, are you up to the challenge?" Zoë sighed and stared at the chili. It's chunky style. The meat in it did look very good. Could the fog have changed her enough so she could tolerate human food? Would it get the others to shut up if she ate something without throwing it up? Zoë always threw up when she tried to eat solid food. Would it be different this time because of the fog? There was only one way to find out.

Everyone gasped as Zoë lunged forward. She speared a piece of chili meat on her fork and had it in her mouth before anyone could stop her.

The meat is very tender, Zoë thought as she chewed. She was pleasantly surprised when the only sensation she felt was a desire for more.

Guy was more than happy to fix her a small bowl of chili. To be honest, when he saw her take the meat he had been certain she was going to heave it.

Everyone watched Zoë eat. This wasn't good. Now they would all have to try something. One by one, they did with the same results.

"I'm sorry," Zoë said after they had finished eating. "I just wanted to shut him up." She could tell that this development upset most of the Romance Group. Most of them had no memory of ever having eaten human food before. It would be an unnerving experience for them.

"We quite understand. We were thinking of doing something to quiet him ourselves." Alfred nodded diplomatically. Of course, his solution would have more along the lines of throwing Guy out an airlock. Aimee and a few of the others had no problems with the meat. Alfred usually got sick just by smelling meat cooking. He had no idea why now was different. He would give Max and a few of the others the task of finding out why. That was their job. "It is a very good meal. I heard they got the recipe off the internet."

+++++++++

Holly played with her hair as she stared at her notebook. "Now let's do a basic outline. How and where do we want to start and end? What happens in between? Roughly how many chapters, pages do you think we'll need?"

"It should start in England and end in New Orleans. They should stop in New York somewhere in between." Gregori watched Holly write this down.

"Are they being chased? Or are they just going where the action is?"

"I'm not sure. What other characters will be in it?"

Holly sighed. "How will they travel from England? Planes are faster, but ships offer more character development. Will they drive from New York to New Orleans? Or take a cruise ship? Or maybe even another plane? I'm not very good at outlining things."

"You'll do fine Babycakes. Let's have them take a plane for all the traveling. I want to concentrate on the places not how they got there."

"No, wait. They can't take planes. They didn't exist in that time. They have the same problem with driving. No cars back then."

"Okay. We'll have them travel by ship and train."

"Okay then, let's have Mina, Quincy, Dracula and Lucy to start with." Holly marked the sheet. "We'll start with them and then add people as we need them. They'll be our core characters. Does that sound good to you?"

"That sounds very good. When can we start writing?"

"Now, if you want. Just tell me where they are in the first scene and what they're doing." They were still working on this when Doug and Bruce brought the children home to eat dinner.

"How's it going?"

"We've decided to kill Zoë again."

"Zoë's not in this novel. I don't think you're funny Holly." Bruce had a thing for Zoë. "Why do you dislike her so much?"

"Cause she's perfect."

"Just like you" Bruce laughed. "Come on Holly, we all know Zoë is an idealized you. Why don't you just admit it?"

"Humph, I don't have to admit to anything. But if you think I'm perfect then you are senile."

"Bruce has never seen the Nile. Maybe can go there on our next tour." Doug scooped Jen up and strapped her into her highchair. That was the only thing keeping Holly from throwing something hard at his head. Bruce coughed. "I don't understand what you have against Zoë. Don't you like happiness?"

Holly hesitated as she set the table. This was difficult, but she wanted to be honest. "I don't know. Happiness is not something I'm use too. I'm still working on it right now. I don't remember ever being as happy as I am right now. I keep expecting to wake up and find it's all a dream."

"I know what you mean." Bruce helped Doug bring in the food once the children were in their highchairs.

"But we've got to let go of the fear and just live our lives in the moment. Do you see what I mean?"

"I've lived so long without getting in touch with my emotions, I just don't know. I've denied them for so long. What happens if I can't control myself? I don't even know how to recognize them."

"Babycakes" Gregori wrapped his arms around Holly. "That's what I'm here for, to help you with those things."

Holly held Gregori tight. That she was sure of the one thing, she did love him.

Platitudes, Bruce thought. One had to deal with the frightened child within. It had to do with their inner frightened child and its fear of abandonment. He tried to explain it to Doug once. He had responded by promising never to leave Bruce. Bruce's inner child had not been reassured.

"I know that, but sometimes this inner panicky feeling just takes over and...."

Gregori placed his finger over her lips to stop her. "We can deal with anything that comes our way. Even that panicky feeling of yours, okay?"

Holly made a noncommittal noise.

"You've just got to learn to deal with each moment as it comes. Okay?"

"Will you be there to help me?"

"Always."

"Then I'll do my best."

"You always do."

They both whirled around when they heard clapping behind them. If it was Bruce or Doug, she was going to kill them. Instead, they found Jen and Johnny clapping. They were teaching Janis and George how to clap. It was a new game for them.

"Dinner Mommy, dinner Daddy," Jen was quite pleased with herself.

"Meatloaf, mashed potatoes and tomato cabbage" Doug announced as he and Bruce set the food on the table. "Let's say grace. Grace. Now let's eat."

Dinner went smoothly. They discussed Holly and Gregori's new book. They came up with the tentative title of Quincy II. It wasn't very original, but was helpful enough for them to start writing it

Chapter 23

Zeus stormed into his and Zoë's living room.

"What's the matter now?"

"Did you see this? They're going to have that asshole Steven Grams play me in the movie version of For the Dead Travel Fast. He's an old cow."

Zoë thought hard for a moment. She didn't watch many movies, which made it difficult to remember what he looked like. "He's in Quincy?"

"Yes, he played Holmwood."

"Oh yes, I remember now. What's wrong with him?"

"He looks nothing like me. And he's a horrible actor to boot."

Zoë remembered him as being cute. He had an excellent ass. She wisely kept that to herself. "So why don't we just go over there and have a talk with them?"

Zeus stared at her. It was pure genius. Why hadn't he thought of it? "You mean to see Holly and the people making it? Right?"

"Of course silly, who'd you think I meant? Mark Cornridge?" Zoë frowned. It would be like him to think that. "You weren't thinking of beating up Steven Grams? Were you? Tell me you weren't."

Zeus gave Zoë his most innocent smile. The smile didn't fool Zoë. They had to arrange for their trip. "I'll ask Alfred if he knows someone who's willing to house-sit for us. I don't want anyone stealing the place while we gone."

Zeus thought of all the things that they had to do before the trip as they prepared to enter the real world. A term he knew Zoë hated. A member of the Romanian Group would pick them up and escort them south where the film crews were staying.

Zoë grabbed Zeus's hand and pulled him threw.

"Oh Paul, Rose, I'm so glad to see you. You remember Zeus?"

"Of Course we do. Let the two boys here take your luggage." Two young men stepped up and took their stuff. "We'll be traveling directly to Rollywood. That's what they call the movie center here." Paul gestured to the small transport that would take them south. It looked roomy and elegant.

"We've been keeping a close watch on Holly during this pregnancy. She thinks Gregori is the father. He's more than happy to let her keep thinking that." Rose watched Zoë rub her extended belly. She looked like she was due at any moment. Hell, she looked like she was going to explode.

"I know what it looks like, but Max says I have another six weeks." Zoë rubbed her belly. She was huge. No one believed she could make it another week, let alone six.

Rose nodded her head in sympathy. "Her dear, rest your feet on these cushions." She watched as Zeus helped Zoë get comfortable and began to massage her ankles. Rose hadn't thought him to be the kind to do that.

"Have you heard about the dinner? Zoë ate human food. Now everyone is doing it."

"I'm sorry. I just wanted that idiot Guy to shut up about it. I really hoped that if I threw up on him he'd just drop it."

"Hush Babycakes, you don't have to apologize for anything. He has shut up about it. Hasn't he?"

"Yes. I think he is as shocked as everyone else when I didn't puke all over the place." Zoë suppressed her laughter. The sight of Alfred and Max eating their first human food was priceless. She shared this memory with Paul and Rose. They were both revolted by the sight and amused by the expressions on Max and Alfred's faces.

"This is caused by the fog? This eating human food is caused by the fog?" Paul couldn't believe this.

"Probably, but we wouldn't have known if Guy hadn't kept pushing it. And I hadn't jumped in."

Paul nodded his head. They had been through this before. The last group to join them had told them all about it. He watched Zeus cover Zoë in a warm blanket. He would never believe the man could be so tender with anyone.

"Zeus, do you mind if I examine Zoë. I just want to reassure myself that's she's doing well."

"As you wish, she's been having some problems with her ankles. Haven't you babe?"

"A bit, they tend to be sore when I rise. My right ankle and heel have been tender lately. Max says I need to exercise them. He suggested I wear weights on them for a couple of hours a night."

Paul examined her quietly. Then Rose did a follow up exam. They remembered from the literature that Zoë was prone to carry multiple babies. In all her pregnancies mentioned in the books, she had carried from two to five at a time. Twins to quadruplets, this time it is sextuplets. "I made some adjustments so you'll be more comfortable. You shouldn't retain so much water."

"Do you think it's the human food doing it? I only eat once a week and then only one small meal."

"Well, we don't know for sure. Max tells us that you and the others tolerate human food quite well. Your doctors told you that your pregnancy is causing the water retention. It should disappear shortly after you give birth."

"I hope so. Their sleeping now, ugh, but they like to be rocked." Zoë shook her head. "Do you remember where we can find some reliable sitters? Cause we're going to need them."

Dorothy and Joseph Morris entered the transport. "We're sorry we're late. Our Great-grandchildren didn't want us to go."

"I don't blame them." Zoë yawned. She felt much better since Paul and Rose examined her. "Are you going to be checking any structures while you're down south?"

"Yes" Dorothy smiled. "They just opened a water park there and they want us to check it out. That's why the Great-grand kids wanted to come with us."

"I love water parks. Don't you?" Zoë pulled the blanket around herself. She hopes it is much warmer where they were going. Being cold was making her tired. Soon she drifted off to sleep. She had pleasant dreams. She woke when she felt Zeus carrying her off the transport. They spent the day at Paul and Rose's place.

Zeus and Zoë looked enough like Gregori and Holly that they had no difficulty getting into the press conference.

At the press conference, Holly looked nervous. She stood close to Gregori, her eyes wandering around as if seeking someone out. She had been nervous and restless all day. The babies had been kicking and punching all day. They seemed to be expecting someone.

Zoë and Holly made eye contact from across the stage. Holly dug her fingers into Gregori's arm. Zoë did the same to Zeus.

"Babycakes, you're hurting me."

"Look at that woman over there. She looks like me, over there, by the man that looks like your father. Is that your father?" Holly felt confused. The couples were making their way over to them.

"My father is in Rome getting impregnating your sister while my Mum watches his daughters." Gregori managed through gritted teeth. He spotted the couple for the first time. The man did look like his father, buy there were differences. In any, his father had called from Rome several times. He had called with the news that Jasmine and Sophia were pregnant. He had called twice after that to tell him that he was the father of Jasmine's baby and maybe Sophia's. He wasn't certain if they had actually slept together. Gregori had had to point out to him that polygamy was still illegal.

Laura stepped in front of the approaching couple. "May I help you?"

"Yes. I'm Zeus and I don't want that asshole Steven Grams playing me. Ever," his voice reverberated around the auditorium, followed by gasps of astonishment. "And this is my wife, Zoë."

Zoë walked around Zeus and took Laura's hands. "I'm so pleased to finally meet you. Perhaps we can go somewhere and talk this over." It wasn't quite a question.

"I am not an asshole." Steven Grams gestured hostilely at Gregori.

"He didn't call you an asshole, asshole. I did." Zeus whirled Steven away from Gregori. Face to face with Zeus, Steven's eyes went wide.

"Who are you? Are you Gregori's twin brother?"

"He wishes. I'm the illegitimate offspring of his wife's fertile imagination and a bad Dracula movie his father was in it." Zeus steamed. Steven Grams had the IQ of a gnat.

Zoë talked quietly to Holly. Zeus could just make out something about a baby shower to make up for the embarrassment.

Holly came forward. "I can see his point of view. Neither of the actors we chose looks anything like them. I think we should go someplace quiet and talk this out."

"No. Let's fight it out right here." Steven was really pissed off about Zeus calling him an asshole. No one blamed him. If they did, they were too polite and professional for a fistfight. They mostly preferred lawsuits to fistfights. Mostly.

Paul exerted his authority. He soon had the combatants off stage and made them sit down and apologize. They didn't sound very sincere to Holly and Zoë who sat huddled on the lone couch in the room.

Chapter 24

Holly looked at the calendar wall by in the booth at their favorite bar, The Bad Moon. In a little over a month, she would give birth and maybe get her normal desire for food back. She doubted it would happen, but she could still hope. Sighing, she slipped another piece of chicken to MareMoo who sat drooling on her feet. MareMoo loved her. Holly fed MareMoo her dinner. Gregori and the others were less than thrilled by this.

Gregori sat glaring at her now. She tried to look innocent while slipping MareMoo her last piece of chicken.

"I've had enough. I think I'll go for a walk now. Anyone want to join me?"

"You haven't eaten anything. You feed all your food to MareMoo." There was an angry note to Gregori's voice, which he couldn't control. Holly was not eating, except maybe once a week, if that. Gregori was at wit's end.

She had to eat. Everyone agreed on that point. All of her doctors, but they couldn't tell him how to get her to do it.

Holly tried to look hurt by his accusations and failed miserably. She couldn't stand human food anymore. Not even her beloved mozzarella sticks would stay down. She willed herself to play at eating for Gregori's sake. "I can't help it. I've no desire for food or need to eat this kind of food. I don't want to do it anymore. Maybe it will change after I give birth."

"What do you want to eat?" Bruce sounded so worried about her. He could tell she was being honest. She had no desire or need for food. The thought of eating normal human food made her sick.

"That cute guy with the tight ass, I want to consume him like a sugar stick." Holly licked her lips as he walked by. "I bet he has the sweetest tasting blood."

"Sugar stick?" Doug popped a mozzarella stick into his mouth.

"She means those paper or plastic filled tubes of flavored sugar. You rip the one end open and then pour the sugar into your mouth. I use to get sugar highs from them." Bruce smiled rapturously. He got high just thinking about them.

"Oh, so you want to have sex with him." It wasn't quite a question. It was an accusation.

"No. I just want to drain him of blood. I'm not like those Romance Book People who only need a mouthful of blood. I need at least a quart or two. I have to think of my growing babies." She added. Maybe to make herself sound less like a murderer, which was what everyone with her thought she might be planning on becoming. "Not that I'd actually do that. Of course I would never actually hurt anyone." Holly crossed her fingers under the table as she said this.

MareMoo licked Holly's fingers. She wanted more chicken. She wagged her tail happily when Bruce slipped her some of his chicken.

Holly chugged a bottle of synthetic blood the waiter had brought to the table. Someone had invented it because it was against their religion to drink human blood. It was a big hit. Holly preferred hers from the tap, not the bottle.

"You do not even taste it when you guzzle." Gregori frowned. "It's really not that bad once you get used to it."

"So you say. But I know better." Watching Gregori carefully, she began to sip her drink. She had to sleep with the person she had just angered. She hated sleeping on the couch though it was more comfortable than the bed.

Zeus and Zoë strolled in holding hands and laughing. They quickly looked around until they spotted Holly's group. "Hi Holly, you're looking so well these nights. Will you be joining us at the baby shower?"

"Of course I'll be there. Who else will be coming?" Holly patted the seat next to her ignoring the loud groan from the men at the table. She loved to listen to Zoë and Zeus talk about their party plans. She hated going to parties herself. It was exciting to listen to Zoë and Zeus talk about their plans for one. They always made the parties sound so exciting though they never were. They treated it as a military operation with everything planned in precise detail.

They were just getting ready to leave when Abraham Van Helsing entered the restaurant. Holly suddenly threw herself in front of Gregori. She felt a sharp pain spread from the center of her chest. Then she felt nothing at all.

How strange, she thought as she found herself looking down at Gregori as he rocked her lifeless body in his arms. Tears streamed down his face and a wicked looking knife was wedged into her chest. That must be painful, Holly thought, not really understanding that she was looking at herself.

Abraham Van Helsing stood frozen to the floor. He had meant the knife for Gregori. He had no idea how he had hit Holly instead.

Doctors and medical people who had been dining were swarming around Holly. Holly approved. A group of motorcycle enthusiast closed in around Van Helsing as they realized what happened. Van Helsing was going to be very sorry for killing a pregnant woman. Their anger assuring that no one would find Van Helsing's body when they were finished with him.

Holly felt bad. If she died, she would never see her children and Gregori grow up. She watched Zoë bite her own wrist and pour the blood over Holly's chest wound.

I've come full circle. When this started, I was dying and now I'm dead. For a moment, she felt surrounded by love, and then a pain grew in her chest.

Gregori watched people working on his Holly. He never felt such pain in his entire life, not even the time when he had broken three ribs, his collarbone and both legs in a skiing accident. A black hole had taken the place of his heart and sucked everything into it. He focused all of his attention on Holly. He ignored everyone else. The doctors were saying something about maybe saving the babies. An angry group of men dragged a screaming Van Helsing out.

Bruce and Doug huddled around Gregori as they took Holly to the nearest hospital.

Erik and Mina watched as they wheeled Holly out. Zoë stationed herself at Holly's side with Gregori following behind them. Bruce and Doug were practically carrying Gregori. Zeus followed all of them. Erik and Mina grabbed Zeus who was taking care of MareMoo, and he quickly told them what had happened. By the time he had finished, they were in a crowded waiting room to wait while doctors worked on saving the babies.

Time stopped for them. It seemed so. The wait kept everyone on edge and nervous. Zoë entered the room. She had gone in with Holly. Heading straight for Gregori, she grabbed his hands.

"The babies are doing well. They're going to make it, and so is Holly. Once the babies were born, she regained consciousness. She wants to see you if you aren't too angry to see her." The last part was not quite a question.

"Why would he be angry?" Bruce asked for him. Gregori felt himself to be completely numb.

"She thinks you'll be angry with her for getting herself hurt again. You told her not to do that anymore."

Zoë yelled after Gregori as he tore into the hospital.

Gregori scooped Holly into his arms. "I'm not letting you out of my sights ever again."

"Is that a promise? I'm going to keep you to it."

"I love you Babycakes."

"Can we go home now?"

+++++++++

This is dedicated to my sister Dodi, who edited it for me, and my sister Jan and all of my fellow Home Depot associates who have encouraged me to finish. Thank you for believing in me.

Mary Jean Rutkowski is one of eight children. She has 20 nieces and nephews and they have an unknown number of children. Mary lives with her sister, Dodi and dog, Dutch. She is currently working full time as a cashier and part time as a writer. She has worked in retail for the last 26 years and feels that talking about herself in the third person is just too weird.

Proof

7336519R0

Made in the USA
Charleston, SC
19 February 2011